Larry Niven is a Nebula Award winner and has won the Hugo Award five times. He is the author of classics such as *Ringworld*, *The Intregal Trees*, and, most recently, *Destiny's Road* and *Rainbow Mars*. He is also the co-author of bestsellers *The Mote in God's Eye*, *Lucifer's Hammer* and *Footfall*. He is widely acknowledged as one of the most important writers in science fiction. Larry Niven lives in Tarzana, California.

Find out more about Larry Niven and other Orbit authors by registering for the free monthly newsletter at www.orbitbooks.co.uk

RINGWORLD'S CHILDREN

LARRY NIVEN

www.orbitbooks.co.uk

An *Orbit* Book

First published in Great Britain by Orbit 2004
This edition published by Orbit 2005

A CIP catalogue record for this book is
available from the British Library.

ISBN 1 84149 222 1

Typeset in Garamond 3 by
Palimpsest Book Production Limited,
Polmont, Stirlingshire
Printed and bound in Great Britain by
Mackays of Chatham plc, Chatham, Kent

Orbit
An imprint of
Time Warner Book Group UK
Brettenham House
Lancaster Place
London WC2E 7EN

This is for the firemen of California and
neighboring states who fought the fires of October
2003, with particular thanks to those who saved our
house and others in Indian Falls, Chatsworth,
Los Angeles County.

CAST OF CHARACTERS

Recent arrivals

Louis Wu: Earth born. First and second Ringworld expeditions.

Teela Brown: Earth born, of a line bred for luck by Pierson's puppeteer manipulation. Turned protector in *The Ringworld Engineers*, and now deceased. First Ringworld expedition.

Nessus: Pierson's puppeteer, the Hindmost's partner and mate. Led the first Ringworld expedition.

The Hindmost: Pierson's puppeteer, once Chief-in-Command of his species. Led the second Ringworld expedition.

Chmeee, once Speaker-to-Animals: Kzin. First and second Ringworld expeditions.

Roxanny Gauthier: Earth born, Detective-One in the ARM. Served aboard *Snail Darter* and *Gray Nurse*.

Oliver Forrestier: Wunderland born, Detective, ARM. Served aboard *Snail Darter* and *Gray Nurse*.

Claus Raschid: Earth born, Detective-Two, ARM. Served aboard *Snail Darter* and *Gray Nurse*.

Detective-Major Schmidt: Earth born. Served aboard *Gray Nurse*.

Wes Carlton Wu: Earth born, Flight Captain aboard *Koala*.

Tanya Haynes Wu: Earth born, Purser aboard *Koala*.

Ringworld's children

Seeker: species unknown, last seen with Teela Brown.

Acolyte: Kzin, Chmeee's exiled son.

Bram: Vampire turned protector, ruler of the Repair Center for countless aeons until killed by Tunesmith with Louis Wu's help.

Wembleth: species unknown, Ringworld-born traveler.

Tunesmith: Night Person (Ghoul) turned protector.

Kazarp: Night Person, Tunesmith's son.

Hanuman: Hanging Person turned protector.

Valavirgillin: Machine People, represents Farsight Trading.

Proserpina: surviving Pak protector.

The Penultimate: Pak protector, long dead.

Szeblinda: Hinsh. Giraffe People

Kawaresksenjajok: City Builder

Fortaralisplyar: City Builder

PREFACE

The Ringworld is about the same mass as Jupiter. Its shape is that of a ribbon a million miles across and six hundred million miles long, which makes it a bit larger than the Earth's orbit, and a few miles thick. It circles a yellow dwarf star. Its spin, at 770 miles/second, is enough to give it about Earth's gravity of centrifugal force. Walls along both rims, standing a thousand miles high, are enough to hold an atmosphere for millions of years.

Much else derives from these basic assumptions.

The inner surface is a habitat three million times the area of planet Earth. The topography is literally a work of art, carved in by whoever built the thing, so that from underneath the Ringworld resembles the back of a mask.

An inner ring of shadow squares block the sun,

giving periods of night; else it would always be noon. A system of pipes leads from the bottoms of oceans, under the Ringworld floor, up the back of the rim wall and over the edge, to recycle seabottom ooze (or *flup*) into spill mountains. Huge attitude jets stand atop the rim wall, Bussard ramjets using the solar wind of protons for their fuel, to hold the Ringworld against its inherent instability. There are spaceport ledges outside the walls. Two vast salt oceans serve as preserves for seagoing life, and as something more: maps of several worlds at one-to-one scale. The Ringworld floor is of unnaturally strong material, dubbed *scrith*, with other unusual properties.

The sun itself is involved in the Ringworld's meteor defense. A superconducting network embedded in the Ringworld floor generates a superthermal laser effect in a solar flare. The drawback: it can't fire through the Ringworld itself. Thus any meteorite that strikes the Ringworld, such as the one that made Fist-of-God Mountain, generally rams upward from underneath.

Some details become clues to the nature of the Builders.

The plethora of harbors and fjords, plus the shallow oceans (most of them), suggest a race that uses only the top of an ocean.

The nastier life forms — mosquitoes, flies, jackals, sharks, vampire bats — don't exist. Hominids have moved into some of those ecological slots. The Engineers weren't ecologists, they were gardeners.

The inhabitants are hominids in bewildering variety, some intelligent, some not. They fill ecological niches which on Earth are held by almost any mammal, but particularly the nastier life forms, jackals and wolves and vampire bats . . . as if mankind's ancestor, *Homo habilis,* had been protected until they numbered hundreds of billions, then abandoned to mutate endlessly.

You don't know the Ringworld until you've grasped its size.

After the book came out, a friend was going to build a scale model for an upcoming convention. He had a marble, a blue immy, to serve as the Earth, for scale. Turns out he'd need a ribbon five feet tall and half a mile long. The hotel wasn't big enough.

One guy who tried to map the Ringworld told me he ran out of computer space very rapidly. He ran into too many powers of ten.

David Gerrold speaks of a class of novel called 'the Enormous Big Thing.' Today you could fill a fair-sized shelf with them. Arthur C. Clarke's *Rendezvous with Rama* and Bob Shaw's *Orbitsville* are in that class, and so is my own *Rainbow Mars*.

But *Ringworld* came first, published in 1970.

It might have been laughed at. Too big, too improbable. Any normal structural material would be torn apart by its spin. I waited for the reviews in some fear.

James Blish wrote that he thought it would win the Hugo Award, but it *shouldn't*.

The readers gave it a Hugo Award anyway.

The writers gave it a Nebula.

I didn't have a sequel planned. I was not expecting a flood of redesigns.

During one of my speeches, a man pointed out that the Ringworld's mathematics are simple: it's a suspension bridge with no endpoints.

An academic in England pointed out that the tensile strength of the Ringworld frame must be approximately the force that holds an atomic nucleus together. (Hence, *scrith*.)

A grade school class in Florida spent a semester on the Ringworld. Their conclusion: the worst problem is that, without tectonic activity, all the topsoil would flow into the oceans in a few thousand years. (Hence, *flup* and the spillpipes.)

At the 1970 World Science Fiction Convention there were MIT students in the halls chanting, 'The Ringworld is unstable! The Ringworld is unstable!' (Did the best that I was able . . . hence, *attitude jets*.)

Somebody decided that the shadow squares shed too much twilight. What's needed is five long shadow squares orbiting retrograde.

Ultimately there was too much opportunity for redesign. I had to write *The Ringworld Engineers*.

All of these readers had found something worth knowing. The Ringworld is a great, gaudy, intellectual toy, a playground with the gates left wide open.

Some readers just read a book and stop.

Others play with the characters, or the assumptions, or the environment. They make up their own homework. We readers have been doing that for unguessable thousands of years: demanding more data on Atlantis from Plato, inventing Purgatory to put between Hell and Heaven, redesigning Dante's Inferno, writing new Odysseys. An amazing subculture has sprung up around Star Trek.

The Internet opens a whole new metaplayground for such people. A number of Web sites have sprung up (well, at least two) whose topic is Larry Niven's fiction.

In September 1999, tipped off by my lovely agent, Eleanor Wood, I logged onto *larryniven-1@bucknell.edu*. They were arguing about whether you can clone a protector, and whether Seeker and Teela Brown might have left a child behind. If they'd been right I wouldn't have seen a story, but they were off on the wrong foot, and I could fix it. After a few months of following these discussions, rarely interrupting, I had enough material for *Ringworld's Children*.

This is a playground for the mind. It's a puzzle too, a maze. Question every turn or you'll get lost. When you've finished the book, remember not to lock the gate.

'All this was indispensably necessary,' replied the one-eyed doctor, 'for private misfortunes are public benefits, so that the more private misfortunes there are, the greater is the general good.'

— Pangloss, in *Candide*, by Voltaire

2893 A.D.

CHAPTER 1

Louis Wu

Louis Wu woke aflame with new life, under a coffin lid.

Displays glowed above his eyes. Bone composition, blood parameters, deep reflexes, urea and potassium and zinc balance: he could identify most of these. The damage listed wasn't great. Punctures and gouges; fatigue; torn ligaments and extensive bruises; two ribs cracked; all relics of the battle with the Vampire protector, Bram. All healed now. The 'doc would have rebuilt him cell by cell. He'd felt dead and cooling when he climbed into the Intensive Care Cavity.

Eighty-four days ago, the display said.

Sixty-seven Ringworld days. Almost a falan; a falan was ten Ringworld rotations, seventy-five thirty-hour days. Twenty or thirty days should have healed him! But he'd known he was injured. What with all the general bruising from the battle with Bram, he hadn't even noticed puncture wounds in his back.

He'd been under repair for twice that long the first time he lay in this box. Then, his internal plumbing systems had been leaking into each other, and he'd been eleven years without the longevity complex called *boosterspice*. He'd been dying, and *old*.

Testosterone was high, adrenalin high and rising.

Louis pushed steadily up against the lid of the 'doc. The lid wouldn't move faster, but his body craved *action*. He slid out and dropped to a stone floor, cold beneath his bare feet. *Stone?*

He was naked. He stood in a vast cavern. Where was *Needle?*

The interstellar spacecraft *Hot Needle of Inquiry* had been embedded in cooled magma when last he looked, and Carlos Wu's experimental nanotech repair system had been in the crew quarters. Now its components sat within a nest of instruments and cables on a floor of cooled lava. The 'doc had been partly pulled apart. Everything was still running.

Hubristic, massive, awesome: this was a protector's work. Tunesmith, the Ghoul protector, must have been studying the 'doc while it healed Louis.

Nearby, *Hot Needle of Inquiry* had been filleted like a finless fish. A slice of hull running almost nose to tail had been cut away, exposing housing, cargo space, docking for a Lander now destroyed, thruster plates, and the hyperdrive motor housing. More than half of the ship's volume was tanks, and of course they'd been drained. The rim of the cut had been lined with copper or bronze, and cables in the metal led to instruments and a generator.

The cut section had been pulled aside by massive machinery. The cut surface was rimmed in bronze laced with cables.

The hyperdrive motor had run the length of the ship. Now it was laid out on the lava, in a nest of instruments. Tunesmith again?

Louis wandered over to look.

It had been repaired.

Louis had stranded the Hindmost in Ringworld space by chopping the hyperdrive in half, twelve or thirteen years ago. Dismounted, it looked otherwise ready to take *Needle* between the stars at Quantum I speeds, three days to the light year.

I could go home, Louis thought, tasting the notion.

Where is everybody? Louis looked around him, feeling the adrenalin surge. He was starting to shiver with cold.

He'd be almost two hundred and forty years old by now, wouldn't he? Easy to lose track here. But the nano machines in Carlos Wu's experimental 'doc had read his DNA and repaired everything down through the cell nuclei. Louis had done this dance before. His body thought it was just past puberty.

Keep it cool, boy. Nobody's challenged you yet.

* * *

The spacecraft, the hull section, the 'doc, machines to move and repair these masses, and crude-looking instruments arrayed to study them, all formed a tight cluster within vaster spaces. The cavern was tremendous and nearly empty. Louis saw float plates like stacks of poker chips, and beyond those a tilted tower of tremendous toroids that ran through a gap in the floor right up to the roof. Cylinders lay near the gap, caged within more of Tunesmith's machinery. They were bigger than *Needle*, each a little different from the others.

He'd passed through this place once before. Louis looked up, knowing what to expect.

Five or six miles up, he thought. The Map of Mars stood forty miles high. This level would be near the roof. Louis could make out its contours. Think of it as the back of a mask . . . the mask of a shield volcano the size of Ceres.

Needle had smashed down through the crater in Mons Olympus, into the repair center that underlay the one-to-one scale Map of Mars. Teela Brown had trapped them there after she turned protector. She had moved the ship eight hundred miles through these corridors, then poured molten rock around them. They'd used stepping disks – the puppeteers' instant transport system – to reach Teela. For all these years since, the ship had been trapped.

Now Tunesmith had brought it back to the workstation under Mons Olympus.

Louis knew Tunesmith, but not well. Louis had set a trap for Tunesmith, the Night Person, the breeder, and Tunesmith had become a protector. He'd watched Tunesmith fight Bram; and that was about all he knew of Tunesmith the protector. Now Tunesmith held Louis's life in his hands, and it was Louis's own doing.

He'd be smarter than Louis. Trying to outguess a protector was ... futz ... was both silly and inevitable. No human culture has ever stopped trying to outguess God.

So. *Needle* was an interstellar spacecraft, if someone could remount the hyperdrive. That tremendous tilted tower – forty miles of it if it reached all the way to the Repair Center floor – was a linear accelerator, a launching system. One day Tunesmith might need a spacecraft. Meanwhile he'd leave *Needle* gutted, because Louis Wu and the Hindmost might otherwise use it to run, and the protector couldn't have that.

Louis walked until *Needle* loomed: a hundred-and-ten-foot diameter cylinder with a flattened belly. Not much of the ship was missing. The hyperdrive, the 'doc, what else? The crew housing was a cross section, its floor eighty feet up. Under the floor, all of the kitchen and recycling systems were exposed.

If he could climb that high, he'd have his breakfast, and clothing too. He didn't see any obvious route. Maybe there was a stepping disk link? But he couldn't guess where Tunesmith might place a stepping disk, or where it would lead.

The Hindmost's command deck was exposed too. It was three stories tall, with lower ceilings than a Kzin would need. Louis saw how he could climb up to the lowest floor. A protector would have no trouble at all.

Louis shook his head. What must the Hindmost be *thinking?*

Pierson's puppeteers held to a million-year-old philosophy based on cowardice. When the Hindmost built *Needle*, he had isolated his command deck from any intruders, even from his own alien crew. There were no doors at all, just stepping disks booby-trapped a thousand ways. Now ... the puppeteer must feel as naked as Louis.

Louis crouched beneath the edge of some flat-topped mass, maybe the breathing-air system. Leapt, pulled up, and kept climbing. The 'doc's repairs had left him thin, almost gaunt; he wasn't lifting much weight. Fifty feet up, he hung by his fingers for a moment.

This was the lowest floor of the Hindmost's cabin, his most private area. There would be defenses. Tunesmith might have turned them off ... or not.

He pulled up and was in forbidden space.

He saw the Hindmost. Then he saw his own droud sitting on a table.

The droud was the connector between any wall socket and Louis Wu's brain. Louis had destroyed that . . . had given it to Chmeee and watched the Kzin batter it to bits.

So, a replacement. Bait for Louis Wu, the current addict, the wirehead. Louis's hand crept into the hair at the back of his head, under the queue. Plug in the droud, let it trickle electric current down into the pleasure center . . . where was the socket?

Louis laughed wildly. It wasn't there! The autodoc's nano machines had rebuilt his skull without a socket for the droud!

Louis thought it over. Then he took the droud. When confused, send a confusing message.

The Hindmost lay like a jeweled footstool, his three legs and both heads tucked protectively beneath his torso. Louis's lips curled. He stepped forward to sink his hand into the jeweled mane and shake the puppeteer out of his funk.

'Touch nothing!'

Louis flinched violently. The voice was a blast of contralto music, the Hindmost's voice with the sound turned up, and it spoke Interworld. 'Whatever you desire,' it said, 'instruct me. Touch nothing.'

The Hindmost's voice – *Needle*'s autopilot – knew him, knew his language at least, and hadn't killed him. Louis found his own voice. 'Were you expecting me?'

'Yes. I give you limited freedom in this place. Find a current source next to—'

'No. Breakfast,' Louis said as his belly suddenly screamed that it was empty, dying. 'I need food.'

'There is no kitchen for your kind here.'

A shallow ramp wound round the walls to the upper floors. 'I'll be back,' Louis said.

He walked, then ran up the ramp. He eased around the wall above a drop of eighty feet – not difficult, just scary – and was in crew quarters.

A pit showed where the 'doc had been removed. Crew quarters were not otherwise changed. The plants were still alive. Louis went to the kitchen wall and dialed cappuccino and a fruit plate. He ate. He dressed, pants and blouse and a vest that was all pockets, the droud bulging one of the pockets. He finished the fruit, then dialed up an omelet, potatoes, another cappuccino, and a waffle.

He thought while he ate. What *was* his desire?

Wake the Hindmost? He needed the Hindmost to tell him what was going on . . . but puppeteers were manipulative and secretive, and the balance of power in the Repair Center kept changing. Best learn more first. Get a little leverage before he reached for the truth.

He dumped the breakfast dishes in the recycler toilet. He climbed around the wall, carefully. 'Hindmost's Voice,' he said.

'At your command. You need not risk a fall. Here is a stepping-disk link,' and a cursor arrowhead showed him a spot on the floor of crew quarters.

'Show me the Meteor Defense Room.'

'That term is unknown.' A hologram window popped up in the portside wall. 'Is this the place you mean?'

Meteor Defense beneath the Map of Mars was a vast, dark space. All the stars in the universe ran round an ellipsoidal wall thirty feet high, and the floor and ceiling. Three long swinging booms ended in chairs equipped with lap keyboards, and those stood black-on-black before the wall display.

Past the edge of the pop-up window, under a glare of light, knobby bones had been laid out for study. This was the oldest protector Louis knew of, and Louis had named him Cronus. In the far shadows stood pillars with large plates on top, mechanical mush-rooms. Louis pointed into the window. 'What are those?'

'Service stacks,' the Hindmost's Voice said, 'each made from several float plates topped by a stepping disk.'

Louis nodded. The Ringworld engineers had left float plates all through the Repair Center. If you stacked them, they'd lift more. Adding a stepping disk seemed an obvious refinement . . . if you had them to spare.

Louis saw a boom swing across the starscape. It ended in a knobby, angular shadow.

All protectors look something like medieval armor.

The protector was watching a spray of stars. His cameras would be mounted on the Ringworld itself, maybe on the outside of the rim wall, looking away from the sun. He didn't seem aware that he was being spied on.

Louis knew better than to expect asteroids or worlds. Unknown engineers had cleared all that out of the Ringworld system. This drift of moving lights would be spacecraft held by several species. Now the view focused on a gauzy, fragile Outsider ship; now on a glass needle, a General Products' #2 hull, tenant unknown; now a crowbar-shaped ARM warship.

Tunesmith's concentration seemed total. He zoomed on starscape occluded by a foggy lump, a proto-comet. Tiny angular machines drifted around it, marked by blinking cursor circles. A lance of light glared much brighter: some warship's fusion drive. Here came another, zipping across the screen. No weapon fired.

The Fringe War is still cold, Louis thought. He'd wondered how long that could last. A formal truce could not hold among so many different minds.

The protector's arms jittered above the keyboard.

In the corner of Louis's eye, sunlight glared down. Louis spun around.

Above *Needle* the crater in Mons Olympus was sliding open, flooding the cavern with unfiltered light.

The linear accelerator roared; an arc of lightning ran bottom to top.

The crater began to close.

Louis turned back to the display. Looking over Tunesmith's shoulder, he watched fusion light flare from offscreen and dwindle to a bright point. Whatever Tunesmith had launched was already too far to see.

Tunesmith had joined the Fringe War!

A protector could not be expected to do nothing, even if the alternative was to bring war down on their heads. Louis scowled. Bram the protector had been crazy, even if supremely intelligent. Louis must eventually decide if Tunesmith was crazy too, and what to do about it.

Meanwhile this latest maneuver should keep the protector busy. Now, how much freedom had Louis been allotted? Louis said, 'Hindmost's Voice, show me the locations of all stepping disks.'

The Hindmost's Voice popped up three hundred and sixty degrees of Map Room. The Ringworld surrounded Louis, a ring six hundred million miles around and a million miles wide, banded in blue for day and black for night and broad fuzzy edges for dusk and dawn. Winking orange cursor lights were displayed across its face. Some were shaped like arrowheads.

This pattern had changed greatly since Louis had last seen it. 'How many?'

'Ninety-five stepping disks are now in use. Two failed. Three were dropped into deep space and probes launched through them. The fleets shot them down. Ten are held in reserve.'

The Hindmost had stocked stepping disks aboard *Hot Needle of Inquiry*, but not a hundred and ten! 'Is the Hindmost building more stepping disks?'

'With his help Tunesmith has built a stepping-disk factory. Work proceeds slowly.'

The blinking orange lights that marked stepping disks were thick along the near side of the Ringworld, the Great Ocean arc. The far side looked sparse. Two blinking orange arrowheads had nearly reached the edge of the Other Ocean. Others were moving in that direction.

The Other Ocean was a diamond shape sprawling across most of the width of the Ringworld, one hundred eighty degrees around from the Great Ocean. Two such masses of water must counterbalance each other. The Hindmost's crew had not explored the Other Ocean. *High time*, Louis thought.

Most of the stepping disks were clustered around the Great Ocean, and of those, most were in a tight cluster that must be the Map of Mars. Louis pointed at one offshore from Mars. 'What is that?'

'That is *Hot Needle of Inquiry*'s lander.'

Teela the protector had blasted the lander during their last duel. 'It's functional?'

'The stepping-disk link is functional.'

'What about the lander?'

'Life support is marginal. Drive systems and weaponry have failed.'

'Can some of these service stacks be locked out of the system?'

'That has been done.' Lines spread across the map to link the blinking lights. Some had crossed-circle *verboten* marks on them: *closed*. The maze was complicated, and Louis didn't try to understand it. 'My Master has over-ride codes,' the Voice said.

'May I have those?'

'No.'

'Number these stepping-disk sites for me. Then print out a map.'

As the Ringworld was vast, the scale was extreme. His naked eye would never get any detail out of it. When the map extruded, he folded it and stuffed it in a pocket anyway.

He broke for lunch and came back.

He set two service stacks moving and changed a number of links. The Hindmost's Voice printed another map with his changes added. He pocketed that too. Better keep both. Now, with luck, he'd have avenues of travel unknown to Tunesmith.

Or it might be wasted effort. The Hindmost, when he woke, could change it all back in a moment.

The Voice refused to make weapons. Of course the kitchen in *Needle*'s crew quarters hadn't done that either.

Tunesmith was still at the end of a boom, still tracking whatever he'd launched.

'Where are the rest of us?' Louis asked the Voice.

'Who do you seek?'

'Acolyte.'

'I do not have that name—'

'The Kzin we shared this ship with. Chmeee's child.'

'I list that LE as—' blood-curdling howl. Louis had to pry his fingers loose from a table edge. 'Rename him Acolyte?'

'Please.'

The map was back, and a blinking point next to Fist-of-God . . . a hundred thousand miles port-and-antispin from Fist-of-God – four times the circumference of the Earth – and twice that far to spinward of the Map of Mars. The hugeness of the Ringworld had to be learned over and over. The Voice said, 'Here we set Acolyte, with a service stack, thirty-one days ago. He has since moved by eleven hundred miles.' The point jumped minutely. 'Tunesmith has altered the setting for the stepping disk. It sends to an observation point on the Map of Earth.'

Home to Acolyte's father. 'Has he used it?'

'No.'

'Where are the City Builders?'

'Do you mean the librarians? Kawaresksenjajok and

Fortaralisplyar and three children were returned to their
origin—'

'Good!' He'd meant to do that himself.

'To the library in the floating city. I note your
approval. Who else shall I track?'

Who else had been his companions? Two protectors.
Bram the Vampire protector was dead. Tunesmith
was . . . still busy, it seemed. In the Meteor Defense
Room the protector's telescope screen was following a
receding point, the vehicle he'd launched earlier. Its
drive was off . . . flared brilliantly and blinked off again.

That was a warship. Reaction motors were still
needed for war; modern thrusters couldn't switch on
and off as fast.

Louis asked, 'Have you kept track of Valavirgillin?'

The map jumped. 'Here, near the floating city and
a local center of Machine People culture.'

Good, and she was well away from vampires. They
had not met in twelve years. 'Why did you track her,
Hindmost's Voice?'

'Orders.'

Carefully, 'Who do you take orders from?'

'From you and Tunesmith and—' a blast of orchestral chaos, piercingly sweet. Louis recognized the
Hindmost's true name. 'But all such may be counter-
manded by—' the Hindmost's name again.

'Is Tunesmith restricted from any interesting levels
of this ship?'

'Not currently.'

The Hindmost was still in wrapped-around-himself catatonia. 'How long since he's eaten?' Louis asked.

'Two local days. He wakes to eat.'

'Wake him up.'

'How shall I wake him without trauma?'

'I saw him in a dance once. Turn that on. Prepare food for him.'

CHAPTER 2

The Hindmost

The Hindmost dreamed of perfect safety.

He did not dream that he was Hindmost again, ruler of a trillion of his own kind. He'd been mad to be so ambitious. Always he had known that that was no stable state, that his Experimentalist faction could lose power in a moment. As it had.

He dreamed that he was young again. That was so long ago that all detail had been smoothed from his mind, and he only remembered a generic sense of being little and protected and unique.

He dreamed that no tool would ever bite his hand.

And then the dance began —

The illusion was marvelous.

Louis stood in a vast hall. The floor was all broad, shallow steps. A thousand aliens moved around him; two thousand throats uttered orchestral music that was also conversation, unbearably complex. Wolfgang Amadeus Mozart would have gone crazy. The Beatles . . . started out crazy, but futz, so did Mozart.

Kick, slide, left heads brush fingerlips; hind leg kicks, partner shies. The Hindmost kicked. A flat one-eyed head emerged from beneath his torso. *Spin, kick;* the Hindmost lurched to his forefeet and tried to turn. Was this a dance or a martial art?

The Hindmost whistled. The dance dissipated. 'Louis,' the puppeteer said.

'How long were you out?'

'I sleep much. Where is Tunesmith?'

'Fighting a war, I think.'

A head turned to the display of the Meteor Defense Room. 'I watched him build that vehicle. The Fringe War grows ever hotter. Have they invaded the Ringworld?'

'I have no idea. Hindmost, how did *Needle* come to be in this state?'

'Recall that Tunesmith accepted me as his teacher, on your advice.'

Tunesmith, the Ghoul musician, had been newborn as a protector and thirsty for learning. 'He needed training, and fast,' Louis said. 'I thought that the more he learned from us, the more we could guess what he'd do. Did you try to keep secrets?'

'Yes.'

'And you barred him from the flight deck, of course.'

'I did,' the puppeteer acknowledged. 'I taught using your displays in crew quarters. I taught well, but he learned faster, always faster. He demanded access to my tools. I refused. Six days after you entered the 'doc, I woke to find him standing over me *here* where I thought he could not reach. I gave him everything.'

'When did he chop up your ship?'

'Some time afterward. I was in fear-coma for eleven days. I woke and found this. Little has changed since. Louis, he has repaired the hyperdrive!'

'A fat lot of good—'

'He will reassemble the ship. When he does, I flee. Be aboard.'

'When?'

The puppeteer's eyes looked at each other.

That meant confusion, or amusement, or any form of internal conflict. Louis asked, 'What's he been doing? Building a warship—'

'Yes, and tracking the Fringe War, delving the secrets of my machinery – he wouldn't trust me to teach him – and ridding himself of my allies and yours. The Machine People are sent home. Acolyte is sent to spy on nothing at all. You, he kept safely asleep in the Intensive Care Cavity, and did extensive experiments there too. Louis, I must instruct you. You shall know everything you might need.'

Louis asked, 'Why?'

'We are allies!'

'Why?' The droud was gone from its place, a bulge in Louis's pocket. Would the Hindmost mention it?

'Tunesmith has us enslaved! Can't you see what he plans for you?'

'I think so. He'll make me a protector.'

Protector was the adult form of the human species.

Child, breeder, protector. At middle age – younger for some species of hominid, older for a few, around forty-five for humans – a breeder can become a protector. His/her skin thickens and wrinkles to armor. The brain case expands. A second two-chamber heart grows where the femoral arteries run into the legs. Joints grow bulky, giving a greater momentum for greater leverage in muscles and tendons.

There are psychological changes too. A protector loses the attributes of gender. A protector will protect his/her progeny, identifying them by scent. Mutations are left to die. A protector with no surviving children usually stops eating and dies . . . but some may choose to protect and nurture their entire species. That can work, if there is a perceived threat.

But none of it happens without the virus that lives in tree-of-life to trigger the change.

Tree-of-life did not grow properly on Earth. On the Ringworld it had been found only in chambers beneath the Map of Mars. The hominids of Earth, and of the

Ringworld too, had evolved as breeders, an unfinished form, like axolotls.

Too young a hominid does not react to the smell of tree-of-life root. The root will poison an elderly hominid. Louis Wu had been too old until Carlos Wu's autodoc changed him, and now he was too young.

'I'm safe for at least a quarter century,' he said.

The puppeteer said, 'Longer than that, if you use Carlos Wu's autodoc in time. The 'doc rejuvenates you. Tunesmith will stop you from doing that.'

Good point. Louis said, 'And what if he waits that long before he puts *Needle* back together?'

The puppeteer spoke in mournful music. 'Then I am lost. Severed from my family, my home. Slave to a creature shaped by his evolution to hold nothing of worth beyond his own bloodline. Louis, you face the same. You are not of Tunesmith's species.'

'On the Ringworld I'm not of any species.'

'Yes, Louis, *yes*,' in crescendo, 'don't you see the implication? He will feed you tree-of-life. You will be a protector. He will not give you power over *him*. You are to be only a prisoner and advisor, a talking head, the protector who has no descendants to guard. You will be the Voice that speaks for the safety of the Ringworld itself!'

'Yes,' Louis said patiently, 'but not for twenty-five years. I've been rebuilt young. I don't react to the smell of the root. I'm not old enough to make the change.'

'But do you want that?'

'No. Nonono. What can you do for me? I've been studying your placement of stepping disks. I made a few changes.'

The Hindmost whistled up the Map Room display, the Ringworld and stepping disks, and vectors and all. He turned a complete circle, heads held wide apart for extreme binocular vision. 'Good.'

'I expect you could reset everything. Understand though, Hindmost, if a service stack isn't where I expect to find it, that could kill me. You should give me access codes.'

'Yes.'

'By now Tunesmith must know everything about the 'doc. What don't I know?'

'You would not have the mental capacity.'

Louis was silent.

'Carlos Wu built an experimental nanotech-based medical system more than two hundred years ago. The United Nations considered him a proprietary genius. They claimed his work too. He took the 'doc when he disappeared. Carlos Wu was never found. The 'doc reappeared six years later on Shasht-Fafnir. My agent, Nessus, was able to buy it. My research team modified it to accommodate Kzinti and Pierson's puppeteer physiology and to make it more versatile and dependable.

'Now Tunesmith has rebuilt the machine. I expect it will accommodate Night People too. He's mastered this form of nanotechnology and is using nanomachines to make more stepping disks. What else must you know? The 'doc is set to rebuild certain life forms from their genetic codes.'

'Let's talk about *Needle*. Has he added weapons?'

'Yes, and mastered mine, and boosted my thrusters beyond sane safety limits—'

'What's he doing now?'

In the pop-up window, the black silhouette of Tunesmith wasn't doing anything. All the action was in deep space, where a point was moving away from the Ringworld at high speed. The ships of the Fringe War hadn't found it yet.

'A very agile ship with a miniature cabin. A small Hanging People protector is the pilot,' the Hindmost said. 'Little fuel, large thruster and reaction motors, weapons not from my library. As you saw, launched via linear accelerator. Onboard fuel is used only to dodge and decelerate. Tunesmith names it *Probe One*.'

Probe One was hard to see when its motor was off, but the motor was sputtering now as it dodged plasma weapons and missiles and, somehow, even lasers. Tunesmith's instruments followed it out toward interstellar space.

The Ringworld system retained its outer comets. All the near masses – planets, moons, asteroids – had been stripped from Ringworld system long ago, but comets must have been judged no threat to the Ringworld.

After all, there were no big masses to change their orbits and hurl them inward.

Ships of half a dozen species had been hiding among the comets ever since Chmeee and Louis revealed the Ringworld's existence nearly forty years ago.

Now ARM ships – human-built, the police and military branch of the United Nations – streaked in from offscreen. They looked more like tethers than ships, some with smaller ships attached. *Probe One* lit like a flashbulb – *guessed wrong about a laser!* – and vanished.

Tunesmith's screen swung wide, following nothing obvious.

Louis hadn't seen any debris.

'Hanging People' was a generic designation for hominids who lived a monkey lifestyle. Some weren't sapient. A Hanging People protector would still gain human intelligence or better. Hastily trained for space-flight, it might outguess ARM defenses, but Tunesmith would still outthink it, would still keep control. Being a protector was all about control.

Tunesmith's telescope swung half around the sky, a hundred and eighty degrees, or nearly that. Tunesmith's viewpoint focused on a fuzzy object . . . a comet, loosely packed ice drifting apart. Then on a spacecraft emerging from within the cloud.

It was lens shaped, painted black with vivid orange markings in the dots-and-commas of Kzinti script.

'Markings name this ship *Diplomat*,' the Hindmost

told Louis. 'We've observed. *Diplomat* seems well armed, but it never comes close to the Ringworld star. Always it lurks among the comets. Always it can flee in hyperdrive.'

'That doesn't sound like Kzinti.'

'They learn. I deem *Diplomat* the command ship for the Patriarchy fleet.'

Probe One was back. It had circled halfway around Ringworld's sun through hyperspace in less than thirty minutes. Its huge intrinsic velocity had pointed away from the sun; now it carried the ship inward, straight toward *Diplomat*.

Word from the other side of the sky would not have reached *Diplomat* yet. Minutes passed before the ship's Kzinti crew reacted to the intruder. Then threads of interplanetary dust glowed a bit in *Diplomat*'s laser fire, and a handful of small ships zipped out of the ice cloud.

Probe One began dodging. A laser: *Probe One* flared brilliantly. Louis squinted against the glare. Tunesmith's screen wasn't built to protect viewers from blindness. *Probe One* dodged out of the beam and into a scintillation of impacts and was still going.

Louis asked, 'General Products' hull?'

'That, under a layer of Ringworld floor material.'

Another ship popped out nearby, just long enough for Louis to get a good view. It was much larger than *Diplomat*, a transparent sphere with complex machinery packed tightly inside the hull . . . gone now, like the soap bubble it resembled.

'*Long Shot*,' Louis said, anger rising.

'I saw it,' the Hindmost said.

'They ran. Kzinti don't do that.'

'*Long Shot* is being used for courier service. It's too valuable to risk, and the Patriarchy will not have found room for armaments.'

'ARM and Patriarchy were supposed to *share* that ship. Chmeee and I gave it to them with that understanding.'

Probe One was too near the lens ship, accelerating sideways to get around it while fighting energy displays and lesser ships. Suddenly there was actinic light. Louis blinked hard. When he could see again, *Probe One* was gone.

'What the futz was that?' he demanded.

'Antimatter bullet. The newer ARM ships are all powered by antimatter, but we had not seen it used by the Patriarchy. They must manufacture their own in a particle accelerator somewhere. The ARM has a source, an antimatter solar system.'

'Antimatter. Hindmost, that makes the Fringe War a *lot* more dangerous. The Ringworld is too fragile for this.'

'Agreed.'

'What's he doing now?'

The shadow of a protector leapt from its chair, arced

like a ballet superstar across the view of comets and warships, touched down at one focus of the elliptical room, and was gone.

A hand like a sackful of ball bearings closed on Louis's forearm. He spasmed like a man electrocuted. 'Louis! Good, you're awake,' Tunesmith said briskly. 'Without you this would have been difficult. Hindmost, come out of there. Danger does not await our convenience. Louis, are you all right? Your heartbeat sounds funny.'

CHAPTER 3

Recruiting

Tunesmith was a *young* protector.

A Night People male of middle age had been lured into a cavern that grew tree-of-life. Tunesmith had emerged from his cocoon state a hundred and ten days ago: a tremendous mind demanding to be trained, in a hominid body hardened for endless war.

At first he must have satisfied himself with the Librarians' incomplete knowledge, and Acolyte's, and with what came in niggardly driblets from the Hindmost.

Tunesmith would not have begun his intrusions in any tentative fashion, Louis thought. The Hindmost might block that. Tunesmith must have built this heavy equipment and programmed it at his leisure, then set it moving all at once, after he'd picked the Hindmost's locks.

Fait accompli: suddenly he's standing over the puppeteer in his own living quarters. Suddenly he's filleted the Hindmost's spacecraft and is removing components as a fisher guts a trout.

Protectors of any species would be manipulative. Intelligence *was* manipulative, wasn't it? A superior intelligence would want to *control* his teachers. Knock them off balance from time to time. The differences between ally, servant, slave, and sled dog blur when the difference in intelligence is great enough.

A moment ago Louis had been spying on a protector. Suddenly the protector was beside him, gripping his wrist.

Louis said, 'I'm fine. Much too young to have a heart attack.'

The puppeteer's heads and legs were buried under him.

'Work on him,' Tunesmith said. 'I'm going to be busy.'

'Two questions,' Louis said, but the protector was gone.

The Hindmost eased a head into the open. No part of the neck showed, only eye and mouth.

Tunesmith could be seen sprinting about outside *Hot Needle of Inquiry*, working controls, then shouting into thin air. Heavy machinery began to move. The rebuilt hyperdrive motor was in motion. Unequal halves of the ship's hull began to close. The top of the linear accelerator began to track across the underside of Mons Olympus.

The Hindmost whistled. 'I was right! He's—' The head ducked back under him. Tunesmith was back.

He stooped to work controls on the hidden stepping disk. Then he picked up the curled-up puppeteer, evading the hind leg as it lashed out. They weighed about the same, Louis guessed. 'Louis, follow,' he barked, and stepped forward and was gone.

Just for an instant, Louis Wu rebelled.

It was a test, of course. Would Louis Wu follow him without question? This was all just too familiar.

An alien mastermind bursts into Louis Wu's life, assembles a crew, and hares off on a mission known only to the master. First Nessus, then the Hindmost, then the protector Teela Brown, then Bram, now Tunesmith, each chooses Louis Wu for reasons of convenience, drops him into the middle of a situation he doesn't understand, and runs him like a marionette. By the time Louis finishes playing catch-up, he's committed to something on the far side of sanity.

Pierson's puppeteers were control freaks. A true coward never turns his back on danger.

Being a protector was all about control.

Where would he be, what would Louis Wu have done, by the time he knew anything?

The instant passed. If he didn't follow, he'd be out of the action entirely. Louis stepped forward, onto a stepping disk that looked like the rest of the floor, and flicked out.

A flood of sunlight made him squint.

He stood on a high peak, on a stack of six float plates and a stepping disk. Tunesmith and the Hindmost stood below him on a translucent gray surface. Louis looked first for the Arch, to orient himself.

The Arch – the far side of the Ringworld – arced from horizon to horizon, broad above the haze at the spinward and antispin horizons, narrowing toward noon where it passed behind the sun. Louis hadn't seen the Arch in some time.

Fist-of-God Mountain loomed to port like a lost moon, poking far out of the atmosphere. Around its foot the land was more moonscape than desert, hundreds of millions of square miles of lifeless pitted rock. Fist-of-God was an inverted crater. A meteoroid had punched up through the Ringworld floor from underneath, hundreds of years ago. The blast had flayed soil from the high places, even this far away. Naked scrith was dramatically slippery.

Closer were silver threads of river and silver patches of sea, and the dark green tint of life gradually encroaching. The land below the hill was a broad jungle, and cutting through it, a river miles across.

'Watch your footing,' Tunesmith said. Louis lowered himself carefully onto naked scrith.

It was worth remembering: beneath this shell of landscape was nothing but stars and vacuum. There would be no springs hereabouts, no groundwater, nothing to support life. No busybody to wander by, to fiddle with the controls on an abandoned service stack. Exposed as it was, this was an excellent hiding place for high-tech tools such as these.

Louis asked, 'Are you going to explain what's going on?'

Tunesmith said, 'Briefly. As a breeder I knew little but remembered a great deal. Coming out of my transition from breeder to protector, the first thing I was sure of was that the Ringworld is terribly fragile. I knew that I was reborn to protect the Ringworld and all its species.

'That has come in steps. I whiffed Bram, of course, and knew I had to kill him. I spent some time learning from the Hindmost and his library, and watching the Fringe War develop. Then for a time it seemed best to work alone or with a few Hanging People protectors. Now I must assemble a team.'

'To do what?'

Tunesmith touched controls. The service stack lifted. Four float plates detached from the bottom and eased apart. Tunesmith boarded a stack of two, leaving one each for the puppeteer and the man.

The puppeteer was looking about him. He said,

'Downslope, one could survive. Ringworld folk are generally hospitable to strangers. Tunesmith, you never accept my word when you can test it. Why do you involve *me*?'

'And for *what*?' Louis demanded.

Tunesmith floated off downslope. Louis and the puppeteer boarded and followed. The protector's voice carried easily. He spoke Interworld with no trace of accent, projecting his voice from deep in his belly, fearing no interruption, like a king.

'The Fringe War grows more intense. The ARM is using antimatter instead of hydrogen fusion to power their motors and weapons. Louis, the Ringworld cannot survive this. Something must be done.'

'See if you can describe it!'

'Louis, to shape a *plan* I need to learn more. Did the Hindmost tell you of a courier ship? Of puppeteer manufacture, with an experimental drive—'

'*Long Shot*. I've flown it. The warcats have it!' He hadn't called a Kzin a warcat in a very long time.

'We're going to take it back. We have time to recruit Acolyte,' Tunesmith said.

They were nearing the edge of the jungle.

'Why would Acolyte join you?'

'I expect you will tell him to. Acolyte's father sent him to you "to learn wisdom".'

'Joining you on a piracy expedition, is that wisdom?'

The puppeteer asked, 'Do you need us? Do you trust us? Could you fight alone?'

The protector said, 'I must leave someone to fly *Hot Needle of Inquiry*, or else leave *Needle* abandoned and adrift among the comets.'

The Hindmost immediately said, 'I can fly *Needle*.'

'Hindmost, you would run.'

'Louis and I will be pleased to—'

'Louis flew *Long Shot* once before. He will again. You and Acolyte will fly *Needle*.'

'As you will,' the Hindmost said.

Tunesmith said, 'Louis, you swore an oath. You must protect the Ringworld.'

In a mad moment Louis Wu had sworn to *save* the Ringworld. He'd done that, twelve years ago, when the Ringworld had drifted off center . . . but Louis only said, 'I won't force Acolyte.'

'Then I must await developments.'

There were long-tailed Hanging People in the jungle. They threw sticks and dung. Louis and the Hindmost rose above the treetops, but Tunesmith's float plates dropped near the forest floor. They heard him whoop and saw him flinging missiles. Stones and sticks flew faster and more accurately than Hanging People could dodge. In less than a minute they'd vanished.

Tunesmith rose to join them. 'Tell me again why Ringworld species are always hospitable!'

'Tunesmith, those were apes,' Louis said. 'Hominids

aren't always sapient, you know. Is this what you picked
to pilot your probe?'

'Yes, made into protectors. Sapience is relative.'

Louis wondered if a protector really didn't see the
difference between these apes and Louis Wu. A
protector's lips and gums hardened into something like
a beak; he could not frown, or smile, or sneer, or grin.

It was jungle all the way, trees and vines that Louis
couldn't name, and a species of elbow root growing in
chains at sixty-degree angles, big enough to match
sequoias.

Louis switched his faceplate display to infrared. Now
lights on the ground wove about each other, lurked,
charged, merged. Thousands of tiny lights above him
must be birds. Larger lights in the trees would be sloth
and Hanging People and – Louis swerved to dodge a
fifty-pound flying squirrel with a head that was all ears
and fangs. It cursed luridly as it passed under him.

Hominid?

Nice day for a float.

Tunesmith settled in a circle of elbow trees. The
ground was uneven, humped here and there, and overgrown with a tangle of grass. The Hindmost descended
and Louis followed, still seeing nothing . . . and then
an abandoned float plate. How had that gotten here?

His own disk settled. Louis stepped off, and they were

surrounded. Weird little men stepped out of the elbow trees and women popped out of the ground. All were armed with short blades. They only stood heart-high. Louis, wearing impact armor, did not feel threatened.

Tunesmith hailed them and began talking rapidly. Louis's translator device had never heard this language; it and he could only listen. But he could see through torn grass into a burrow that ran deep underground. The grass was torn just so in fifty places.

He was standing on a city.

Hominids – descended from the Pak who must have built the Ringworld – had occupied every possible ecological niche, starting half a million years ago with a population already in the trillions (though the numbers were pretty much guesswork.) This group were burrowers. They wore only their own straight brown body hair, and carried animal-skin pouches. They had a streamlined look, like ferrets.

They were looking less defensive now. Some were laughing. Tunesmith spoke and more laughed. One stepped to a rise of ground and pointed.

Tunesmith bowed. He said, 'Acolyte is hunting a daywalk or three to spin of port. Louis, what shall I tell them? They offer rishathra.'

He was tempted for an instant, then embarrassed. 'Louis isn't in season.'

Tunesmith barked. The Burrowing People laughed hysterically, looking at Louis with myopic eyes.

Louis asked, 'What was your excuse?'

'I've been here. They know about protectors. Board your disk.'

CHAPTER 4

Acolyte

The smells were stunningly rich. Hundreds of varieties of plants, scores of animals. Kzinti could survive in style here, until their numbers grew too great. Acolyte, millions of miles from the nearest Kzinti, did not miss their company; but Acolyte resolved to tell his father about this place.

He sniffed, seeking an elusive smell: anything large or lethal.

It wasn't there. Only the smell of brachiating hominids.

His father's hunting park had been more dangerous. The danger level of father's park was as carefully measured as the placement of each bush. Kzinti needed a threat to bring them alive, and to keep their numbers down too.

Pak protectors didn't think like that.

Louis Wu had explained it thus: protectors had spread life across this land in imitation of the life patterns that evolved on Ball Worlds, but they had left out anything that harmed *or annoyed Pak breeders, from carnivores down to parasites and bacteria. Whatever attacked today's bewildering variety of hominids had evolved over the million years, the four million falans, that followed.*

Of course Louis was guessing. He'd said that too.

So, here was a safe place to play. One day Tunesmith would call, or Louis, and Acolyte would find danger enough. The lights in the night sky were not all stars.

A blotch in infrared, bigger than other blotches, went from perfect stillness to a blur of speed, leapt into a tree, merged with a smaller glow, paused –

Tunesmith yowled.

A returning yowl seemed muffled. Louis's dawdling translator caught up; it said, 'Acolyte!' 'Here. Wait.' Then: 'Louis!'

'Hello, Acolyte!' called Louis.

'Louis! I was worried! How are you?'

'Young. Hungry, antsy, not quite sane.'

'You were forever in the healing box!'

Tunesmith said, 'Acolyte kept bothering me for updates until I had to find work for him elsewhere.'

Louis was touched. Acolyte had worried . . . thinking that Louis remained in the 'doc because there was more to be done for him. More likely Tunesmith was just keeping Louis out of the way; or he might have been refining the rejuvenation process, or using Louis as a test subject to study nanotechnology, tanj him. A twelve-year-old should not be forced to such cynical thinking, even a twelve-year-old Kzin.

The massive cat was halfway up a tree trunk, eating, while Hanging People threw hard fruit from a distance. Tunesmith separated his float plates and hovered one next to Acolyte.

Chmeee was a Kzin chosen by the puppeteer Nessus to join his exploration team, decades ago. Acolyte was Chmeee's eldest son, cast out by his father and sent to 'learn wisdom' from Louis Wu. He stood seven feet tall, shorter than his father, furred in orange and dark chocolate: dark ears, dark stripes down his back, a smaller chocolate comma down his tail and leg. Three parallel ridges ran down his belly, possibly his father's legacy; Louis had never asked. On a huge tilted trunk under green-black foliage, he looked utterly at home.

He asked, 'Are we finally ready?'

'Yes,' said Tunesmith.

Acolyte judged the distance above a drop of fifty feet. He had to make a twisting leap. He hit the disk on all fours. The disk dropped under his weight, and Acolyte slid, scrambled, and had his grip.

A Kzin's hands were good, but with his claws extended his fingers would have slid off. Anger might have killed him. It was a jest, or a test – and Tunesmith had been dropping past him, ready to catch him.

'I should reclaim my float plate,' Acolyte said. He

dropped toward the forest floor and took off through tilted trunks along a path Louis couldn't find.

A float plate floated above a display of huge, gorgeous orange flowers. Acolyte eased the disk he was riding down over the other float plate, and with a magnetic *click* they locked.

'I left one with the Underpeople, their toy until I need it,' the Kzin said. 'I mass too much. I have to be too careful when it's just one floater.'

The double disk took off, Tunesmith followed, and they were racing.

Louis tried to keep up, but it was a hairy ride. They were leaving the Hindmost far behind. Tunesmith called, 'What have you learned?'

The Kzin bellowed, 'Nothing since we spoke. Teela's path ends with the Mechanics, two months after she left Louis and my father. I have dwelt among five civilizations, six species – interesting symbiotic culture, Mechanics, and a variety of Hanging People. None tell any tale of Teela Brown, or Seeker, or weapons that throw light, advanced medicine, famine averted, a flycycle— Whatever I thought of, they never heard of it.'

'Were you lied to?'

'Who would dare? Who would care? Teela's path is discontinuous. I never tracked her through the sky! I only found places where she and Seeker landed. The Mechanics remember her from two or three falans after

a floating building passed over, a hundred and fifty
falans ago. Have you sought rumors of flying devices?
Or assessed conflicting reports?'

'Yes.'

'Louis—' Acolyte looked back, then slowed.
Tunesmith slowed too: the race was over.

'Louis, I was asked to track Seeker and Teela Brown.
I found little. They disappeared for seventy or eighty
falans. Then the Vampire protector Bram tells us they
entered the Repair Center as breeders. The man died
of tree-of-life – too old – and Teela woke from coma
as a protector.'

Tunesmith said, 'I want to know how breeders could
find their way into the Map of Mars. I want to know
why Bram let Teela wake. It would have been so easy
to study her in her coma, then kill her. They may be
trivial questions, but I wonder.'

Louis shrugged. He'd wondered too. Bram had had
little respect for human life, breeder or protector.

Acolyte asked, 'Are you caught up with what's
happening?'

'Tanj, no. Tunesmith is driving me crazy with his
secrets.'

The protector said, 'I'll talk as we go.

'Louis, you made me. You saw that a Vampire
protector was unfit to decide the Ringworld's fate, or
else that Bram himself was unfit. You thought a Ghoul
would serve. You lured me into the Repair Center. A

tree-of-life garden made me a protector. You expected me to kill Bram, and I did. I assume you considered implications.' No anger, no bitterness showed. A protector's face was like hardened leather.

'Consider this implication: no protector ever evolved to stand aside when his descendents are in danger. You saw that a Ghoul's children must benefit where other hominids survive well, but did you see that too? We must act, sensibly or not. The Fringe War was bad enough when you entered the 'doc, Louis. Now the ARM has brought antimatter-powered ships, twenty and counting. Now it seems the Kzinti have stolen the puppeteers' Quantum II hyperdrive ship. To use it for courier service tells us interesting secrets, doesn't it?'

Louis agreed. 'They don't dare endanger it. They don't know how to duplicate the drive. There's still only one ship.'

Tunesmith asked, 'Hindmost, could *you* build another *Long Shot*?'

'No. My research team could, but trial and error played a large part, and the cost . . . broke my power, drove me into exile, as much as any of my other mistakes.'

They circled Tunesmith's service stack, then landed. Tunesmith said, 'I can't do nothing. If I can understand *Long Shot*— Here, let me reset our destination. Acolyte, this setting would take you to your father. Were you tempted?'

'I have nothing to offer him yet.'

'Follow me through.' Tunesmith stepped from his float plate and was gone.

They came out underground, where float plates waited. The air smelled of the caverns beneath the Map of Mars. Tunesmith showed off his toys as they drifted through tunnels and caverns.

A dozen float plates carried a huge laser cannon at a walking pace. 'I made this from specs in the Hindmost's records,' the protector said, 'with a few improvements. I'll mount it on Mons Olympus. I've heliographed the design to protectors along the rim wall. Soon we won't have to depend on the sun to let us talk. I should mount one on Fist-of-God too.

'Here—' He reached out and down to snatch up a nest of tubing. He put one end to his mouth and wild music emerged. 'What do you think?' He blew again, and what the futz, Louis danced on the float plate with an imaginary partner.

Tunesmith stopped to examine massive machinery, then reworked some superconducting circuitry with a spray gun. The mass crept away on sixty or seventy float plates. 'Meteor repair kit,' he said. 'Finished, but now it's got to be moved to the launcher.'

Stepping disks were growing in a vat while instruments monitored the metal content of the fluid.

Tunesmith used a finished stepping disk to flick them into the Meteor Defense Room.

Louis had no idea where he'd been.

No idea what they were doing.

It seemed to Louis that the protector's mind was like a vast maze, and Louis lost within it. Working with Bram had been no different. The Vampire protector had committed an intolerable crime, and Louis had found him out. Louis had taken steps to replace him with a Ghoul, a Night People. Well and good, but had he expected to suddenly attain freedom?

Protectors themselves didn't have freedom. If Tunesmith could always see the right answer, why would he ever choose otherwise? And all that a poor stupid breeder could do was ride along. But if Louis didn't get some answers soon—

The Fringe War was all laid out on the floor-to-ceiling screen circling the Meteor Defense Room. Ships and bases were marked with blinking cursors in neon colors. Kzinti and human ships were numerous. Others manifested a presence: puppeteers, Outsiders, Trinocs, ships and probes Tunesmith hadn't identified. The Ringworld was of interest to any entity who learned of it.

A Kzinti ship fell through the inner system, rounding the sun without a challenge.

Tunesmith said, 'An ARM attempted to talk to me,

but I chose not to answer. No other faction has. There were early attempts to invade. The meteor defense stops everything but microprobes, but those must be everywhere. I've intercepted what must be messages between ships, too well encrypted even for me. By *Needle*'s database I can identify ships and habitats in the inner comets belonging to ARM, Patriarchy, Trinocs, an Outsider ship, and three Pierson's puppeteers all hanging well outside the system, and thousands of probes of unidentified origin. I had best assume that everyone knows everything that anyone is doing. Even for me, keeping a secret will be tricky.'

He zoomed the display. 'Louis, what is this?'

A dot was light-amplified to a blurred view of a ghostly torus made of black lace, all intertwining threads, a tiny point-source of yellow-white light at the center, no obvious spacecraft drive. 'Thirty-two Ringworld radii distant—'

Louis said, 'Another Outsider. They don't always use light sails. We bought hyperdrive technology from them, but they've got something even better. The good news is, they've got no use for liquid water and high gravity, so they've no interest in human worlds.'

'And this?' A battered cylinder, flared at the tail, windows glinting about its waist.

'Mmm? The design looks like United Nations work of a long time ago. Maybe a slowboat retrofitted with hyperdrive. It might be from Sheathclaws. Would they try to deal themselves in? That planet was settled by Kzinti telepaths and humans.'

'Sheathclaws. A threat?'

'No. They couldn't afford serious weapons.'

'Good. Hindmost, did you show him *Diplomat*?'

'Yes. We watched your *Probe One* break up a rendezvous between *Diplomat* and *Long Shot*. *Long Shot* retreated to hyperspace.'

'Louis, Acolyte, Hindmost, I need a sanity check,' Tunesmith said. 'Is this a story you can believe? My *Probe One* frightens *Long Shot* away from a scheduled rendezvous. *Long Shot* jumps in hyperdrive, not far, then observes from a safe distance, a few light minutes away, until the pilot sees no further threat. Now he returns to exchange data and packages with *Diplomat*, but he's late.

'He returns to the Patriarchy still behind schedule and trying to catch up. *Long Shot* must report directly, because who else could? Every other ship is too slow. The Kzinti homeworld is two hundred thirty light years from here. That's three hundred minutes each way. We start with ten hours to play with before *Long Shot*'s pilot can return to Ringworld space, and he will still make his next rendezvous in haste. Yes?'

'Kzinti would do that anyway,' Louis said. 'Charge right in.'

Acolyte bristled. 'We do not worship clocks and calendars, Tunesmith. This ship *Diplomat* was attacked. They will be wary.'

Louis said, 'Spaceborn always worship clocks and calendars. Orbits are like that.'

'Hindmost?'

The puppeteer asked, 'What are you risking on this guesswork?'

'Too much,' Tunesmith said, 'but I must gamble. Fringe War activity accelerates toward a singularity. My worst move is no move.'

'What do you intend?'

'I will capture *Long Shot*.'

Louis saw that he'd been right: a crazy mission. He pointed out, '*Long Shot* is three thousand times as fast as us in hyperdrive, and never enters the Ringworld singularity.'

'They can't use hyperdrive if they're docked with another ship. Follow me.' Tunesmith strode forward and was gone. And again, Louis followed.

CHAPTER 5

Hanuman

As best he could tell, Probe Two *was a perfect machine. Hanuman continued working on it anyway. Of all the fascinating machines in Tunesmith's domain, this was the one he felt justified in making his own. His own life would ride this ship.*

He had watched Tunesmith at work on the Meteor Reweaving System.

Tunesmith talked while he worked. Hanuman almost felt he understood it. Inside a Ringworld puncture, vast numbers of minimally tiny components would weave strands of scrith out of lesser matter, pulling the vast structure back together, closing the holes. Something else would be going on while the nanomachines worked. Similarly tiny components would weave magnetic cables thinner than the hair on Hanuman's body, following superconducting cables already in place inside the torn floor of the Ringworld.

A protector's nature was to act. It was all Hanuman could do, to stand away from the Meteor Reweaving System, to keep his hands off machines that could save the Ringworld and every species on it, including Hanuman's own. He dared not touch what he didn't understand.

For fifteen hundred turns of the sky, Hanuman had lived in trees with others of his kind. He had loved; had sired children; had grown old. Then a knotted creature sheathed in leather armor had given Hanuman a root to eat.

Hanuman had only been intelligent for a falan or so. He knew this much: Tunesmith was a superior intellect. Hanuman's touch on Tunesmith's machines could only ruin them unless he were explicitly directed and guided.

But he could work on Probe Two. *This was the machine that might kill him. He was hoping to understand it better. Tunesmith – as much Hanuman's superior as he was superior to his species' breeders – didn't quite understand it either.*

Hanuman heard a puff of air and turned around. Tunesmith had arrived, with visitors.

They were in the cavern beneath Mons Olympus. Tunesmith strode toward an individual half his height. He said, 'Hanuman, these are friends. Folk, this is Hanuman, pilot for *Probe Two*.'

The stranger's voice was high-pitched but not childish. 'Acolyte, Louis Wu, Hindmost. Hello.'

Louis said, 'A pleasure. *Hanuman?*' Still trying to

decide what he was seeing. The stranger wouldn't weigh more than fifty pounds. Three feet tall, with two feet of tail, swollen joints and swollen skull and skin like cured leather pleated in folds. 'You'd be a Hanging People protector?'

'Yes. Tunesmith made me and named me. "Hanuman" is a literary reference from the library in *Hot Needle of Inquiry*.' Hanuman switched to another language: Ghoulish, spoken far too fast. As he and Tunesmith chattered, Louis's translator caught a word here and there.

'– haste –'

'– lower that into place.'

'A single theory to be tested. If your vehicle survives—'

A cylinder waited beside the linear accelerator. It looked too small for a passenger, but the nose was fully transparent, and the magnet coils behind it – the linear accelerator – were more than a mile across.

Machines had already mounted the rebuilt hyper-drive motor in *Needle*'s belly. Now *Needle*'s missing hull section crawled forward to rejoin *Needle*.

Needle's sliced-off wall had been breached. A drum-shaped cylinder ran into and through it. The outer, hull side of the intrusion was opaque, painted with more of that bronze stuff. As the hull section moved to join *Hot Needle of Inquiry*, the intrusion eased into what had once been the garage for *Needle*'s lander.

The intrusion was an airlock, Louis saw. A big one, big enough to transfer a dozen humans at a time.

The bronze edges matched. Then the bronze edging oozed away, coiling on the lava like a snake. The bronze splotch on the airlock remained in place.

Louis said, 'I can't stand it. What is that bronze stuff?'

Hanuman said, 'Glue.'

Louis waited.

Tunesmith spoke with a touch of reluctance. 'It's more complex than that. Do you know about General Products' hulls? Each variation is a molecule with its interatomic bonding artificially enhanced. It's very strong, but if the molecule is cut, it comes apart. I've engineered a substance to replace the interatomic bonds. It does more than allow me to slice up a hull. I can bond one General Products ship's hull to another. Hanuman, are you ready?'

'Yes.'

'Only fulfill your mission, then save yourself if you can. Go.'

Hanuman scampered across the stone floor, climbed into the tiny missile, and closed the transparent nose. His ship dropped below floor level.

Hanuman spared a moment to wonder about Tunesmith's companions. One was a breeder, species unknown, but all three

*showed their alien state. Starborn, alien to the Ringworld.
Hanuman knew a little about them from* Needle *and its
computer files.*

Where did they stand with regard to Hanuman?

*'Glue,' Hanuman had said, to see if Louis Wu would
extrapolate the rest. He didn't. Not that bright.*

*Hanuman was brighter than a Hanging People, but he
couldn't see what Tunesmith saw: the right answer, every time.
Louis Wu had chosen Tunesmith. Did that make him bright
enough to trust? The big hairy alien was a youth; he'd have
little to say. The two-headed one was as old as seas and
mountains . . .*

*Probe Two was ready to launch, and Hanuman had his
instructions. But if he survived, he must come to know who
to trust.*

Hydrogen fuel flooded into *Needle*'s tanks.

Tunesmith waved at the tower of rings. 'Bram built
this to launch meteor defense and repair systems. I've
altered it. It will give us higher initial velocity than
our fuel and thrusters would buy. Board *Needle* now,
don pressure suits, strap down. Hindmost, up front
with me. We should launch behind *Probe Two*.'

Now *Hot Needle of Inquiry* was sliding across the lava.
Louis wondered if they'd have to run after the ship, but
Tunesmith led them to a stepping disk that flicked
them aboard. The Hindmost and Tunesmith moved to

the control room; Acolyte and Louis stayed in crew quarters.

While Louis was getting into his suit, *Probe Two* launched in a flare of lightning and was gone into the sky. The launch system was inefficient, Louis thought. Bad for the environment. Tunesmith must have power to throw away.

Needle sank toward the base of the launcher.

Tunesmith was suited up much faster than the others. 'Eat before you close your helmets!' he shouted. 'There's time.' He raced through some diagnostic programs, then began using stepping disks to flick through the ship, stopping to observe, to fiddle. In two or three minutes he was back.

Needle's control cabin had been given place for a copilot. Tunesmith's bolted-in seat was a layer of plates that moved to accommodate him. He glanced around at his crew – in place, webbed down, the Hindmost beside him – and launched.

CHAPTER 6

The Blind Spot

'Another one!' *Forrestier shouted.*

'Tec Roxanny Gauthier looked. In the wall display, what was rising past the edge of the Ringworld was no more than a blurred point. Gray Nurse *was on patrol among the inner comets, far, far away from any Ringworld action.*

Roxanny asked, 'Did you see where it came from?'

'Same as the other. One of the big salt oceans, an island cluster.'

The fighter-recon crews didn't actually know anything. They were watching a wall display relayed from Control. The officers in Control could feed them any data they liked. That didn't stop crewfolk from speculating.

Roxanny said, 'The first one was too small. So's this one. They're not ships, they're just probes.'

'Fast, though. 'Tec Gauthier, what's that?'

That, rising from the same Great Ocean island, was a

larger dot, elongated, moving with the same amazing speed as the probe.

'That's a ship,' Roxanny said. Headquarters would have to respond to that! Gray Nurse herself would not fight. She was a carrier. She was long and slender, built for spin gravity in emergencies, and she carried twenty fighter-recon ships. Roxanny belonged to the crew of the fighter Snail Darter.

Crewfolk numbered about two men for every woman, all between forty and eighty years old. Younger than forty, Command wouldn't trust your reflexes. Older than eighty, why hadn't you been promoted? In Sol system they'd been the best. Here, in this strange place, some were startled to find themselves average.

Roxanny Gauthier was fifty-one, and still one of the best. Lack of action didn't bother her. For two years she'd enjoyed Gray Nurse's modest rec facilities, kept herself in shape, competed ferociously in war simulations, and worked on her education. She enjoyed dominance games. Some of the fighter crew found her intimidating.

The Fringe War couldn't last forever. The forces involved controlled energies that were too powerful. If the Ringworld itself was getting involved, nothing would last much longer.

Gray Nurse came under power. Her nose swung around. The voice of Command – placid, not quite soothing – said, 'All fighter-recon crews, we will be passing through the inner system in fifty to sixty hours. You're on down time until then. Eat, sleep, wash. After you launch, you'll wish you had.'

One or two crewfolk blew raspberries. Gray Nurse *hadn't launched a fighter since their arrival ten months ago.*

Launch was ferocious. Louis heard a whine from the cabin gravity generators, and a planet's mass settled on him and squeezed out all the air. That wasn't supposed to happen! Then

discontinuity

the view jumped, navy blue masked by flame colors around a black disk. The flames died, leaving the sun a deeper black disk on black sky.

He could breathe again.

The ship's wall protected them from unfiltered sunlight by imposing a black patch on the sun. As Louis's eyes adjusted, he could make out stars, and here and there a spear of fusion light. A sudden starship zipped past, an advanced ARM design, too close.

Tunesmith said, 'Sorry. I reworked the stasis field generator. The stasis effect was holding for too long. It would have left us vulnerable, but now it doesn't become active fast enough. I'll fix it. Is everyone all right?'

'We could have been crushed!' the Hindmost whimpered.

'Where is Hanuman?' Acolyte asked.

A virtual window appeared, and zoomed. 'There, ahead of us.'

The Fringe War was starting to notice Hanuman's tiny ship and the larger craft following four minutes behind. Tunesmith jigged and jogged to avoid dangers unseen. Ahead of them, Hanuman's *Probe Two* was jittering all over the sky. The black patch that covered the sun was expanding.

Tunesmith used the thrusters for a sustained surge; veered in the midst of the burn. The forward view went black, then cleared.

Probe Two was gone.

Louis had never had a chance to know the little protector. He asked, 'Now, what did that accomplish, Tunesmith?'

Pyrotechnics sought them out, Fringe War weapons following *Needle*'s jittery path. Tunesmith ignored all that. 'What you've seen buys us nothing yet—'

Probe Two was *back*. It had moved, pulled ahead by a crazy quarter of a million miles. *Tanj dammit, what has Hanuman done?*

Tunesmith said, 'We are constantly testing each other, aren't we, Louis? Let me *show* you what I have learned.'

The puppeteer's orchestral scream drowned out Louis's, 'Wait!' Tunesmith's hands moved.

*   *   *

There was color and flow. Shapes weren't there, just flow patterns of light and a few tiny dark comma shapes.

In the Blind Spot, in hyperdrive, Louis had never been able to see anything.

To go into hyperdrive this close to a sun was insane, but Hanuman's *Probe Two* had done it anyway. And somehow popped out again. And Tunesmith was about to do that too! They screamed at him but he did it. He went into hyperdrive while too close to a sun.

Born and raised on the Map of Earth, Acolyte hadn't even guessed the danger. Launch must have been scary enough. In this nightmare of scrambled light and dark darting commas, he was only drawing breath to roar when they were out again.

Stars. The singularity hadn't eaten them, it had spit them out. Louis looked around, savoring his ability to see. Close behind him was a black half-moon rimmed in fire: the sun chopped in half.

Hyperdrive gone wrong might, in theory, take them anywhere. Louis had not expected to see a black arc of Ringworld eclipsing half the sun – out of all the quintillions of suns in the universe, he had not thought he would still be next to *this* one – but it was there.

Tunesmith said, 'Hindmost . . . no? Louis, then. Will you tell me if that was the Blind Spot your histories speak of?'

Louis said, 'The Blind Spot is what you don't see in hyperspace. If you try to look through a window, you're blind. You can only see what's inside the cabin. It's why most pilots use paint and curtains to cover up a General Products' hull. There are freaks, though, people and other LEs who can at least use a mass detector without going nuts. I can do that. Hindmost?' The puppeteer was in footstool mode. 'Acolyte?'

The Kzin said, 'Tunesmith, if you can't see while flying in hyperspace, this will be a fun ride.'

'But that's not the point!' Louis tried to explain the obvious. 'Ships just disappear if they drop into hyperspace too near a big mass. The space is too warped. What happened? We should be dead, or somewhere else in the universe, or in some other universe. Why aren't we? We're still in Ringworld system!'

Tunesmith said, 'I found no convincing theory anywhere in the records. I must evolve one. "Hyperspace" is a false term, Louis. The universe accessed through the Outsider drive corresponds to our own Einstein universe, point-to-point, but there are fixed velocities, quantized.

'You're aware that you can map any part of a mathematical domain onto the whole domain? For every point in one domain, you can place a unique point in the other. I thought the relationship here might be point-to-point except that space warped by nearby masses isn't represented. A ship that tried what Hanuman tried would go nowhere. Then I thought of an alternate model. We'll have to look at the recordings

to know if I'm right, but after all, Hanuman *did* get
in and back out— Excuse me,' Tunesmith said, and
turned to his controls.

Hot Needle of Inquiry began to dodge.

The war wasn't letting them through.
Thermonuclear fireworks bloomed outside the ship. The
ship surged, and protective blackness washed across the
walls.

Louis's inclination was to beat Tunesmith over the
head with something heavy until he talked, but that
would not be prudent while he was flying them through
a firestorm.

Tunesmith said, 'Notice that we didn't travel far in
hyperdrive. Hanuman didn't either. A light year in
three days is characteristic of mass-free space. This close
to a star's mass, space isn't flat. I'm not sure we even
exceeded lightspeed.

'We launched at point one C. We'll be among the
comets in a few hours. We can safely use hyperdrive
then. Hindmost, will you take the controls?'

One head poked above the jeweled mane. 'No.'

'Then get into ship's memory and summon up what
information we collected.'

A mass pointer can't record, because the user's mind is
a necessary component. Tunesmith had built something
better, something that took pictures in hyperdrive.

A virtual screen showed the streaming colors Louis remembered, and a deep violet dot expanding into a tadpole shape. Tunesmith said, 'This explains why we didn't travel far. Too close to the sun's mass—'

'Inside the singularity,' Louis said.

'Louis, I don't think there's a mathematical singularity here at all. I found reference to a mass pointer in the Hindmost's library. Have you used a mass pointer?'

'There's one in front of you. It only works in hyperdrive.'

'This?' A crystal sphere, inert now. 'What do you think you see with it?'

'Stars.'

'Starlight?'

'. . . No. A mass pointer is a psionics device. You perceive, but it's not with your usual senses. Stars look bigger than they should, as if you're seeing a whole solar system.'

'You've been perceiving *this*.' Tunesmith waved into a recorded view of neon paint streaming through oil. 'Dark matter. The missing mass. Instruments in Einstein space can't find it, but it huddles close around suns in this other domain you've been calling hyperspace. Dark matter makes galaxies more massive, changes their spin—'

'We rammed through that?'

'Wrong picture, Louis. My instruments didn't record *any* resistance. We'll test that later. It might have been different if *this* had reached us.' A deep violet comma-shaped shadow. 'We find life everywhere we look in this universe. Would it be surprising if an ecology has grown up within dark matter? And predators?'

Maybe Tunesmith *was* mad. Louis asked, 'Are you suggesting that ships that use hyperdrive near a star are *eaten?*'

Tunesmith said, 'Yes.'

Crazy. But . . . the Hindmost continued his work with the recordings and *Needle*'s instruments. He hadn't flinched at the notion of predators eating spacecraft.

The puppeteer already knew.

'I only held us in hyperdrive for a moment,' Tunesmith said, 'but these hypothetical predators only have one speed, Louis, and it's *fast*. "Singularity" is a mathematical term. Certainly there are mathematics involved, but they may be more complex than just places where an equation gives infinities. Inside this morass of dark matter, the characteristic speed may be drastically lowered. The proof is that we live.'

'We are being observed,' the Hindmost said. 'I sense ranging beams from ARM and Patriarchy telescopes and neutrino detectors. Ships begin to accelerate inward. The ship from Sheathclaws houses telepaths of both species, though they can't reach us yet. I've found the comet cluster that hides the Kzinti flagship *Diplomat*. It's across the solar system, seven light-hours away and receding behind us. Tunesmith, do you have a plan?'

The Ghoul protector said, 'I have the simple part. We will observe the Fringe War as we coast outward. Let our velocity carry us beyond the danger zone, the dark matter zone where predators lurk. Then swing around the system in hyperdrive. Approach *Diplomat* from the other side of the system. Await developments.'

Hours passed. The Fringe War made no further test of *Needle*'s defenses. When the sun was only a bright point and the Ringworld was barely more than that, Tunesmith asked, 'Hindmost, can you perceive hyperspace directly?'

'Yes.'

'I can't. But if you can't fly for terror, I must fly *Needle*.'

The puppeteer uncoiled. He took *Needle*'s controls. 'Where shall I fly?'

'Take us ten light-minutes outward from *Diplomat*'s last position.'

Human beings can't look into the Blind Spot. Most would go mad. Some can use a mass pointer to steer through hyperspace and keep their sanity too. Some Kzinti can perceive hyperspace directly; their female kin have mated into the family of the Patriarch for half a thousand years.

This time there was nothing. Not darkness, not featureless gray, not even the memory of sight. Louis fumbled until he could opaque the hull in crew quarters.

Acolyte said, 'I don't know enough to ask intelligent questions, Louis.'

'We're okay. I understand this. This is hyperdrive the way I'm used to seeing it. We're outside the . . . borderline,' Louis said. 'Even if I have to unlearn everything I know.'

All his life he'd thought in terms of a mathematical singularity. In such a system, the realm of heavy masses – suns and planets – would be undefined in hyperspace. Ships couldn't go there.

'What we're doing is a standard maneuver. We have a velocity, right? We were flung up from the Ringworld, toward the sun and past it and outward. We still have that huge velocity, straight out from the sun.

'But the Hindmost is taking us halfway around the system in hyperdrive. When he comes out, we'll have the same velocity we started with, but pointed back toward the sun and the Ringworld.'

'We're out,' the Hindmost said. They were in black space with one overbright star. They'd been in hyperdrive about five minutes.

The Hindmost said, 'The Fringe War doesn't

normally reach this far out. We're safe for the moment. Our velocity vector `is inward, toward *Diplomat*. We should act within ten minutes, before *Diplomat* can see our neutrino wake and Cherenkov radiation.'

'Get me a view,' Tunesmith ordered.

Ten light-minutes is further than the distance between Earth and Sol. The virtual window popped up, and zoomed, and wiggled a loose-packed comet out of the starscape, and zoomed . . .

A lens of steel and glass was the Kzinti command ship *Diplomat* emerging from its cometary nest.

That larger sphere just popping into view was *Long Shot*, close and closing.

Tunesmith barely glanced at the view. 'They'll be a few minutes matching. We have time. Hindmost, show us what we recorded in this last hyperdrive jump.'

The hypercamera's record was blank. Louis snickered.

Tunesmith reproved him. 'Louis, there's nothing to see. We're outside the envelope of dark matter that collects around our star. Where there almost isn't any dark matter, there almost isn't space either! This is why we can travel faster than light does in vacuum, because distance in this domain is drastically contracted.

'Now I need only learn why there is more than one characteristic velocity. I'll get that by studying *Long Shot*. Hindmost, take us in range of *Diplomat*.'

'Two fighting ships guard the near side of the comet.'

'I see them. Use hyperdrive. We'll beat our own light.'

The Blind Spot flashed for only an instant.

Their target was still too far away to see, but the virtual window nailed it: a loose dark fluffy comet, icy puffball satellites drifting around it, and four ships, two linked. Tunesmith's knotty hands danced. *Needle* surged: the cabin gravity motors were whining again. The larger ships, *Diplomat* and *Long Shot* locked together at the airlocks, were coming up fast. Slowing. Slowing.

'I'm taking the controls,' Tunesmith said.

Diplomat fired lasers: crew quarters went black.

The virtual window was looking at something other than light. A flock of dim points was coming at them. *Needle* didn't have rocket motors; Tunesmith was using only the sluggish thrusters. Now the virtual window disappeared, and the hull was slapped sideways, then backward.

Louis just had time to realize that they were mated. Then *Needle*'s cabin gravity surged uneasily while the generators whined. Three ships, locked together, tried to turn round their common center of mass.

Diplomat ripped loose, tumbling, dwindling.

Hot Needle of Inquiry was using full thrust to push *Long Shot*. *Needle*'s overbuilt thrusters against *Long Shot*'s sizeable mass would give, what, around ten gravities? And *Long Shot* hadn't had cabin gravity when Louis flew it. In all that packed space there hadn't been room for extra machinery, or so he had assumed. Ten gravities would flatten any Kzinti aboard, knock them out or kill them.

Diplomat, the Kzinti command ship, fired a cloud of missiles, then disappeared in a black-cored fireball.

The missiles twinkled. Tunesmith was exercising his marksmanship. The warrior ships didn't fire – for fear of harming *Long Shot*? Tunesmith exploded the ship that tried to take up escort. The other fell behind.

A *ship carrying antimatter is very vulnerable*, Louis thought. Was that reassuring, or just scary?

Needle's thrust died. Tunesmith was out of his seat shouting, 'Lander bay!' He reached a stepping disk and was gone.

Acolyte followed before Louis could quite get moving. The wall had become a window again, and *Long Shot* was a planet jammed against *Needle*'s hull, with the cabin right up against *Needle*'s new airlock, the view blocked by bronze 'glue'. Louis was out of his web, weapon in hand, running for the stepping disk. He saw Tunesmith race through the hangar, dive into the airlock, look, open the second door, leap, with Acolyte right behind. Then Louis flicked into the hangar.

He was ten feet behind Acolyte, moving at a dead run, leaning forward because he was about to enter free fall, a laser weapon in one hand. *Pirate!* he thought, elated, expecting no real resistance.

But light sputtered where Tunesmith disappeared. Acolyte stopped suddenly, then leapt out of sight.

In free fall now, Louis dug his feet into the wall and jumped behind his extended weapon.

Generated gravity slammed him to the floor.

That was confusing, if he'd had time to think about it. *Long Shot* hadn't had gravity generators.

Long Shot's life support system was only the pilot's cramped cabin and a cramped sleep-and-rec room above it, now occupied by Tunesmith and three Kzinti. Two Kzinti were sprawled in pools of orange blood, chopped and seared and dead. A third was fluffed out like a yellow-and-black cloud with teeth. Louis held his aim on that one until he was sure it was Acolyte.

Tunesmith's voice spoke in Louis's helmet. 'Time presses. Louis, take your place as pilot. Acolyte, return to *Needle*. Hindmost, go with him. You have your instructions.'

Louis wriggled past Acolyte and took the pilot's chair.

Acolyte pushed the dead Patriarchy warriors into the recreation space. He sprang toward the airlock. The puppeteer had gone ahead of him.

Tunesmith's communicator voice followed them. 'Hindmost, what does it mean if we found cabin gravity aboard *Long Shot*?'

Silence.

'Hindmost!'

The puppeteer was reluctant, but he spoke. 'It suggests that the Patriarchy has solved some of our secrets. Some of what we packed *Long Shot* with was data-collecting instruments. Some was mere misdirection. The Patriarch's science team must have learned how much superfluous space is there. They've used it to install a cabin gravity generator and who knows what else. What would human or Kzinti warriors do with so fast a ship if they knew there was extra space for thrusters, fighter ships, and weapons? Tunesmith, if you can't imagine that, ask Louis.'

'Louis?'

'Just be glad this ship is ours again,' Louis said. He studied *Long Shot*'s control system. A crude second control panel had been set beside the first. All the indicators had been reworked in Kzinti dots-and-commas.

Gravity rolled uneasily. They were in motion, and *Long Shot*'s cabin gravity generator wasn't happy with the unbalanced configuration.

Tunesmith was behind Louis's shoulder, his jaw against Louis's neck. 'Can you fly it?'

'Yah,' Louis said. 'I may have to close my eyes—'

'Do you read the Heroes' Tongue?'

'No.'

'I do. Make room. Join your companions aboard *Needle*.'

'I can fly *Long Shot*. I remember the controls.'

'They've been changed. Go!'

'Can you fly this ship?'

'I must try. Go.'

When Louis entered *Needle*'s hangar, Acolyte was already gone.

Louis took a moment to contain his fury. Typical of a protector, to bet his own life and everybody else's on his own not-yet-formed abilities, on nebulous theories, on risks Louis wouldn't have taken even in his teens and twenties. But that wasn't enough. He'd bet Louis Wu's life because he might need him . . . and now he didn't. What the futz, just another gamble that hadn't paid off.

Inhale through the nose, hold it, flatten that abdomen, exhale . . . it felt remarkably good to be back in his teens and twenties. Lovely if he could live through it.

Needle lurched and separated from *Long Shot*.

Louis found the hidden stepping disk and flicked to crew quarters. Acolyte was there. The Hindmost was on the flight deck, his back to them. He said, 'We must make our way separately. Louis, Acolyte, strap down.'

Acolyte said, 'I was to be copilot.'

'Plans change,' the Hindmost said without turning around.

Louis didn't even wonder how the Hindmost had gained control of the bronze 'glue' that linked the hulls.

Tunesmith didn't hesitate either. From *Long Shot* he said, 'As you will, Hindmost. Your enemies in this part of space include every ARM and Patriarchy ship and very likely all strangers. I've sheathed *Needle*'s hull in scrith, giving two layers of defense, but antimatter is still a danger. Make your way to the Map of Mars as best you can.'

The Hindmost didn't answer. *Hot Needle of Inquiry* turned toward interstellar space.

CHAPTER 7

End Run

Acolyte asked, 'Louis, are we pointed the wrong way?'

Four fusion rocket motors glowed blue on *Long Shot*, grown tiny now. The great ship didn't have much acceleration, and that was all fusion flame, conspicuous against a sky full of enemies.

Would the ARM, would the Patriarchy, try to destroy *Long Shot*? Not while there was a ghost of a hope of capturing it. The Quantum II hyperdrive was just too valuable, Louis thought. Unless another faction looked ready to make a capture. Then what?

How could the protector expect to hide the great ship? A mile in diameter . . . but that was tiny against the scale of deep space.

But none of Tunesmith's problems had any relevance to what the Hindmost was doing: turning toward interstellar space, toward his home.

Louis hadn't answered at once. Acolyte said, 'My father often assumes that I know things I don't. He learned them too early. They must seem obvious. Spherical geometry, centrifugal force, seasons, the way light falls across a Ball World—'

'He's trying to escape,' Louis said.

'Escape?'

The Hindmost was certainly able to listen, and Tunesmith might hear this too, but what did Louis have to hide? 'The Hindmost has an intact spacecraft now,' he said. 'He sees the Ringworld as fragile. It makes him feel trapped. Now he's out. He'll run for the Fleet of Worlds . . . the Ball Worlds where the puppeteers live.'

'Then I am kidnapped! *Hindmost*!'

The puppeteer didn't answer.

'I'm kidnapped too. Relax,' Louis said. 'We have time. This ship couldn't reach human space in less than two years. Even the Fleet of Worlds is months away. We've got time to think.'

'Louis, what will you do when you finish teaching me patience?'

Louis smiled. 'Mount you as a statue in your father's palace.' It was their private joke.

So, the Fleet of Worlds might be the Hindmost's target. Then again, Fleet of Worlds politics had ousted him from the supreme position . . . years ago, but puppeteers thought in much greater time spans.

The Hindmost might not be welcome among his own kind.

One could hope.

As for Louis Wu, the United Nations wanted him for holding proprietary knowledge . . . for the crime of knowing too much. The UN held great power among the worlds of human space. Still, they didn't rule everywhere. Their rule only included the Earth and Moon – and all targets which might threaten that domain.

The Hindmost had found Louis Wu on Canyon and snatched him away, some fifteen years ago. The local government or the ARM would have claimed his possessions there. His homes on Earth were forfeit. So. Where? There *had* to be a place of safety.

He hadn't really seen this day coming.

Louis said, 'I'll have to be persuasive. Maybe I can get the Hindmost to drop us somewhere in human space. Then I'll find a way to get you home. I'll show you some of human space first. Could be fun.'

'Why human space? Take us to the Patriarchy! Let *me* guide *you*.'

Louis had been an interspecies hero, briefly, when they brought back *Long Shot*. He said, 'I've been in the Patriarch's palace and hunting park. Have you?'

'Guide me then. Show me where my father grew up.'

'I'm afraid to go there. I could show you recordings I made, if I could get to Earth or Canyon . . . but even that's too risky.' Even in a daydream, the ARM would have claimed his possessions. 'But I could read up on the Fringe War before we come back here. Tunesmith doesn't know enough. Maybe nobody does. It'll be like the War of the Roses, or the Vietnam War, or Avenge Mecca: it could last forever. Nobody knows how to turn off a war.'

'Stet, take me to human space. Will they grant me my place, my rights?'

Louis laughed. 'No. Stick to Interspeak, the way Chmeee and I taught it to you. We'll claim you're from Sheathclaws or Fafnir, grown up in a Kzin-and-human community. They'd *expect* you to be a little strange. Tanj, why haven't we moved? *Hindmost!*'

Long Shot was lost in starscape and sunglare, and *Needle* wasn't doing anything at all.

Louis shouted, 'Do *something*, Hindmost!'

The puppeteer squawked. Then, tonelessly, 'Louis. Acolyte. The carrion eater has disabled my hyperdrive motor.'

Louis had nothing to say.

The puppeteer said, 'I could have circled in hyperspace to hide my point of return into Ringworld system! Now every telescope in the system will be watching while I try to reach safety. We'll be under fire for . . . two days as a most optimistic estimate. Tunesmith has much to answer for.'

'You would have run,' Louis said.

The puppeteer snorted an orchestral dischord. *Needle* swung about.

Clouds of missiles and a score of ships began drifting in from the comets an hour after the Hindmost started his run. They watched it all coming while *Needle* accelerated toward the sun.

The Hindmost remained on the flight deck. Acolyte and Louis were sealed in their own quarters. They talked of this, voices low, as if they couldn't be heard that way.

Louis watched the Fringe War coming.

The faster missiles weren't a danger. Nothing with high thrust would carry antimatter. You couldn't risk antimatter jarring against its containment. Some ships, particularly those elongated ARM ships, might carry antimatter bullets and a linear motor to fire them, but those ships would be slow, too slow to catch *Needle*.

Tracking *Long Shot* gave the invaders no problem at all. The mile-wide sphere was conspicuous and undefended.

On the second day missiles began to arrive. Most of them gathered in a cloud around *Long Shot*.

Tunesmith had added a laser turret to *Needle*. The Hindmost shot down the few scores of missiles that sought *Needle* out. The sun grew large. Louis wondered if more ships waited in the inner system.

'Shouldn't we be making turnaround, Hindmost?'

'That's just what they'll be expecting,' the puppeteer said.

Louis wondered what the puppeteer intended. Then, looking ahead, he knew.

How dangerous could it be? Puppeteers are cowards, right? Louis Wu couldn't show fear before a Kzin. Better if he could persuade himself that he was having fun. *It's a ride!*

But the Hindmost was more afraid of his pursuers than of what he was doing.

Louis took a moment to consider his words. Then, 'Hindmost, everything new about *Needle*, even the hyperdrive, has been built or rebuilt by Tunesmith and never tested afterward. Do you still trust it all? Even the stasis field?'

'I must,' the Hindmost said. 'Out here I'm prey. Any creature with a telescope might have seen our attack on *Long Shot*. Are we a mere diversion? Will Tunesmith throw our lives away for misdirection? Louis, he is your kind more than mine!'

Being asked for his opinion of Tunesmith, Louis gave it. 'Don't trust him. Take your best shot. Assume he reacts very fast.'

'Even if we can reach the Ringworld, I'm still his prisoner,' the Hindmost said. 'But I will not accept that. I will not. I tire of being put at risk for purposes I don't understand.'

'*Tell* me about it.'

* * *

Hot Needle of Inquiry had picked up considerable velocity and was still accelerating as it passed the rim wall. As it did, ships lifted from the Ringworld's black underside. Then *Needle* was inside the Ringworld's arc in a glare of sunlight and a halo of thousands of tiny probes.

Louis heard a howl to melt bones and a rhythmic thudding sound, but he didn't walk around the kitchen wall to see. It was just Acolyte attacking a wall, getting some exercise.

The ship was jigging and jogging across the sky, but only the jittery starscape showed that. *Needle* had tremendous acceleration, but its cabin gravity was up to the challenge. Then again, so were the probes. Nothing was attacking *Needle*, but every species wanted to look.

What would they see? A #3 General Products hull, puppeteer made, and a puppeteer in the command section. *Needle* should be safe. Most LEs wanted to avoid frightening a puppeteer.

The black spot that hid the sun was growing larger. It was going to be a hell of a ride.

A sudden glare blinked white-black. Acolyte asked, sarcastically, 'Missiles don't carry antimatter?'

'Maybe it's a ship hit by an antimatter bullet. The light looked right. I'm guessing, of course. Hindmost, keep dodging.'

The puppeteer's voice sang, 'As opposed to *what*? Distract yourself. What if they kill Tunesmith? Will you choose another protector? Or choose none?'

'How's he doing?'

The Hindmost popped up a virtual window.

Shoals of missiles and ships were converging in a shell around the mile-wide crystal sphere. Lasers and bombs sparkled among them. Against all sense, a ship had fired on *Long Shot*, and now others were firing too. The sphere turned, bright-dark-bright in laser light, its four archaic rocket motors flaring.

Then *Long Shot* was gone.

'Dodged into hyperspace,' Louis said. 'Crazy bastard. He'll lose them if he didn't get himself eaten.'

'What will you do if Tunesmith is dead?' the Hindmost persisted.

'There's too much tree-of-life around. I have to do something,' Louis said. 'Otherwise the protectors on the rim wall will take over everything. *That's* no good. They're evolved too far out of the mainstream of hominid development, and they don't know enough. Hindmost, a Ghoul is still the best choice. They live a jackal lifestyle. Whatever lives is theirs eventually. They do best for their own kind by making life better and safer for everyone. Aside from that, their heliograph system is wonderful. We need it.'

The Hindmost said, 'Tunesmith is arrogant and manipulative.'

The black blotch covering the sun expanded and swallowed them.

discontinuity

CHAPTER 8

Try an Anti-matter Bomb

For two days Gray Nurse had been accelerating, then merely falling toward the sun and the Ringworld. The carrier would whip past the rim wall in a few hours. In that moment there would be an option. A linear motor ran the length of Gray Nurse's hull. Fighter-lurker ships could be backfired into range of the Ringworld itself.

The crews waited.

Whatever had gone on in that Kzinti-held patch of comets and vacuum, it took place far above Gray Nurse, half-hidden in a fog of ice crystals. Fighter crews could speculate, of course. Explorer probes were on their way to do forensic work. Meanwhile the attackers were in view and running.

'The little one is a GP hull,' 'Tec-Two Claus Raschid said. 'Might be anyone.'

'Anyone but puppeteers,' Roxanny said. 'They'd never have the nerve.'

'But the big, slow one, that's Long Shot.'

The rest of the Fringe War had taken notice. Both ships were now surrounded by probes from half a dozen civilizations. Feeds were shown on the common-room monitors. A Pierson's puppeteer was at the helm of the GP#3 ship. Long Shot's pilot looked like a man.

'Long Shot's ours,' Claus said. 'This might be our chance to get it back.'

The crewfolk watched the feeds. A sudden burst of firepower surrounded Long Shot — threatening an experimental ship of inestimable value — and Roxanny smiled at their cursing. Her smile slipped and the cursing stopped when the crystal sphere simply disappeared.

The voice of Command spoke at last. 'Board your ships! All fighter crews board your ships now!'

Gone like a soap bubble, Roxanny thought. How? But she was scurrying along the corridor toward her station, flinching from burly hot shots who thought they could fly in these narrow confines.

Her station was Snail Darter. She crawled through the lock and took her assigned seat. Claus Raschid followed her through. The third crewman— 'Where's Forrestier?' she rapped.

'Tec Oliver Forrestier swung in and took his place. The three were back to back, looking into their wall displays. Oliver asked, 'Think they'll launch us this time?'

Roxanny Gauthier grinned. She liked this: herself and two males in an environment that couldn't possibly rid the air of all pheromones, in conditions too cramped to do anything beyond flirting. Claus and Oliver already found her intimidating. 'We'll launch,' she said. 'Depending on what those ships do, we could see the Ringworld close up. We might even get down to the surface. Gird up thy loins, Legal Entities! We are going in.'

The ship jerked, and Louis jerked too, as everything around them shifted. *Needle* was out of stasis.

Views to the side showed fearsome coronas above a black horizon of blocked-out sun. Aft was only black: the sun, receding.

Louis couldn't see what the Hindmost's cabin displays saw. *Good.* If he could see graphs and false-color representations, he would *feel* the hull temperature rising. There was that about Pierson's puppeteers: they never ignored danger, never pretended it wasn't there. Never turned their backs on a threat except to kick.

Ahead, arcs of glowing coronal gas streamed past. The stars were hidden in a ruby glare that might actually be *Needle*'s invisible hull giving off black body radiation.

The ships of the Fringe War . . . were not to be seen. The puppeteer had lost their pursuers by aerobraking his ship through the sun.

They were already nearing the ring of huge rectangles that cast shadows of night across the Ringworld. The Hindmost drifted his ship behind a shadow square, then boosted to some ferocious acceleration and ran for it.

Louis wondered idly if Tunesmith had turned off the meteor defense. Once before, the meteor defense had fired on Louis. *Lying Bastard* in stasis had smashed into the Ringworld floor and plowed a furrow across the land. They'd survived without a bruise . . . but this time Tunesmith had futzed the timing on their stasis field.

This time the Ringworld's sun-powered superthermal laser didn't fire, or didn't fire quick enough to catch *Needle.*

But the Fringe War found them. 'We're being followed,' Acolyte said.

The Hindmost sang, 'I'll lose them. Don't distract me.'

The Ringworld came up like a vast fly swatter. *Needle* dove straight toward a long strip of nightbound land. Louis could see the Other Ocean almost below, a vast diamond dotted with clusters of islands, easing off to the side as *Needle* came down. The Hindmost aimed at lightning-lit cloud laid out like a flattened hourglass in a pattern several times larger than the Earth.

An eyestorm is the visible sign of a puncture in the Ringworld floor.

It's the Ringworld equivalent of the hurricanes and tornados that form on planets. Air draining through the puncture produces a partial vacuum. Air flowing from spinward slows against its spin velocity; it weighs less; it wants to rise. Air from antispinward speeds up, grows heavier, wants to sink. From overhead the pattern is a sketchy flattened hourglass with a puncture at the throat. From port or starboard the storm takes the appearance of an eye, upper lid and lower lid and a horizontal tornado whorl in the center, and perhaps an eyebrow of high cirrus.

A Ringworld protector, Tunesmith or Bram before him, would have filled in any large puncture by now. Lost air is hard to replace. The meteor crater at the heart of this storm would be a small one, and old: these storms took generations to form.

The Hindmost dove toward the whirling throat of the hourglass, slowing hard, with one large and two smaller ships still in his wake. Then *Needle* plunged into the black whirlwind as if in suicidal frenzy, and out. Out through the meteor crater into black interstellar space, looping hard around and up. The Hindmost fired a laser at the Ringworld's black underside. A ruby glare lit an array of spillpipes broken by another ancient meteor.

Have to tell Tunesmith, Louis thought. *The Ringworld is wearing out. It's losing air and water. Everything needs repairs, underside, rim walls, landscape. Yah, in our copious free time.*

They were driving through a plume of ice crystals now. A block of frozen seawater was being boiled away. Acolyte suddenly demanded, 'Louis, stop saying that!'

'Sorry.'

'I know what "It's a ride" means. Billions of your kind pay a sum for the privilege of being scared out of their wits under conditions of assured safety. A hero must risk real danger!'

'You did that when we fought Bram. *Here* we go,' as *Needle* surged upward. *It's not a death trap. It's a ride.*

The foamy black sea ice was nearly boiled away. *Needle* rammed up through a smashed drainhole, through a last barrier of ice, and into the sea above.

Hot Needle of Inquiry settled through black water and came to rest.

'And here the ship may stay,' the Hindmost said. He popped up the lip of a stepping disk and went to work on its controls.

Louis asked, 'How much of this were you expecting?'

'Contingencies,' the Hindmost said. 'If Tunesmith ever gave me a chance to move *Needle*, I'd need a place to hide it. Here, Louis, this link leads to the Repair Center. The stepping disk network is open to us.'

Acolyte's ears were up. He watched them like a tennis match.

Louis thought it through. The ocean around them would drain until an ice plug formed. Tunesmith could find them by the plume of water vapor, if he had the leisure. But *Long Shot* was slow in normal space, and if hyperdrive near a star was no longer sure death, it was still tanj dangerous. Tunesmith and *Long Shot* would be hunted across the sky for days yet.

So *Hot Needle of Inquiry* was . . . 'Hindmost, you can't *hide* the ship.'

'I have.'

'We need access to *Needle* for food, beds, showers, pressure suits. We need a stepping-disk link, and that's all Tunesmith needs too.'

'I can hide its location, Louis.'

The Hindmost was searching for the illusion of control. It seemed futile, but hey, Louis was doing the same. 'Think now,' Louis said. 'While Tunesmith is watching *Hot Needle of Inquiry*, why don't we steal *Long Shot*?'

'How?'

'I have no idea. But I'm tired of being run around like a marionette *by him or you*, Hindmost. There has to be some way out of this box!'

'While Tunesmith is occupied, we might yet have a day or two to accomplish something.'

They flicked to the Meteor Defense Room.

Daylight had swept across the eyestorm. Louis was looking across a hundred and ninety million miles, past the rim of the sun and the black edges of shadow squares.

Silver knots and threads still marked rivers, lakes, seas; but time and a puncture wound had desiccated this land. Three ships dodged and weaved in and out of a flattened hourglass made of storm. These must be the ships that had followed *Needle* down. The big ship was Kzinti, and the smallest was an ARM fighter, and the third was ARM too. They'd be able to detect each other through cloud, as anyone could given deep-radar.

Lightning flickered sporadically in the constriction, but a sudden sputter was too bright to be lightning.

'The trouble with an antimatter bullet,' Louis surmised, 'is that the crew will use any excuse to get it off the ship.'

Both ARM ships were chasing the Kzin ship. The Kzin dove back into cloud. Louis could track its deep-radar shadow through the axis of the eyestorm, one ARM ship in its wake, one darting ahead through open air. Then the Kzin ship was gone, down through the drainhole and out.

Two ARM ships now commanded perhaps a trillion square miles of Ringworld. They spent the next several hours quartering the area, returning every so often to the eyestorm.

'Guarding the puncture against entry,' the Hindmost suggested. 'You and Chmeee blurted that secret to all of known space, didn't you, Louis? Enter and leave the Ringworld through any meteor puncture. Otherwise face a solar-pumped superthermal laser meteor defense.'

'If they find *Needle*,' Louis said, 'they'll have access to the stepping-disk network. Hindmost, is that technology easy to copy? The United Nations never had the chance. It's a lot more advanced than transfer booths.'

The Hindmost didn't answer, of course.

Louis found himself staring at the display of the Other Ocean. The vast expanse of water and land looked like tapestry on a castle wall. Clusters of islands . . . continents; they'd be that big, as big as the maps in the Great Ocean, one of which was a one-to-one scale map of Earth. These were more thickly clustered, and they seemed all identical.

'Hindmost, was the Ringworld built by Pak?'

'I don't know, Louis.'

'I thought you might, by now. I wondered if there might be real Pak, somewhere among all these variant hominids. We've never seen anything of Pak but old bones.'

The puppeteer said, 'We can deduce a good deal about Pak breeders. They slept or hid during the day and night. They hunted and did their business at twilight. They lived above a shoreline.'

Louis was startled. 'How can you know all that?'

'Your partial baldness suggests that your ancestors swam regularly, and I've watched you in the water, too. As for twilight, this Ringworld gets far more twilight than a planet would, and it's wholly unnecessary. Let me show you.'

The Hindmost boarded a chair, clumsily. His questing mouth found controls. The wall display jumped, became a featureless blue. The Hindmost began to draw in white lines. A blob of white: the sun. A circle: the Ringworld. A much smaller ring, concentric: thirty-odd shadow squares moving a little faster than orbit, held in a net of cables. 'This is the way the Ringworld was designed,' the Hindmost said. 'A thirty hour day with ten hours blacked out, and more than an hour of a sun partly blocked. Instead—'

He sketched in five long shadow squares sliding retrograde, against the Ringworld's spin. 'This model would avoid the long, long twilight period and give equal day and night. The builders didn't want that. Whoever built the Ringworld must have wanted endless summers and long twilights. We surmise they were Pak protectors, and we surmise that the Pak world was like that.'

Louis studied the picture. *Or else*, he thought, *they built an advanced model somewhere else.*

The Hindmost said, 'I'm hungry. Will you keep watch?'

'Hungry,' the Kzin agreed. 'Hurry.'

Time had slid by unnoticed. Louis realized he was half starved.

A puppeteer must eat more often than a carnivore. The Hindmost was gone for most of an hour. He returned with jewels sparkling in a newly coifed mane. A float plate heaped with fodder followed him.

'We'll regret the time we're wasting,' he said. 'Our last hours free from Tunesmith, but what can we do with them? My plans didn't reach far enough. Look, more warships.'

Three Kzinti, then an unfamiliar larger craft, then three more ARM ships danced around the inner ring of shadow squares, not firing yet.

Louis said, 'Acolyte, go feed yourself.' Who wants to be around a hungry Kzin?

Louis and the Hindmost watched the warships at play. 'They won't all have stasis fields,' Louis speculated. 'Stasis fields are expensive and not too dependable, and of course they take a ship out of the action. So they'll be leery of the Ringworld's meteor defense, but Tunesmith turned that off, and they're starting to realize that. So,' as three Kzinti ships began a long dive toward the Ringworld surface, 'here come Kzinti to stop the first ARM ships, and more ARMs to stop *them* – tanj dammit!' A brilliant streak inside the atmosphere ended in a flash against desert.

'That was an antimatter bullet,' said the puppeteer.

'And now it's a little eyestorm. Tanj, this isn't even the main event! What they want is *Long Shot*. *Needle* is nothing.'

'A *Needle* in a haystack? What you describe is mostly your imagination,' said the Hindmost. 'Much of a war goes unseen. That larger ship, I have identified it. Lure of Far Lands Limited, the Kdatlyno and Jinx business alliance. They won't fight, they will only observe. Here is Acolyte. Louis, go eat. Bathe.'

Louis jerked awake. Something had disturbed him . . . a flash of light from the screen?

Acolyte and the Hindmost were asleep, sprawled far apart on the hard floor beneath the Meteor Defense Room walls. It was good to be clean; he'd eaten like an army; sleeping plates would be good too. But anyone who slept aboard *Needle* would miss something.

Louis sat up. Nothing hurt! He grinned, remembering what an older woman had told him at his two hundreth birthday party. 'Dearest, if you can wake in the morning with no pain in your joints and muscles, it's a sure sign that you have died in the night.'

The Hindmost had reset the wraparound screen. It showed a skyscape with windows in it, views of an eyestorm and the Other Ocean. Around the windows stars moved uneasily: ships of the Fringe War. All views were quiet now.

It did bother him, that he couldn't think of anything to do except watch. He was trying to outthink a protector. What chance would he have later if he couldn't find an angle now, while Tunesmith was being hunted across the system?

On the Ringworld were millions of seas. Louis couldn't guess where the Hindmost had put *Hot Needle of Inquiry.* He could get there by a stepping-disk setting. The first pair of ARM ships hadn't found it, and now they were too busy maneuvering. The war above the eyestorm had been quiet for hours, but ships continued to shift position.

Sudden light splashed around the Farland ship: antimatter bullets intercepted in transit. The Farland ship was accelerating away from the action. Its new course would miss the Ringworld. A ruby laser lit it brilliantly, but diffused, its attacker already deep in atmosphere. Ships tens of millions of miles apart had some chance to defend themselves.

But the war above the eyestorm was getting too tight.

Fire burst into the clouds where two ARM ships were hiding. Louis cried, 'Wake up! Wake up! You're missing action!'

The others stirred.

Tunesmith's deep-radar window showed one ARM ship diving through the puncture hole — leaving hard-won turf abandoned, but safeguarding data from its explorations, unless some ambush waited beneath the Ringworld floor. The other accelerated hard, running down the storm's axis in a channel of clear air, the pupil of the eye.

Kzinti had deep-radar too. Two lens ships were diving. Fire followed them down.

The eyestorm flashed to a blue-white glare.

The Hindmost killed the zoom window before it could blind them. On a less expanded view – Tunesmith must have a camera on one of the shadow squares – a star glared near the Other Ocean, as big as . . . too big . . . far too big.

The puppeteer said, 'I believe one of the ARM ships exploded. Antimatter. We'll have a hole the size of . . .' The Hindmost thought it through, then folded into himself and was silent.

The eyestorm was gone, blasted apart. Cloud patterns showed an expanding ring of shock wave crossing seas and gray-green land. A hemisphere of cloud enveloped a dimming fireball.

'What has happened here?'

Tunesmith and the little chimp-protector were on the stepping disk: a sorcerer confronting wayward apprentices, demanding explanations. Louis's throat closed on him. It felt like he should have stopped this. It felt like Tunesmith would, *should* blame him.

'Antimatter explosion,' Acolyte said.

'Is there a hole under that cloud?'

The question was already silly: the dome of cloud was dimpled in the center. It was being sucked into interstellar space. When Acolyte didn't answer, Louis said, 'There was already a hole—'

'Of course. We have to move fast,' Tunesmith said. 'Come.' He had the lip of the stepping disk up and was redirecting it.

Louis found his voice. 'Sure, *now's* a good time to move fast. You've brought the war home! And now the air's draining out of the Ringworld!'

What had been a fireball was nearly gone. The Ringworld floor was naked scrith within a slowly expanding ring of cloud. Clouds streamed toward the hole.

And Tunesmith had Louis by the forearm. He walked them to a stepping disk.

Hanuman's eyes took it all in in one sweep:

He'd bent the laws that governed this universe and a hypothetical other. His mission was a total success. And none of it mattered. The Ringworld held everything worth saving, and the Ringworld floor was ripped open.

The puncture was on the far side of the arch. That was both good and ill. Death would be a long time marching around the curve to reach them here; but Tunesmith's countermeasures would have to cross that same gap.

The aliens saw it too. The most alien was the eldest, the most experienced, perhaps the wisest, and that one had shut down his mind. The hominid had lost hope. The youngest, the nothing-like-a-big-cat, was — like Hanuman — waiting for someone to solve it.

Tunesmith?

Tunesmith was in motion while Hanuman was still catching up. The Ghoul protector showed no doubts. When

*Tunesmith and Louis Wu vanished, the little protector
followed. Tunesmith would fix it.*

Machinery on a Brobdingnagian scale had been moved
into the workstation under Mons Olympus.

Tunesmith dropped Louis's arm and moved among
his instruments at a sprint. The little protector,
Hanuman, scampered after.

Acolyte popped up next to Louis. 'Louis, what's
happening?'

'The air's draining out of the Ringworld.'

'That would be . . . the end of everything?'

'Yah. Starting on the far side. We might have days,
but only because the Ringworld is so endlessly *big*. I
have no idea what Tunesmith thinks he's doing.'

'What is that massive structure? I've seen it—'

Hanuman rejoined them. 'That is a meteor plug,
largest version. Of course it was never tested.'

It was the shape of an aspirin tablet and roughly the
size of the Twin Peaks arcology or a small mountain,
still small compared to the puncture in the Ringworld.
Louis said, 'I remember. It was in one of the caverns.
He set it moving here on big stacks of float plates.'

They watched it slide into the hole in the floor and
fall, guided by magnetic fields toward the base of the
linear launcher. Tunesmith was at the edge, watching.
Louis and Acolyte went to join him.

Forty miles from the roof to the floor of the Repair Center ran the loops of the linear launcher. It was way overbuilt for something as small as *Hot Needle of Inquiry*. It would better accommodate something like this half-mile-wide package of Tunesmith's. The launcher's bottom sat on an array of float plates, and that was moving to adjust its aim.

The package was near the bottom now, still falling, but slowing.

Tunesmith saw them watching. Immediately he hustled them away from the hole in the floor.

Lightning roared at their backs. Louis turned to see something tremendous flash past, out through the crater in Mons Olympus and gone.

Acolyte's ears were curled into tight knots. Hanuman lifted his hands from his ears and said something inaudible. Louis couldn't hear anything. His ears still held the roar and agony of that lightning blast.

Louis didn't lose his deafness for some time. Acolyte recovered much faster. Louis could see the Kzin discussing . . . whatever . . . with Tunesmith and Hanuman while they all followed the action in a wall display of the Meteor Defense Room. The Hindmost remained in footstool mode.

Louis could only watch.

Tunesmith's meteor-plug package drifted toward the

sun. *Needle* had been launched at a tenth of lightspeed; the launch system was capable of that. But over such a distance the package's fall seemed sluggish.

In a zoom window the puncture showed as a black dot on landscape that looked lunar: clear and sharp and barren of water's silver or the dark gray-green of life. Louis guessed the puncture was sixty to seventy miles across. A ring of fog surrounded it, bigger than the Earth and still growing.

The Ringworld was not yet aware of its death. Air and water would flow into the hole and out into vacuum, but first it all had to move . . . from up to three hundred million miles around each arc before the shock could reach the Ringworld's far side, the Great Ocean, *here*. Not much would be lost in a hundred and sixty minutes, while Tunesmith's package crossed the Ringworld's diameter. Even the Other Ocean wouldn't have begun to boil yet.

Hanuman wandered over. He said – loudly, spitting his consonants; it was fun to watch his lips – 'I have been in this state for less than a falan. I still cannot grasp the scale of things. I did not grow up in a universe fifty billion falans old, on a ring spinning around one fleck of light among ten-to-the-twentieth of flecks. There were not that many of anything! My world was small, cozy, easily grasped.'

'You get used to it,' Louis said. He could barely hear himself. 'Hanuman, what is that? What can it do? We're losing our atmosphere!'

'I know little.'

'Share it with me,' Louis demanded.

'Two bright minds with similar goals will solve problems in similar ways. The Vampire protector Bram saw a need to plug meteor holes. His first meteor plugs were small, but his mass driver under Mons Olympus is hundreds of falans old and hugely overbuilt. The Fist-of-God meteoroid impact must have frightened Bram witless.

'Tunesmith builds bigger yet. That package is his biggest effort.' Hanuman was constantly in motion, bouncing around Louis as he spoke, arms swinging. 'We shall see it in action. Tunesmith wants us to observe on site. If there is partial failure, then we must see what must be redesigned.'

'This double-X-large meteor patch, how does it work?'

'I would be guessing.'

'It's never been tested?'

'Tested when? You were stored in the 'doc for less than a falan. Tunesmith made and trained four Hanging People protectors, built a nanotech factory to make bigger meteor plugs, monitored the Fringe War, designed several probe ships, built a stepping-disk factory, redesigned your *Hot Needle of—*'

'He's been busy?'

'He's been crazy as a stingbug hive city! And if the plug doesn't work, it's all for nothing.'

'Do you have children?'

'Yes, and they have children. Since Tunesmith made me, I've not had the chance to count them, nor even to sniff them. Of course they are all forfeit to Tunesmith's schemes and the Fringe War.'

'Aren't we all. Should Tunesmith have taken such a risk?'

'How should I judge?' Hanuman's frantic dance, the hands pounding his chest, would have been an uncontrollable rage in any human. 'Tunesmith implies that the greatest risk was not to act. Louis, how can you remain so still?'

'Fifty years . . . two hundred falans of yoga. I'll teach you.'

'I *must* act,' Hanuman said, 'but not because to be still is wrong. It may be that way with Tunesmith. How can I know? I am enraged with no target.'

The sun's gravity was bending the package's course minutely.

Tunesmith and Acolyte walked over. Tunesmith asked, 'Louis, do you have your hearing back? Have you rested?'

'I slept. Where did you land *Long Shot*?'

'Why would I tell you that?' Tunesmith waved it off. 'You and Acolyte and Hanuman must observe my plug in action. Has Hanuman told you anything?'

'It's a double-X-large-size meteor plug.'

'Good. I have a stepping disk in place—'

'You saw this coming,' Louis said.

'I did.'

'Could you have stopped it?'

'How?'

'Don't steal *Long Shot*?'

'I need to understand the Quantum II hyperdrive. Louis, you must *see* that the Fringe War would never have stayed in the comets. These Ball World species covet the technology that made the Ringworld. It isn't the Ringworld they want to preserve. They want the knowledge, and to keep it from each other.'

Louis nodded. It wasn't a new thought. 'Scrith armor. Cheap fusion plants.'

'Trivia,' Tunesmith said. 'The Ringworld engineers needed motors to spin this structure up. They must have confined a hydrogen mass equivalent to a dozen gas giant Ball Worlds, then fed it all through force fields arrayed to act as hydrogen fusion motors. Your Ball World bandits don't have decent magnetic control, and what they have won't scale up. They might learn something by studying our motors on the rim wall. They would study the Ringworld. They need not preserve it. Am I talking sense?'

'Maybe.'

'Louis, I want you in place to observe the meteor patch as it deploys.'

'Tunesmith, it bothers me to be expendable.'

'I don't use the word, Louis. I don't use the concept.

All life dies, all life resists dying. I would not put you in unneeded danger.'

'Interesting word.'

'I have a stepping disk in place from which you may observe. A sight not to be missed. Hanuman will go. Will you? Acolyte, will you go? Or will you rest here in comfort to learn if all we know has been destroyed?'

Acolyte looked to Louis.

Louis threw up his hands. 'Stet. You want us in pressure suits?'

'With all my heart,' Tunesmith said. 'Use full gear.'

CHAPTER 9

View from a Height

They geared up in *Needle* and flicked from there. The Hindmost wasn't with them. They'd left the puppeteer in a depressed and uncommunicative state.

At lightspeed via stepping disks, they'd arrive ahead of Tunesmith's plug package.

Acolyte wore Chmeee's spare pressure suit, retrieved from *Needle's* stores. He looked like a bunch of grapes. Hanuman, in a skintight suit with a fishbowl helmet, went first. Louis stepped onto the plate.

The bottom dropped out.

Louis hadn't expected free fall. He hadn't expected to be thousands of miles up, either. He snatched at something: Hanuman's hand. Hanuman pulled him to the stepping disk.

The Ringworld, two or three thousand miles below, skimmed past at ferocious speed. It looked infinite in all directions. The rim walls were too distant to show as more than sharp lines.

Acolyte yowled.

Louis didn't dare reach for the thrashing, terrified Kzin. Acolyte's father's spare pressure suit was all balloons, but there were waldo claws on all four limbs. It would have been like reaching into a threshing machine.

'It's all right. You have attitude jets,' Louis shouted. 'Use them when you feel like it.'

The yowling stopped.

Louis's magnetic soles held him down. Hanuman had turned the stepping disk off. Otherwise they'd be back aboard *Needle*.

'Plenty of time, Acolyte,' Louis said. 'We're orbiting the sun.' Louis held his voice calm, soothing. *He's only twelve.* 'Essentially we're standing still, and the Ringworld goes at the usual seven hundred and seventy miles per second, so we'll see the whole thing go under us in seven and a half days. Hanuman—?'

'Eight,' Hanuman said. 'Eight stepping disks are now in orbit. Tunesmith intended more. This was the nearest. I've committed the stepping-disk system to memory. If we need to reach the surface, there's a service stack not too far, but meanwhile we can see it all. Can you pick out the puncture?'

'I don't see it yet.'

'Look antispin.'

'It's *behind* us? Stet, I have it. It looks like a target.' Airless moonscape rimmed with cloud, scored with lines pointing inward toward a black dot.

The land racing below them still had river networks lined with the dark green of life. Through the land a white streak ran to antispin. Louis thought he knew what that was, but it was less urgent than the puncture. 'Acolyte—?'

'I see the wound. I do not see the plug package.'

'I haven't found that either,' Hanuman said. 'Too small. Tunesmith, are you with us?'

'Half hour delay,' Louis reminded him. 'Sixteen minutes each way, lightspeed.' This was a *protector*? But upgraded from an animal. You didn't expect a protector to forget things . . . and Hanuman must be very accustomed to Tunesmith's guidance.

Acolyte bounced against the stepping disk. Magnetic boots clung. He stood uncertainly. 'My father tried to tell me about free fall,' he said. 'I don't think he ever feared it.'

Tunesmith spoke from sixteen minutes in the past. 'I've sent the signal to deploy the double-X-large meteor plug. Tell me what you see, all three of you. Be free to interrupt each other, I can sort your voices.'

A lamp lit above the target.

It didn't look much brighter than a street lamp, but its size . . . Louis squinted past the glare. 'Something unfolding. Tunesmith, it looks like fire salamanders mating . . . or a balloon inflating . . . it's bulking up into a shape like a sailing ship's life preserver. Jets firing at fusion temperatures. What have you got there, Tunesmith?'

Acolyte: 'It's settling. Slowing. A torus. It's much wider than the puncture, a thousand to two thousand klicks across. Was this what you wanted to hear?'

Hanuman: 'The scrith foundation that holds the Ring together demonstrates tremendous tensile strength. I've done the numbers. The forces that hold scrith together would generate showers of quarks if pulled apart. A bag made of such material would be strong enough to confine a hydrogen fusion explosion. There's risk, Tunesmith, but it seems to be holding.'

Acolyte: 'It's settling—'

Louis: '– enclosing the puncture. Leaving the puncture exposed like a bull's-eye on a target. I'm guessing your balloon stands fifty miles tall, so it'll confine the atmosphere as long as it holds.'

Hanuman: 'Tunesmith, how good an insulator is a scrith balloon? We wouldn't see it if it weren't leaking energy. When it cools enough, it'll collapse. Tunesmith, it will leak air. The ground beneath will be uneven.'

Answer came there none. Tunesmith's reaction was a Ringworld diameter away.

So he must have spoken sixteen minutes ago. 'Watch for the second package,' the protector said. 'Tell me if it settles inside the ring.'

Acolyte: 'I don't see anything. Louis? Hanuman?'

Louis: 'There won't be a meteor trail—'

Acolyte: 'Rocket! I see it. Fusion, by its color. Settling slowly at the edge of the hole. It's down.'

Louis: 'We're drifting too far. I can't see the puncture any more.'

Hanuman bent over the rim of the stepping disk. 'I'll fix that. The next stepping disk is thirty degrees around the Ringworld arc. Ready?'

They flicked.

The Ringworld flowed beneath them. They'd jumped thirty degrees, about fifty million miles. Louis, looking ahead of him, found a line of white several worlds wide, and a brighter line peeping above its center. Acolyte said, 'There it is. We can't see detail, Tunesmith. We won't be over it for half a day.'

Louis: 'There's a zoom function in our faceplates. Tunesmith, I don't see any change. Your balloon plug is still inflated. Everything outside the balloon is fog. We've lost a . . . few percent of the Ringworld already.'

Around the edges of the fog, the land would be ravaged by shock waves running through air, sea, earth, and the scrith foundation. Weather patterns would be shattered. . . . Louis realized he was being optimistic. He was assuming that Tunesmith would plug the hole, stop the loss.

He had once estimated the Ringworld's population at thirty trillion, with hominid species in every possible ecological niche. That vast plain of fog would be water droplets condensed by a drop in pressure. Ecologies under that fog blanket would be dehydrated and suffocating. Around it they'd soon be ravaged by climate change.

But only if Tunesmith made a miracle.

'I think a ship in stasis crashed to antispin of the puncture,' Louis said. 'I can't see it from here.'

Hanuman said, 'We won't be over it for half a day. I'm going to flick us home.'

A moment later – plus a quarter hour – they were aboard *Needle*.

Moments afterward, so was Tunesmith. 'Hanuman, report,' he said.

'Your device deployed. It will hold for days, but it will leak. What are you expecting?'

'I sent a reweaving system to make more scrith. I based my design on nanotechnology from the 'doc aboard *Needle*. A complicated matter, this. The system must replace not only the scrith floor but the superconductor grid within.'

Hanuman said, 'There are species whose breeders evolved intelligent. Their protectors would be bright enough to help you with such problems.'

'Bright enough to quarrel, too, and to hold the Ringworld hostage for the advantage of their own gene pool. Louis, tell me what you saw of a downed spacecraft.'

'Just a streak,' Louis said

'Different from other streaks?'

He spoke too patiently. Louis flushed. 'We saw it from a long way away, but – I reached the Ringworld aboard a ship in stasis. *Lying Bastard* came down with a horizontal velocity of seven hundred and seventy miles per second, like anything that brushes the Ringworld. We left a streak of molten lava and bare scrith. Now I've seen one just like it. I think when one ship exploded, another got knocked down.'

'We'll have to find it.'

'That's easy, but not now,' Louis pleaded. 'Your orbiting stepping disk won't be in view of the puncture for twelve hours anyway. Let us get some sleep.' He was ready to weep, exhausted physically and emotionally.

'Sleep, then.'

They slept aboard *Needle*. Louis shared sleeping plates with Hanuman. The little protector just had to try it.

CHAPTER 10

A Tale to Tell

They woke, they breakfasted, they returned to the work-station under Olympus where Tunesmith was waiting.

Tunesmith had added to their gear. The new gear included two flycycles.

Nessus and his motley crew had carried four flycycles: flying structures built something like a dumb-bell with a seat mounted between the weights. They'd all been ruined on that first voyage. These two must have been modeled on the wreckage; but they were longer, each with two seats and a big luggage rack.

Louis inspected one of the vehicles. The kitchen converter would store in the luggage rack or swing out. Mounts on the dash carried a flashlight laser and some other tools. Nessus's team had reached the Ringworld with gear similar to this, some of puppeteer make, some purchased off shelves in human space.

'I reworked the sonic fold too,' Tunesmith said. 'Orbiting Stepping-Disk Eight will be almost in place, Hanuman. You can take it from here.'

'Stet.' To Acolyte and Louis, Hanuman said, 'Get into your pressure gear, then stow your baggage. We'll push the flycycles through first.'

'Where's the Hindmost?' Louis asked.

'He's still in a depressed state,' said Tunesmith. 'That worries me. He may be suffering a chemical imbalance. I'll put him in the 'doc after you're gone.'

Louis didn't comment. They geared up and went.

And out into free fall with the Ringworld blazing below. The Kzin, the protector, Louis, and two flycycles drifted apart. Riding lights flashed on the flycycles.

Orbiting Stepping-Disk Eight had drifted in the night, twenty degrees, thirty-three million miles. Louis was looking almost straight down into a black hole with a glitter at the rim, in a quasi-lunar landscape marked with radial streamlines and glittering threads of frozen riverbed. A torus the size of a mountain range, glowing ruby from within and beginning to sag, was its border. It looked like God had dropped one of his toys. A plane of white cloud surrounded the torus, bigger than worlds.

To antispin, where cloud cover became patchy, a white scratch ran across the land.

Louis pointed it out. 'A ship dug that gouge. We'll find it at the antispin end, the far end. I don't see it yet, so it'll be small. Hanuman, shall we start decelerating?'

'Yes. Board a flycycle, I'll take the other, Acolyte rides with whom he will. Acolyte?'

'With you,' Acolyte said.

'Stet. Keep your altitude until your relative velocity is low, Louis. The sonic fold won't take more than a few times sonic speed. I'll keep you in sight. Guide us down to the ship.'

A grid of superconducting material ran beneath the Ringworld floor. Nessus's flycycles had flown by magnetic levitation. With maglev for lift, thrusters didn't have to be powerful . . . but these redesigned machines did deliver some serious push. When his velocity relative to the landscape had decreased to something reasonable, Louis eased down into atmosphere until he could hear a thin whine in the sonic fold. He could see a lacework of water vapor around the other flycycle. His own shock waves were barely visible.

Tunesmith spoke suddenly in his earphones. 'Your mission is to seek out a crashed ship. Louis, guide them. Report to me at every step. Watch for more than one ship down. The crash grooves they carve would be close together and parallel.

'I want to know the species and what to expect of them. Don't throw your life away to find out. Don't kill any LE if you can avoid it, but if you must, leave no sign. If possible, negotiate. I'll make any guests glad they met me.

'I worry for what I might forget to tell you.

'Louis, remember that information storage is easy. All of human knowledge is probably stored aboard every ARM spacecraft, with blocks to restrict secrets. The right officer will know the right passwords. Acolyte, if you find a Patriarchy ship instead, give up. The knowledge may be there, but no hero will give it to you—'

Louis said, 'A telepath might,' but Tunesmith's monologue droned on.

I worry for what I might forget to tell you ... that it's a three hundred million mile walk home, and the stepping disk is orbiting beyond your reach, and the Hindmost will be in the 'doc. So you can't count on him for an ally, and you can't use the 'doc to rejuvenate, Louis. In the fullness of time, I'll make you a protector ... Not likely that Tunesmith would say any of that. Louis concentrated on flying.

Far behind them was the low wall of fog. The ship they were tracking had skipped across a sea, a river, another river. A ridge showed a glittering notch of bare scrith where the ship must have bounced aloft. The arrow-straight canyon resumed further on, scrith rimmed with splashed lava. Following it was easy. It ran across forest, a white sand beach, a long, long stretch of veldt . . . there . . .

So small a thing to have wrought so much damage.

Against another ridge lay an elegantly contoured half-cylinder, flat along one side, no cabins, no windows, no breaks in the reflective surface, except near one end. Louis zoomed his faceplate.

'Is that an ARM ship?' Acolyte asked. 'Or Patriarchy? Smooth as it is, it might be puppeteer. But they'd use a General Products' hull, wouldn't they?'

Closing now at several mach. The protrusion at one end looked like a bee's stinger.

'It's a drop tank,' Louis said.

'Explain,' Hanuman rapped.

'It's not a spacecraft. It's part of a spacecraft, the part that carries extra fuel, the part you can throw away.' He was furious with himself, and then, suddenly, elated. 'The ship whapped down in stasis. After the stasis field collapsed, they still had a working space-craft.'

Working spacecraft!

Keep talking. Somehow he held his voice steady. 'They drop the tank when they want agility or longer range. I'd say they were getting ready for a dogfight.'

But a working spacecraft!

Hanuman said, 'Flup. We have to find that ship. Were you expecting this?'

'No. *Lying Bastard* was a different design. After we hit, we were grounded. Now what?'

'Possibilities suggest themselves,' Hanuman said. 'First, I'm linked to Tunesmith. Tunesmith, you have Louis's assessment. Shall we wait for the ship to return for its fuel? Is it ARM or Kzinti or something else? Must we negotiate or challenge?'

Louis said, 'ARM.' Kzinti would have marked their property. Pierin or Kdat or Trinocs wouldn't challenge Kzinti or men; Kzinti had owned them. Puppeteers wouldn't directly challenge anything. Outsiders wouldn't get this close to a star. 'Might be some other human branch, or Kzinti bandits, or Trinocs . . . but call it ARM.

'That's a little tank, so we're looking for a little ship. A fighter won't carry antimatter fuel. Energy stored in a battery. Water for reaction mass because it's easy to store and pump. They might have anti-matter weapons. It's surprising that a little ship would have a stasis field. Maybe the UN is getting better at building them.'

Any part of a warcraft would have dot-sized cameras all over it. 'If they're not watching us, they might still record us,' Louis said. 'So what shall we be?'

The little hologram heads of his companions looked blank.

Louis explained. 'We're operatives working for a superintelligent protector who used to be an eater of the dead. That's too scary. Any military LE who heard *that* might shoot us out of hand. An ARM ship will have records of what a protector is. That'll scare them too.

'So, what do we want to be? We're a Kzin and a man and a Hanging People protector. We don't want to be Patriarchy. They're scary too. We can't show ARM identification—'

'Ah,' Hanuman said. 'You want to lie.'

'Hanuman? A new concept?'

Acolyte rumbled in dissatisfaction. Hanuman said, 'My species' breeders aren't sapient. I've been able to think and speak for less than a falan. Who would I lie to? Tunesmith?'

A dog will try to lie to its human master, Louis thought, *but getting away with it* – 'Stet, but we *do not* want to confront them with a protector. Hanuman, do you remember how you behaved as a breeder? Can you do it again?'

'You would make me a *pet monkey*?'

'Yah.'

'Stet. If I can't talk, I can't be caught in a lie. Acolyte's pet, I assume. What of you?'

Louis said, 'I think Tunesmith saw this coming. Our gear is pretty close to what Nessus brought aboard *Lying Bastard*. Let's be the Hindmost's new crew. With the puppeteer leading from wayyy behind, as usual. It would explain flycycles. Hanuman, any thoughts?'

'We're telling a story. Better if they do not learn that Louis Wu made a protector and set him in charge of the Ringworld. You would seem too powerful and too undefended. Best if we do not mention an experimental medical system using nanotechnology, either. That was stolen from the United Nations, even if eight hundred falans ago. They'd want it back.'

'I hadn't even *thought* of that. Stet, let's keep working on this. Acolyte—'

'I am proud of what I am! And I was not taught to lie. We serve a powerful master. Why not simply demand what we want?'

'Maybe this is why Chmeee sent you to me. Acolyte, it's only a fighter, but their mother ship would carry *antimatter fuel*. Hanuman, how many double-X-large plugs does Tunesmith have?'

'One partly completed.'

Worse than he'd thought. The Ringworld couldn't afford another antimatter explosion! 'Acolyte, you're Chmeee's son. Stick with the truth, as much as you can. Just don't talk about the Repair Center or Tunesmith or Carlos Wu's nanotech autodoc. Your father, Chmeee, rules a chunk of the Map of Earth. The Hindmost made you an offer, and you went off with him rather than fight your father again. You're his hostage, but you don't know it.'

'And how did I meet Louis Wu?' the Kzin demanded.

'I . . . hadn't got that far.'

'Land,' ordered Hanuman. 'We'll fill our kitchen slots while we wait for the ship's return. Louis, how long does a dogfight take?'

'Not long. Hours.'

They landed among trees like redwood-sized dandelions. Louis had seen these elsewhere.

Light and noise would alert them if a ship returned. Meanwhile they dismounted, stretched, removed their pressure suits. As soon as Acolyte sniffed the air, he bounded away with a howl, hot in pursuit of something the others never saw.

Louis swung his kitchen converter out on its boom. He loaded grass and small plants into the hopper. Hanuman was doing the same. If the kitchen box was based on what they'd used thirty-odd years ago, it would process local vegetation or animal flesh, make handmeal bricks he could eat, and discard the dross. He'd have to catch something meaty, soon.

It extruded a brick.

'Wrong setting,' Hanuman said. 'Here.' He turned a dial on Louis's kitchen. 'That was for me. Fruit eater.'

Louis broke a chunk off the protector's brick and tasted it. 'Good, though. We eat fruit too.'

It hit him without warning, a rush of nostalgia. He'd

been here before, on unknown landscape in all this Ringworld *hugeness*, sharing a handmeal brick with Teela. He turned away from Hanuman as his eyes filled with tears.

He remembered Teela Brown.

She was tall and slender and walked with the confidence of a centenarian, though she was only in her thirties. He'd first seen her wearing silver net on blue skin; hair scarlet and orange and black, like bonfire flames and smoke, streaming upward. Later she'd put aside flatlander style. Nordik-pale skin, oval face, big brown eyes, and a small, serious mouth; dark and wavy hair cut short to fit into a pressure suit helmet.

She had never stumbled, never had a bad love affair, never been sick or hurt, never been caught in scandal or a public gaffe, until she attended Louis Wu's birthday party. Louis still believed that was a statistical fluke. Among a population in the tens of billions, someone like Teela Brown could surely be found.

But the Experimentalist Party among Pierson's puppeteers believed that they had been breeding the human race for luck. Teela was the descendant of six generations of Birthright Lottery winners. Whatever happened to Teela could be interpreted as lucky:

Falling in love with Louis Wu. Following him here.

Losing her way, in a domain three million times the surface area of the Earth. Finding Seeker, the brawny explorer who could show her so much of the Ringworld's secrets.

Finding the Repair Center beneath the Map of Mars. Finding a cache of tree-of-life root. Falling into a coma while her joints and brain case expanded, gender disappeared, gums and lips fused to horseshoes of sharp bone, skin thickened and wrinkled into armor . . . while she became a protector.

Nessus led us, and I led Teela, to the biggest, gaudiest toy in the universe. How could she not want to make it her own? But only a protector's intelligence could hold the Ringworld safe. And when the Ringworld was endangered, Teela Brown the protector saw that she must die.

Death isn't bad luck to a protector. It's just another tool.

Acolyte returned with his mouth bloody. 'Good hunting here. My father is missing another fine adventure.'

Hanuman asked, 'Louis, can you pass for crew on an ARM ship?'

'*There's* a notion.' Louis thought about it. Did he really remember enough . . . ? 'What I can't pass for is a local. I'm Homo sapiens, Earth origin. Why do I want to be a crewman, Hanuman? Crew of what?'

Hanuman said, 'We must not be servants of a protector. So, I must be a tree-dwelling animal, and you must be a wanderer unless you serve some greater force. If you serve, it must be some aspect of the Fringe War—'

'The ARM, of course. But I don't know ARM protocol, and I'm not in their records.'

'Isn't there a way you could have been missed?'

'. . . No. Let's try something else.'

He munched on a handmeal while he thought. Drop the previous story; start over. Tell something simple. Something Louis Wu can keep straight, and Acolyte also.

He said, 'Let's try to guess what a random ARM fighter has in its computer records.

'They know that we came home – that Chmeee and Louis Wu came home with Nessus injured and no Teela Brown. Suppose Teela lived? She never finds the Repair Center and tree-of-life.

'They might know that the Hindmost landed on Canyon twenty-three years later, and Louis Wu disappeared then. They might have tracked Chmeee too, from one of the Kzin worlds up to where the Hindmost collected *him*.

'So the Hindmost brings us both back to the Ringworld as crew. That's the way it happened, but let's say he planned to rendezvous with Teela. She and Louis Wu have been living together ever since.' It could have been that way. Should have been! Even though the Ringworld would have been torn apart a year later.

Still daydreaming, Louis said, 'They had a child after her implant wore off, and that's me.'

Hanuman said, 'Hypothesis diverges from ARM records.'

Tanj! 'How?'

'When would these events take place? Louis Wu returned here thirteen years ago. Does the ARM know that?'

'. . . Yes, they do. ARM found me on Canyon just before the Hindmost collected me.' Louis had killed two agents. 'Tanj! That would make Louis Wu's son twelve years old at best.'

'Can you pass for twelve?' Hanuman asked.

'Hah hah.'

'Could you, Louis Eldest, have left Teela with a child? The child would be aged a hundred and sixty falans.'

'Almost forty years old. Couldn't happen. Teela must have had her five-year infertility shots. They'd have had to wear off. We never had the time.'

Acolyte asked, 'Can you be a child of Teela and Seeker?'

'Hah! No. Different species.'

Hanuman and Acolyte waited.

Start over. 'At the end of the first expedition, thirty-eight years ago, Chmeee and I came back to known space and the Patriarchy. We turned over *Long Shot* and some information about the Ringworld. We were debriefed by a joint commission, then the ARM asked me a lot more questions. They didn't learn much, because we didn't explore much. Our second expedition was twenty-three years later. What if there was an expedition in between?'

Hanuman asked, 'Who sent it?'

'The Hindmost sent it. Expedition number one-and-a-half. I can fake that. I met a puppeteer named Chiron on the Fleet of Worlds. He was pure white, perfectly coiffed with a wonderful array of classic gems, and a little smaller than Nessus—' His companions had never met Nessus. 'Thirty pounds lighter than the Hindmost. He sounded just like the Hindmost; I suppose they all had the same training.

'So now we can all describe him, stet? The Hindmost puts Chiron in charge. Chiron leaves not long after Chmeee, and I came back to human space. That brings him here . . . mmm . . . at least thirty years ago. He finds Teela. Her infertility shot has worn off. Teela takes up living with one of Chiron's crew. I'm the child.'

'What is your name, child?'

'Luis.' Acolyte might forget, but he'd still sound right: *Loo-iss, Luis*. 'Luis Tamasan,' the first Oriental name he could think of, to account for the epicanthic folds in his eyes. 'Chiron had his records erased. The ARM already knows that puppeteers meddle with their records. There's no Fertility Board record either, because my father . . . mmm. *Horace* Tamasan was born to a freemother, an illegal birth. Lots of bastards go to space.'

Hanuman said, 'A consistent tale. Have we the acting knack to tell it?'

Tunesmith's voice broke in without warning. 'Hanuman, you surmise that an ARM fighter has dropped its add-on tank and gone off to battle. I scan an area bigger than worlds, and I find nothing to fight. My neutrino scan shows no power sources. Battery-powered ships would not register, I assume. Must I watch until they fire lasers or antimatter bullets?'

Louis said, 'That half hour delay is going to drive us nuts sooner or later.'

'Small ships might escape Tunesmith's instruments, but he wouldn't miss a weapons laser or antimatter flash,' said Hanuman. 'Would they fight while refusing to use such weapons? No. I surmise there is no fight at all, Luis.'

Louis mulled that. If the ARMs hadn't been expecting a fight, where had the ARM ship gone? Why had they dropped their tank first?

'The tank might be empty,' Hanuman suggested. 'They wanted greater range. They won't be back.'

Louis said, 'All right, let's rethink. Spinward of us, there's a lot of fog to hide in. Ships could be hunting each other. Ah, flup, never mind.' Both aliens were looking at him. 'If there's nothing to fight, they've gone off to look at the puncture! What else is there? The

Ringworld is dying. They need to tell their mother ship what's happening here, and they might want to run away fast, so they dropped their tank.'

Hanuman thought it over; nodded. 'Don your pressure suits.'

CHAPTER 11

The Wounded Land

Most of the Mouse Eaters were dozing underground after a morning meal.

This wasn't Wembleth's custom. Wembleth was a traveler; he adapted his behavior to his hosts. He'd been living with these nocturnal hunters for several turns of the sky, sharing their meals and their women, teaching them how to make and use tools he'd learned of elsewhere.

Most of the villagers were inside their burrow houses. Older children and elders were cleaning up after the feast, with Wembleth's help, while shadow withdrew from the sun. For him it was a good choice; he needed some sunlight to stay healthy. In a minute they'd all go in—

And the day lit up.

Children began screaming.

Mouse Eaters couldn't deal with mere daylight; what would this glare do to them? His own eyes squinted to teary slits.

Wembleth scooped up two small children, hugged their faces against his chest, and shouted at the rest. 'Get inside!' He darted into the nearest house. The others would have to follow, or find their own houses.

Windows were mere slits in Mouse Eater houses. Wembleth dropped his load of children into the dark, wiggled past more frightened children and out again.

In the horrid light children and elders were running blind. Elder Mouse Eaters tended to lose their sight anyway; it let them move around in daylight. Through squinted eyes Wembleth could still see. They could not. Adults were bigger than he was. Somehow he wrestled them into doorways.

He couldn't guess how much time passed. The light faded. A hot fierce wind blasted across the plaza, scattering coals from the commonfire, and died. Presently a softer wind was blowing the other way. When he couldn't find anyone, couldn't see anyway, he crawled indoors. Indoors was perfect blackness; his night sight had faded, and the horrid light had faded too. Wembleth lay down and gasped for air.

Something would change. Something always did, when things went bad. You had to watch for the opportunity that would follow.

Presently Wembleth realized that he was suffocating.

The blast spit Snail Darter, in stasis, into a rocky cliff above a vast forest. When time resumed, the ship had become part of an immense landslide of shattered shale.

Far, far to spinward, a sea of mist ran all across the horizon, hiding everything up to the base of the Arch. Worlds away, the mist domed upward. The near edge of the mist was a shock wave still moving sluggishly toward Snail Darter.

'It looks like the end of the world. Any world. Lots of worlds,' Oliver said.

'See who's around,' Roxanny ordered.

Detective Oliver Forrestier busied himself with various sensors. Right Whale, the big ARM cruiser, had gone up against a nameless Kzinti juggernaut, just before the fireball and blackout. There had been other ships too . . . but now there was nothing. 'No obvious contrails,' Oliver said. 'The cloud is spitting neutrinos . . . last traces of antimatter, I guess, and diminishing. No point sources. No big ships.'

'The fireball is collapsing. Like it's being sucked *down*,' Claus said uneasily.

'Well,' Roxanny said, 'let's go look. We've run out of enemies, right, 'Tec Forrestier? The blast must have smashed them all. Friends too. So our mission is to collect data. Lift us, Claus.'

Snail Darter *lifted.* 'Tec-Two Claus Raschid asked, 'Just go straight on in, Roxanny?'

'Stay low, take our time. Look around. Claus, there's a hole *at the center of all this. A hole in the Ringworld is a way home.*'

'Roxanny, what has you so cheerful?'

Roxanny Gauthier laughed boisterously. 'We're alive! Isn't that enough? Look at the trail we left! We can follow it right *back to the explosion. Claus, Oliver, for all we know about stasis fields, did you really believe it? Does it make sense that you can stop time and restart it? When I saw the light, I knew I was in an antimatter explosion. I thought we were dead!'*

'This was a city,' Oliver said. He played his instruments along the grid of streets and buildings. 'Big one. Spread out, like Sydney.'

'Claus, slow us down,' Roxanny said. 'I don't see much in the way of corpses. Where are the dead?'

Oliver guessed. 'Inside, taking cover from the shock wave. Look at your displays, Roxanny. Air pressure is down and dropping. They hid from the shock wave and then—'

'Suffocated? The air's draining out.' Claus wasn't stupid; he was only coming out of denial. 'We've killed the whole Ringworld. Hey—'

'We'll be ten thousand years investigating the structure, learning its secrets,' Roxanny said. 'What are you doing, Claus?'

'Landing. I can see a survivor.'

Underground, Wembleth was suffocating.

He clawed his way into the light, but the air wasn't any better.

The light was no more than broad daylight, but there was a weirdness to spinward as if half the world had been taken away, leaving only fog and chaos. Wembleth made his way to the commons, his chest heaving.

An hour ago they'd been feasting. Now there was nobody.

The fires had gone out. Mouse Eaters wouldn't come outside in an emergency, and Wembleth didn't have a better answer than they did.

Something shaped vaguely like a silver vinch's egg was dropping out of the sky.

Wembleth stood up, though he nearly fainted, and waved both arms. When in doubt, ask for help. It was his normal instinct, but his fading intellect backed him up:

Here were folk with the power to fly! Tales told of such power, but these were flying in the winds of a major disaster. Anyone who could do that must know something.

News of this disaster must be carried to other peoples.

Wembleth was on his hands and knees, his vision blacking out, when two men of unknown species descended to him. They wore hard armor, like the mythical Vashneesht. They offered him a bag to crawl into.

Wembleth did.

Air hissed into the bag. He could breath.

He didn't know how to tell the Vashneesht that others needed rescuing. It never occurred to him that Vashneesht — wizards — might be the cause of a world-destroying disaster.

Gravity near a Ball World follows an inverse square law. In contrast, the Ringworld is a plane surface. Gravity does not dwindle as you rise, nor do spin gravity nor magnetic force, until the Ringworld looks less like a plane than a ribbon, from hundreds of thousands of miles high.

The Ringworld engineers embedded a lacework of superconducting cable in the Ringworld floor. The grid allows magnetic manipulation of solar flares to cause a superthermal laser effect, the Ringworld meteor defense; but it also opens the entire Ringworld to magnetic levitation.

Magnetically powered vehicles could rise to any height.

It was night when the skycycles lifted. Sixty miles high, effectively out of the atmosphere, they followed the gouge spinward. Verdant landscape became stormy, in ripples and streams of lightning-lit cloud rather than in whorl patterns. Then it was all unbroken clouds.

The terminator, the shadow of the edge of a shadow square, swept over them. A growing sliver of sun became a noonday glare. How long had it been since Louis saw a sunrise?

They crossed above a tremendous, sagging, faintly glowing tube. Horsetails of mist were flowing over the tube's flaccidities and disappearing into vacuum. Tunesmith's plug wouldn't hold forever.

Soil and rock still clung to the scrith floor. There were pools and ribbons of foamy ice, all ravaged in a radial pattern. They followed it inward toward the puncture.

The rim of the hole glittered. Maybe, maybe Tunesmith's 'reweaving' system was working.

'Spacecraft,' Acolyte said. 'Above the hole.'

There was no exhaust. The ship hovered on thrusters: a cylinder with a flattened belly, a little bigger than the tank it had left behind, but with a bulb of transparent canopy for a nose.

'That's an ARM design, Kittycatcher Class,' Louis said. 'A fighter. Three crew. They'll have seen us by now.'

'Will they fire on us?'

'We must look harmless enough.' Louis was trying to persuade himself.

Hologram miniatures of his two allies blurred, then became two views of a dark-skinned woman in ARM uniform. A contralto voice blared from his speaker. 'Intruders, answer at once or be destroyed! You have entered a war zone!'

'I'm Luis Tamasan,' Louis Wu answered. 'Can you hear me?'

'We hear you, Luis Tamasan. Please approach *Snail Darter*.'

'What are your intentions?'

'We are observers for the United Nations,' the woman said. 'What do you know of events in this region?'

'We came to observe a puncture in the Ringworld floor.'

'Your associate is a Kzin.'

Louis laughed. 'Acolyte is local, a Ringworld native. I'm local too.'

She peered at his hologram. 'You look human.'

'I'm human. Born here. Acolyte was too, and he's Kzin.'

'There are Kzinti here?'

'Archaic Kzinti, in the Great Ocean.' That should rouse their curiosity.

The ARM woman sounded peevish. 'We tried every reasonable frequency. Why are you communicating in a mode used by the Fleet of Worlds?'

'Puppeteers found the Ringworld and puppeteers explored it first,' Louis said with a trace of chill in his voice. 'My parents and Acolyte's father came here with Pierson's puppeteers.'

'Land there at the edge.'

'We came to examine the puncture. May we circle above it?'

'Land *now*, Ringworld's children.'

Louis said, 'Down, Acolyte.' He let his flycycle sink.

The ARM asked, 'Acolyte, do you speak Interworld?'

'Madam LE, I do,' the Kzin rumbled.

'While I serve the United Nations you may address me by my rank, as Copilot or 'Tec, not as Legal Entity. How may I call you?'

'Acolyte, until I earn a more worthy name.'

'What is your connection to the Patriarchy?'

'I hear of them from my father. We see the lights of the Fringe War.'

The skycycles settled on bare scrith.

Snail Darter descended with evident caution, and

touched down. An airlock opened below its rounded tip. A human shape emerged, then a second pulling a bulb of some kind through a door that was too narrow. It got through anyway.

One ARM flew to meet the flycycles while the other lowered the bulb to the desiccated turf. The bulb was a rescue pod, an inflated balloon with a few opaque bulges of life-support gear. The shadow of a walking man showed in the bulb as it rolled toward the flycycles.

'Tec-First Gauthier – easily recognized through her fishbowl helmet – must have had a clear view of Hanuman riding alert in Acolyte's lap. Acolyte attached a line to Hanuman's pressure suit, as if the Hanging Person might scamper away and have to be caught. The pair debarked and joined Louis. Gauthier settled before them.

'I feel small,' Acolyte said uneasily.

This close to the puncture, the floor was polished by the antimatter blast: featureless scrith, translucent and smooth, artificial and infinite. Louis and his companions were tiny. Louis hadn't felt it until the Kzin spoke.

'LE Acolyte, LE Luis,' said Gauthier – courtesy, because Acolyte couldn't ever have been registered as a Legal Entity, nor could Luis Tamasan. '– meet 'Tec Oliver Forrestier and LE Wembleth. I'm 'Tec Roxanny Gauthier.' Her manner had softened.

'Tec Forrestier, the second flyer, was large and pale,

perhaps a Belter raised in low G. Like Gauthier's his rust-colored curly hair was cut close to his scalp. He smiled and touched gloves with the man, then the Kzin. 'We're glad to find you,' he said.

Gauthier asked, 'Can you take Wembleth for us? We don't have room for him.'

'It's a three man ship,' Forrestier explained.

'What's Wembleth, then?' Louis asked. 'Local?'

Wembleth had lagged behind. Rolling a balloon by walking on its bottom didn't seem to bother him, but it was slow going. When he tried to stop, the balloon kept moving; he fell over, and got up without embarrassment.

Could Wembleth hear their communicators? He wasn't speaking.

Forrestier said, 'We found him where the air was disappearing. Corpses and smashed burrows all around him. Do you recognize his type?'

'His species?' Louis studied Wembleth.

Wembleth blinked back as if light hurt his eyes, but they met Louis's without a flinch. He was eight inches shorter than Louis, five feet six or a little more. He was dressed in woven cloth, trousers and a loose shirt with patch pockets, all the color of sand. His feet were bare, large, and horny, with toenails like jagged weapons. His skin was darker than Louis's, paler than Roxanny Gauthier's, and his hands and face and neck were wrinkled. Thick hair, black and white, hid most of his face.

Blue scrollwork on his brow and cheeks might have been ritual tattooing, or might have been naturally evolved camouflage. He was smiling, interested, where any normal man might have cowered in terror.

'I don't know this exact species.' Louis hadn't met any locals within hundreds of millions of miles, but he didn't say that. He hadn't decided how far 'Luis Tamasan' had traveled. He said, 'There are thousands of hominid species on the Ringworld, maybe tens of thousands, and most of them are sapient. Wembleth is about average size. Dark skin's pretty common too. Teeth—' Wembleth smiled; Louis winced.

Wembleth's teeth were crooked and discolored. Four were missing, leaving black gaps. Louis could *feel* what that must be like. Wouldn't he be constantly chewing up his tongue?

Wembleth still had three canines, though. Louis asked, 'Meat eater?'

'Tec Gauthier shrugged. 'We gave him a standard dole brick. There's a setting for raw meat, of course, in case we get a Kzinti prisoner. He ate some of that.'

'We can feed Wembleth, then. Even if his whole ecology is dead,' Louis said.

'Good! Another matter. Tell me anything you can,' Oliver Forrestier said, 'about *that*.' His arm swept a circle.

'The sudden mountain range.' Obvious first question, yet Louis hadn't planned an answer. He improvised: 'We saw it come down. Things of this scale, Ringworld scale, even my parents never have much to say. Chiron sent us to learn more.'

'Chiron?'

'He brought my father to this place. A puppeteer.'

'Stet. Come here, Luis.' Forrestier walked toward the puncture seventy feet away. Louis followed.

Forrestier stopped. His toes were too near the edge. From this viewpoint it was still a bottomless pit ten or fifteen miles across. Shrinking, it was shrinking. The edge was hard to focus on; it blurred and shimmered when Louis moved his head.

Forrestier asked, 'Is this normal?'

'I've never looked into a rip in the floor of the world,' Louis said. 'It's scary.' It was barely a lie. He'd seen Fist-of-God crater . . . but 'Luis' hadn't.

Gauthier said, 'Well, it looks like it's repairing itself. Does it always do that? Over the years we've seen some of those hourglass storms die out. We think those are punctures and air leakage.'

Louis frowned, projecting *Don't understand*. He remembered a word from far away, used as if it meant *magicians*, but it meant *protector*. 'Vashneesht,' he said. 'There are secrets we never learn.'

'Tec-One Gauthier said, 'Oliver, get back from there! Luis, Acolyte, shall we set up a tent?'

*   *   *

Roxanny and Oliver lifted a bulky package out of the ship's lock. They set it on the scrith and moored it with stickstrip edges. The tent inflated itself, writhing and trying to bounce, because of course the stickstrip wouldn't hold on scrith. Roxanny left Oliver to deal with that while she went back for the kitchen 'doc.

Oliver saw what she was doing and exploded. 'LE Gauthier, are you schitzy? We can't lose that!'

'We can live without for a few hours.'

'Why did you try to give away Wembleth? A Ringworld native! He's a wonderful find!'

'Wembleth is a prize, all right. I wish we could take them both, but he's still just a local. He doesn't know enough. I want Luis Tamasan! I'd take the Kzin if I could fit him in the ship, but I can't, so we'll question him first.'

'Roxanny, he's still a Kzin!'

'You're afraid? He's a kid. They're both teen children. Both their parents were on the Ringworld before the Fleet, and the kids must have been hearing about it all their lives.'

Oliver considered. 'What would their parents do to get them back?'

'Maybe we'll find that out too, after we know everything they do.' She grinned. 'Ollie, did you see the look on Luis's face? Like—'

Oliver had, and his voice showed his resentment.

'Like he never saw a woman before. All right, Roxanny, have it your way. We'll crawl into the tent with a Kzin, and by Finagle he's the first that gets fed! But we've got way more data than we were sent for, and the trick now is to get home with it!'

The ARMs were involved with erecting the tent. Nobody was looking at Louis when Tunesmith's miniature bust popped up on his dash.

The protector said, 'I urgently need to know whether my reweaving system is working. Is the hole getting smaller? How drastically must I act to save *something*? I need hardly warn you not to fall into the puncture.'

Was *Snail Darter* or its mother ship eavesdropping? Even if this line were private, little glowing hologram heads would be seen. Louis said quickly, 'The hole is closing. *It's closing.* We have company.' He turned the holoscreen off.

Now Tunesmith could do no more than listen.

The tent had inflated into a tube with a big airlock, an alcove for vacuum gear, a living space, and silver walls that must hide a toilet. Gauthier inside, and Forrestier outside, assisted the rest to enter.

Acolyte carried Hanuman, but left him in his pressure suit. 'The suit takes care of sanitary matters,' Acolyte said. Hanuman ooked.

Gauthier had thrown back her helmet, though she didn't move to strip off her suit. Oliver had done the same. The ARMs didn't seem to be excessively distrustful. Louis and Acolyte opened their own helmets. The varying species settled themselves around a small kitchen box.

Wembleth spoke syllables Louis had never heard. A translator voice spoke from one of his pockets: 'Good, this is much more room.' The hairy man zipped his rescue pod open and wriggled out with a sigh of contentment.

'Wembleth makes number four in a three man ship,' Forrestier explained. 'We found him surrounded by the dead of some larger, hairier species, gasping like a beached fish, but on his feet and pulling himself toward us by any ruined wall the storm hadn't flung away. We had to stuff him in Mission and Weapons and shut it all off. We've questioned him – he knows things we need – but we can't fly like that, LE Luis. We need to defend ourselves.'

'We'll take him someplace he can live,' Louis said.

'We'll find a way to moor his rescue pod to your flying thing. We don't have a suit that'll fit him.'

'Tec Gauthier was handing out dole bricks from the little kitchen. She made adjustments to give Acolyte a brick of drippy red, then something fruity for Hanuman. 'It's the only kitchen we've got, and it's the 'doc too. In flight, in peacetime, this tent buds out from the hull. If we can't deploy it, we barely have room to wiggle. War is hell,' she said lightly. 'Can I give you something to drink?'

'Surprise me,' Louis said. 'Tea? Juice?'

'Beer?'

'Better not. And Acolyte's too young.'

Acolyte growled.

Roxanny laughed. 'So're you, Luis!'

She thought he was a child! He said, 'Yes, LE.'

She passed out squeezebulbs: something cranberry-flavored for Louis, boullion for Acolyte and Wembleth. 'You both grew up on the Ringworld. Did your fathers tell you about planets?'

'We learned physics that way,' Acolyte said. 'Father – Chmeee – tried to show me what a Coriolis storm is, a hurricane. I'm not sure I understand.'

'I'd love to see Earth,' Louis said. A working space-craft! His first chance to defect since the abominable Bram had found him . . . no, since before that. Since he'd sliced up *Needle*'s hyperdrive motor!

There had to be a way to speak to Roxanny Gauthier alone.

Her suit wasn't quite a skintight: it only hinted at a shape that made his heart turn over. A strong woman, an athlete. Her face was severe, with a square chin and a straight-edged nose. She'd be in her fifties, Louis judged, based on body language and the way Forrestier deferred to her . . . unless she ranked him. Her hair was a sparse black puffball; she must depilate or shave her scalp periodically.

It took Louis by surprise, after all the hominids he'd met, how much he longed for the sight of a woman.

But she was asking something. 'Do you know anything about a big transparent ship?'

Louis shook his head. Acolyte was less cautious. 'Like a General Products ship? What would we see, a glass bubble?'

'Yah, a big glass bubble. What do you know about General Products hulls?'

'Luis's father came here in a Number Two,' Acolyte said. He was giving too much detail. He'd be caught in inconsistencies, Louis feared . . . but Chmeee must have described *Liar*, which had been a Number Two, when he told his son of the first expedition.

And Acolyte was enjoying himself.

'A huge glass bubble filled with gear. Massive machines inside,' Gauthier said.

Forrestier said, 'Or four flames moving across the sky. It's got four fusion motors. It was stolen, maybe by your Chiron.'

Louis said, 'Chiron doesn't tell us everything. Or anything.'

Roxanny said, 'Actually it was stolen twice, first by the Kzinti, then from the Kzinti. We didn't see it reach the Ringworld, but we think it's here. We want it back.'

'Tell us about the Chiron expedition,' Oliver ordered.

Louis improvised. 'Dad says it took two years, and it was way cramped.' Stick to what you know where possible – 'My mother came on the first expedition. She says *Lying Bastard* started as a Number Two and just grew out of all proportion, bigger every time a puppeteer thought of another safety feature. In the end *Lying Bastard* was a big flying wing with the General Products cylinder stuck into it. The stasis field enclosed the cylinder, but they lost everything that was on the wing.' All of that would be in ARM records, including Louis Wu's own speculations. They'd find Louis's description of Chiron there too.

'So when Chiron built *his* ship, he wedged everything inside the hull. I've been in it, but not since I was *this* high, and it was already cramped—'

'We would like to talk to Chiron,' Oliver said. 'Where may we find him?'

Acolyte said, 'Chiron has told us most explicitly that we must not tell anyone how to find him.'

To Roxanny Oliver said, '*Long Shot* was in the hands of Kzinti. Puppeteers might find that distressing, don't you think? A puppeteer might act to get it back.' He asked Louis, 'Did Chiron's ship have a name?'

'*Paranoia*,' Louis said without cracking a smile.

'How is it armed?'

'*Paranoia* has no armaments at all,' Louis said, 'barring tools which may be turned to that end. We're not to speak of those.'

'Where on the Ringworld did your *Paranoia* land?

Was it near the Great Ocean, where the first expedition left Teela Brown?'

Louis hadn't decided that either. 'Can't say.'

'Boy, you don't seem to have anything at all to trade,' Roxanny Gauthier said. 'What would you like to know from us? Did Chiron tell you what questions to ask?'

'He wants to know if the Ringworld is going to heal. I can see that the rupture's sealing itself. Even so, what can you tell us about the Fringe War? Is it about to go away?'

'I doubt it,' Roxanny said.

'Or is it going to get so big and violent that it shatters everything?'

'That doesn't have to happen,' she said firmly.

Oliver laughed. Roxanny looked around in annoyance, and Oliver said, 'Just a passing thought. How old are you, Luis?'

Louis had planned to be in his thirties, but both ARMs seemed to think he was just past puberty. For some reason this delighted him. Tanj, why not? He said, 'Eighty falans and a bit.'

'And a falan would be?'

'Ten rotations of the sky.'

'About seventy-five days? Thirty-hour Ringworld days?' Oliver was whispering to a pocket computer, bigger than a civilian version. 'You're about twenty years old, Earth time. I'm forty-six. Roxanny?'

'I'm fifty-one,' she said without hesitation.

'We take boosterspice, of course. It keeps us from getting old. What crossed my mind,' Oliver Forrestier said, 'is that this is the first human woman you've ever seen other than your mother, Luis.'

Roxanny was smiling, a reluctant smile. And Louis was flushing, suddenly aware that his eyes had lingered too long on Roxanny Gauthier; that he'd edged closer to her than the cramped quarters demanded; that he couldn't look at her and talk coherently. The close air must be alive with pheromones . . . Roxanny's and Oliver's too. And as Oliver was the first human male he'd seen or sniffed in twenty-odd years – and no room for a shower aboard *Snail Darter* – it wasn't surprising if Louis felt both horny and threatened.

'Sorry,' he said, and eased back by an inch.

It crossed his mind that intimidation could take many forms. They wanted something from Luis: information Louis Wu would have to make up, but still—

Roxanny laughed lightly. 'Never mind. Luis, would you like to see *Snail Darter*? Acolyte, we can't take you aboard. It's too cramped. Luis can tell you about it afterward.'

Hanuman's eyes met Louis's, but he said nothing. Wembleth and Acolyte had begun a halting conversation. Wembleth found the Kzin fascinating. Louis closed his faceplate and followed the ARMs out.

* * *

The ship was awesomely cramped.

Three seats faced away from each other around a central pillar. One seat was occupied. There was a pucker next to the airlock door for the now-detached tent. A hole in the floor led to a cavity the size of a man: the Weapons and Mission Room.

Roxanny entered first. She slid into the second seat. 'LE Luis Tamasan, meet 'Tec-Two Claus Raschid. Claus, Luis,' she said. 'Not quite a native.'

Claus turned around and offered a hand. He was darker than Roxanny, taller than Oliver, and his arm had a long reach. 'Luis, I'm the pilot. Sit there.'

Louis had hoped to talk to Roxanny alone, or even Oliver alone. They'd both come along, a little too closely agreed for Louis's comfort, leaving Acolyte and Wembleth (and Hanuman) alone in the tent.

Louis slid into the third seat. He felt planes shifting, adjusting to his height and weight and the bulk of his pressure suit. Basic seating: it fit him imperfectly.

Roxanny Gauthier tapped an instruction into her chair arms, using both hands. A crash web held Louis before he could move.

The force field in a crash web would protect a passenger in a collision; it was also useful for police work.

Louis didn't react right away. How would *Luis* react? Frozen in panic, at least long enough for Louis to *think*. And then what?

'For your protection. You did say you wanted to see Earth,' Roxanny said, smiling like a cat.

Oliver slid in through the airlock and then down through the hatch, into the fourth chair. The Mission and Weapons Room fitted Oliver like a tight suit.

Louis wriggled a bit; the field permitted that much. He asked, 'Are we going to Earth?'

'Back to *Gray Nurse*, anyway,' the third crewman said. 'We'll be there in an hour. We'd better be. Roxanny, you left the kitchen 'doc behind.'

'We had to,' she said.

'Stet, but if anything goes wrong — stet. Luis, the carrier *Gray Nurse* is our first stop, and people other than us will decide where you go from there. I expect that's Earth, or at least Sol system. And hey, you can tell us some things while we're on route. Chiron can't stop you now. You'll be the second Ringworlder to reach human space.'

'Don't go through this hole,' Louis said.

All three ARMs turned their heads to look at him. Roxanny asked, 'Why not?'

That was a tough one. Louis Wu was certain that Tunesmith wouldn't allow an ARM spacecraft to escape this easily. Something would block them . . . but why would *Luis Tamasan* say something so out of character?

He said, 'Chmeee says he left the world through Fist-of-God. My father came through a different puncture.

Neither of them saw anything like this . . . shimmer. Fist-of-God Mountain isn't repairing itself, is it? But this hole is.'

Claus said, 'So is Fist-of-God. The crater closed itself weeks ago, before we noticed. We were hoping you could tell us about that.'

Tunesmith must have tested his reweaving system, Louis guessed. Luis said nothing.

Claus Raschid had something on a virtual screen. 'Here we are. Luis, try to follow this. The nearest puncture we know of is a million miles away. Too far. They'll track us across the surface. Every tanj species in the Fringe War will want us as bad as we want you, because of what we might know. But we might escape if we go through *immediately*, *right here*, and with our motors *off*.' The ship lifted. 'Here is where *Gray Nurse* is waiting, our mother ship, in the dark, up against the Ringworld floor—'

Below them Oliver was yelling, 'Raschid! What are you playing at?'

Louis tried to yell louder. Being immobilized was driving him frantic. 'Drop something first! See what happens to it!'

'I'm getting us home,' Raschid told Oliver. The ship eased sideways. Now it was above the puncture. 'All power sources *off*. Luis, if we had the auxiliary fuel tank I'd drop that, but I don't.'

They were falling. Louis glimpsed the tent sitting

alone on the scrith. They'd be all right, he told himself; they had Hanuman to guide them. The hole expanded. It was full of stars.

Snail Darter smashed down into something that gave.

Crash webs caught his captors recoiling upward. Louis felt his brain bounce in his skull. Already in a crash web, he recovered first . . . still immobilized. He could hear Oliver screaming below him.

Claus shouted, 'What did we hit?'

'Get us *out*! Get us *out*!' Roxanny screamed.

Reweaving system, Tunesmith had said. How strong would threads made of scrith be? Strong enough to stop a falling spacecraft? But they'd cut through the hull. The hole must be laced with them.

'The thrusters are dead,' Claus said.

'Where are they?' Louis demanded.

Claus craned around to snarl at him. Louis asked, 'They're on the bottom, aren't they?' It was ancient habit: shipbuilders tended to put thruster motors where they would have put rockets. 'Whatever's in that hole, *mending* that hole, it's cutting the thrusters apart. We'll sink into it. How long before it reaches the power source? What do you use for a power source? Where is it?' Babbling, he was babbling. Why hadn't the stasis field been triggered? But if that happened, they might be here forever.

Claus was slow catching up. Roxanny Gauthier said, 'Midship. It's a battery. If anything cuts into it—'

The ship was indeed sinking inch by inch into the puncture. Worse, it was beginning to tip over.

Claus was staring at them, not getting it. When he did, he yelled in terror. His hands danced above the controls.

Roxanny shouted, 'Wait!'

The hatch in the floor closed. Oliver's yell chopped off.

A rocket motor bellowed. The cabin section detached and rose fast, wobbled, then steadied. Claus took over manually; the cabin tilted far over, fell, tilted upright again.

'You *killed* him!' Roxanny said. 'Oliver!'

'He was sitting in the wrong place.' Claus glared at Louis Wu, who was in Oliver's chair; then at Roxanny. 'Wasn't that you yelling, "Get us out"?'

The tent billowed in the exhaust as the escape pod thumped down. Recoil threw Roxanny and Claus several inches before their crash webs caught them.

Through the wall of the tent Louis could just see that Acolyte and Hanuman were spreading the rescue pod open for Wembleth to enter.

A brilliant light flared from the direction of the puncture. Then that side of the cabin blackened. Louis yelled, 'Roxanny, *let me loose!*'

'Wait it out, Luis.'

A shock wave slammed the cabin.

'They're dying out there! Let me loose! Claus!'

Claus said, 'Here.' His hand moved, and Louis was free. He rolled out of his chair and into the tiny airlock.

The tent was splayed out in fragments like an exploded balloon. The blast had scattered its contents. Wembleth and his rescue pod rolled gently past, Wembleth tumbling like clothes in an Oil Age dryer, as Louis wiggled out of the airlock.

Acolyte was trying to find his feet, falling over, trying again. Hanuman was not in sight. Wembleth must have regained his senses: he was curled in a tight ball now, still tumbling.

'Acolyte? Are you all right? Pressure okay?'

'My suit is holding pressure. Do you see Hanuman?'

'No.'

Wembleth was nearest. Louis flashed his attitude jets, dropped ahead of him, and ran alongside the balloon, pushing to stop its spin. The Ringworlder tried to help. They got it stopped, though Wembleth was unbalanced . . . off balance because Hanuman was clinging tight to him, face to chest. Hanuman still wore his pressure suit.

'Acolyte, I've got them both.'

They walked back toward the ruined tent. Acolyte, Claus, and Roxanny joined them. Roxanny was carrying something heavy, an oblong brick she hugged to her breast.

The kitchen 'doc hadn't been moved. It looked unharmed.

They moored it to Louis's flycycle, and moored Wembleth's rescue pod to Acolyte's. The ARMs gave orders as if they were superior officers. Louis asked at one point, 'Any reason to take your escape vehicle? I don't think flycycle motors are up to that.'

'Leave it,' Roxanny said. 'It's dead.'

The explosion of the fighter ship's battery might have damaged Tunesmith's reweaving system, Louis thought. Tunesmith should be told . . . but he *was* being told, by voice and camera feeds. He just couldn't answer, and that was fine with Louis.

CHAPTER 12

The Giraffe People

The glow in the XXL plug was dimmed. The tube sagged, leaking broad white rivers of tropospheric storm. It didn't matter. They'd left the puncture nearly closed.

The party flew to spinward, directly away from where they had left their fuel tank. 'Leave it as bait. We don't want to be near it,' Roxanny Gauthier ordered. 'Whatever dropped that inflatable mountain range might take an interest. Vashneesht, you said? What do you know of Vashneesht?'

Louis said, 'Vashneesht is just what we say when nobody knows anything. Wizards. Magic.' Interworld words Luis would know from his parents.

She was riding the front saddle of Louis's flycycle. She'd tried to operate the controls, and turned icy when they didn't work. Louis flew from the aft saddle. Neither

Roxanny nor Claus had said so, but it seemed clear they'd been drafted into the ARM.

The other flycycle seemed in good shape. Acolyte rode the front seat; Claus was hidden behind him. The native seemed comfortable enough, slung below the flycycle in his inflated rescue pod, until he began gasping.

'Acolyte!'

'Here, Louis.'

'The rescue pod has run out of air. Wembleth is in trouble.'

Claus said, 'Tanj, it must have been faulty.'

'We descend?'

They landed. Wembleth had fainted.

They kept their suits on. The air was thin fog and hurricane wind; it dimmed their headphone voices. Louis shouted, 'I don't think opening the rescue pod—'

Acolyte: 'Better idea?'

'Get the tree swinger to open his helmet. His suit has a recycling feature.'

The little anthropoid was quick to respond to Acolyte's gestures. He threw back his helmet, sneezed at the stink, but left it open. Concerned, he pushed his face close to Wembleth's and sniffed. Wembleth stirred and presently sat up.

*   *   *

They flew above fallen trees that had grown as puffy tops on tall, slender trunks. The antimatter blast had flattened them with their tops pointing spinward. Further away, the wind from the pressure drop felled them to antispin and left lower growth alive.

Falling pressure was a wave still expanding across this land. The flycycles followed the shock wave, catching up slowly. They crossed tens of thousands of miles of disaster and storm. Now there were standing trees among the fallen in the pufftop forest. The forest ran on, cleaving to the lowlands, mingling with other ecologies.

Louis took them down into a break in the pufftop forest, in a meadow alongside a rushing stream.

Air! They pulled Wembleth out of his bubble before they stripped off their own suits. Wembleth whooped; he danced, though stiffly. He plunged into the water, stripped off his coarse-woven shirt and pants, and began scrubbing himself with them.

Water! Running water, ankle deep, ran down to a deep pool. The ARMs looked at each other; then they stripped off their skintights too and dove in. In midair, Roxanny's laughing eyes brushed Luis Tamasan's. Louis couldn't breathe.

Acolyte plunged in with a mighty splash. With his fur plastered flat he looked wonderfully funny. It broke the spell: Louis laughed.

Hanuman was wrestling with the fittings of his suit.

Louis helped him out. Hanuman, the affectionate anthropoid, hugged him and whispered, 'The ARMs have hand weapons hidden.'

'Surprise,' Louis murmured.

'Ook ook ook. Get naked?'

'My problem—'

'They know. Go in like Wembleth.' Hanuman eeled out of his arms and, four-legged, ran for the water. He dove in without a splash. Louis yelled and chased him, leaping into a cannonball dive.

Cold! He pulled his skintight off in deep water. He made an attempt to rub it clean against himself, then balled it up and threw it onto the rocky shore to drain.

There now. All concerned could pretend not to know that Luis Tamasan was in a state of arousal.

He stayed clear of the ARMs, who were – getting friendly, he'd thought, but Claus was backing off, and Roxanny was talking fast and inaudibly. Quarrel? They'd still want privacy.

Acolyte didn't swim well, but the stream wasn't deep. He scooped up Hanuman and waded up to Louis, who was treading water.

Hanuman spoke briskly. 'I saw a meteorite descend near the puncture. Tunesmith would spot another ship.'

'He can't tell us. I turned him off. I—'

'Good. I will continue riding with Acolyte. Let me lead. I can take us to a service stack.'

A service stack would take them home to the Map of Mars. Louis asked, 'How far away?'

'Orbiting. Tunesmith can direct it toward us.'

'Do we want the ARMs to see a service stack?'

'We'll ask Tunesmith later, when we ask if he's seen other intruders. Your opinion?'

Louis thought about it. 'They'll want to rejoin their ship. We don't mind that, right? As long as they don't learn too much first.'

Hanuman's voice was a whipcrack, barely audible. 'Gauthier rescued their library! I want it! I want to watch them use it before we let them loose. But these ARMs are dangerous companions. No need to risk us all. Louis, what if Acolyte and I escape? We can rendezvous with a service stack. You stay and observe.'

It seemed an astonishing suggestion. 'Why would I?'

'Across the entire Ringworld Roxanny Gauthier is your only possible mate. You don't have a plan of your own, do you?'

Louis shrugged.

Acolyte asked, 'Have you noticed that we have an audience?'

Louis looked around.

The ARMs, upstream, were waist deep and still talking, their body language gone conspiratorial. Louis had to pull his gaze away from her breasts. Wembleth was onshore, on his back on a warm flat rock, soaking up sunlight. Black birds whirled above the puffball forest, and a pair of horn-bearing quadrupeds were watching it all suspiciously.

'I don't see anything human.'

Acolyte said, 'Seven hominids. Three men, four women. I found them by smell. We should decide—'

Something had Wembleth's attention. Wembleth stood up. He shouted into the woods.

A man stepped forth. He walked past the horned beasts; the beasts didn't run. The man stopped a dozen yards from Wembleth. He spoke. His hands were at his side, conspicuous. So were Wembleth's.

They were both naked. The man towered over Wembleth. He'd be taller than Acolyte, eight feet or a little less, and as slender as the trees around them. Every part of him was elongated . . . but not his head. His jaw was strong and square. The hair on his head was the same color as the forest's puffball tops.

Naked in running water, the ARMs seemed at a loss. They waded upstream toward Louis and Acolyte.

'They haven't drawn their weapons,' Hanuman murmured. 'Louis, will they stay calm?'

He meant the ARMs, of course. Louis said, 'Don't know. Someone has to tell them about rishathra.'

Wembleth and the stranger were talking freely now.

Claus came in earshot. He asked, 'Any suggestions?'

'Wembleth is doing fine,' Louis said. 'Let him talk for us. There are more locals.'

'Where?'

Acolyte said, 'In the trees.' He pointed. 'There, all six.'

'He looks like a giraffe,' Claus laughed.

Roxanny said, 'Or a lunie.' It was a rebuff.

Luis Tamasan would never have seen a citizen of Luna. Louis said, 'They'll be peaceful. Look at the jaw: he's an herbivore. Probably picks fruit from these trees. We have to decide—'

'Tanj that. Our translators have to hear them.' Claus waded out. The others trailed after him. Claus picked up his skintight to wipe himself dry, then dropped it, and picked up his backpouch. If nakedness was good enough for the strangers, then Claus didn't need clothes; but the pouch held his translator, and maybe a weapon too.

Six tall, slender humanoids emerged from the tall, slender trees. *Rishathra? We still have to tell the ARMs.*

Wembleth talked rapidly, waving at Acolyte and Hanuman. The tall hominids bowed deeply, and went on talking to Wembleth. Louis and Roxanny fished out their translators and joined the group.

The ARM translators were picking up some speech. It was close to what they'd learned from Wembleth, though this local language would be a long way separated from any speech heard near the Great Ocean.

Wembleth suddenly turned to Roxanny. His speech

sounded no different, but the translators all reacted.
'They want to know what your kind does about—'
something that didn't translate. 'What shall I tell
them?'

Roxanny asked, 'What is it?'

Wembleth tried to explain. The activity that makes
women bear children? But between different kinds it
doesn't? Claus and Roxanny listened, then turned to
Luis for help.

Louis said, 'He's using a different word, but it means
rishathra. Rishathra is sex practiced outside your species
but between intelligent hominids. Not a word you'd
need—'

'Smart-ass boy.' Claus was not amused.

It dawned on Louis that he was afraid of Claus. 'No
joke, Claus. It's the first thing you need to know about
a new species. Look, you can always say you're mated.
Monogamous.'

Claus was looking at the four women. They were as
tall as the men, eight feet or just under. Not lunies,
not giraffes: *Elves*. They were staring as frankly as the
men; but the men were looking at Roxanny, who was
blushing. Louis realized he'd blushed too.

He said, 'Wembleth, tell them Acolyte is not our
kind at all. He doesn't rish.'

Wembleth talked. One of the women laughed.
Louis's translator picked up her 'Think not!'

Louis said, 'But we need to decide. Claus? Roxanny?'

Claus demanded, 'Luis, have *you* done this?'

'Sure!' What would *Luis* say? An adolescent wouldn't admit to being a virgin! He'd exaggerate — 'With more than one species — nothing like these — but I've heard more than that. Why not?' He couldn't quite look at Roxanny, or Claus either. 'It's friendly, it's safe, you can't get pregnant. Infections don't usually cross the species boundary. And who else is there for me? Human women were just rumors, as far away as the stars.'

Wembleth exclaimed, 'Same for me! I was a lost one too. Claus, why are you having trouble with this thought? When folk meet, they always ask this question first. Some kinds use reshtra for birth control. Water dwellers — well, to them it is a joke, unless you can hold your breath far too long. Some species can't resh, or mate with any but a life partner. Some oddly shaped ones don't expect reshtra — rishathra? — only ask for politeness. Some insist. Roxanny, can't you see the Hinsh are puzzled? It's because you haven't answered.'

Louis said, 'Luis' being wistful, 'I'd like to meet a City Builder. They're supposed to be really good at it. They built trading empires around rishathra. They even tried to go interstellar.'

Claus was grinning. 'What if we say no?'

'I can do that for you,' Wembleth said immediately. He began to speak Hinsh.

Claus said, 'Hold up, Wembleth. I'll *do* it,' his eyes flicking toward Roxanny, then away.

Wembleth asked, 'In company, or only two?'

Claus was startled. 'Um. Company. I wouldn't know what to say to just, just one.'

Roxanny Gauthier stepped close to Wembleth. She spoke fast and low. Wembleth nodded. He changed language. Now the translators were picking up a few words of Hinsh speech.

One of the women bent far over. Her long fingers wrapped around a cantaloupe-sized yellow fruit. She bit into it, rind and all, then broke it and offered pieces to Wembleth, then Claus, then the other Hinsh. Wembleth broke his further and offered fruit to Louis and Roxanny. Louis realized that they were labeling themselves. Claus and Wembleth would rish with the women, Louis and Roxanny would not. Hanuman was getting his own fruit: he would not rish.

Do they rish with carnivores? Not by offering melon. But this ritual would eliminate Ghouls, and maybe they want that.

The fruit was red inside. It tasted a little like berries.

The others took it as a signal when the strangers ate: they feasted. There was fruit all around them. They were herbivores, all right: they needed to eat a lot. They fed Wembleth and Claus, and moved into more intimate contact.

Roxanny turned her back and walked away.

Louis picked up a melon, broke it on his knee – tanj, why not? – and followed her. He had hoped to court Roxanny's attention.

She turned and waited; looked down, grinned up at him, and said, 'I told Wembleth to tell them we're courting.' She took half the melon and ate.

Then she stepped into him, on tiptoe, half a head taller than he, and slid the length of her down his body until she was kneeling.

With a hoarse shout, Louis pushed her into the grass and entered her.

It was not the way he would ever have treated a woman. Roxanny was astonished. She wasn't quite ready, either, but she wrapped her arms and legs around him and made him prisoner again. Louis Wu's mind went away.

When he came to himself again, he was babbling, and he wondered if he had blurted secrets. Roxanny, still holding him prisoner in the grip of her legs, was laughing. 'Boy, you are eager!'

And the Hinsh had moved to surround them.

The women knelt to rish. When they mated with their men, both knelt. The men watched the strangers with their women and made graphic half-translated commentary. They found short men funny.

Wembleth, the shortest, was funniest. They learned he was ticklish.

'I'm sorry, Roxanny. I lost control of myself,' Louis said. It felt like he'd mated with one of the Ringworld bloodsuckers: it was that mindless, that intense. He dared not tell her about that!

She patted his cheek. 'Refreshing. Nine years to go on my implant, and it's a tanj good thing.'

'I'm fertile,' Louis said.

''Course you are.' She stood up, her back to him, fists on hips. 'I didn't buy it. Rishathra? You haven't told me every last bit of the truth, Luis. But . . . shall we join them?'

What? 'We're mated! You'd shock them!'

Roxanny picked up a melon, broke it in half, and offered it to an elf.

The elf was shocked. Then he laughed, knelt, and swept her against him. Louis flushed . . . and picked up a melon.

By dusklight – too dark to tell which fruits were perfectly ripe – the Hinsh broke off eating and rishing and mating to introduce themselves: an odd reversal of order. Their names were long and formidable.

Wembleth took Louis aside and said, 'The Hinsh are like others where I have traveled. If strangers plan to stay a short time, they use short names, quick to learn.

This can mean, *go away soon*. But do you see all this fruit? The wind shook hundreds of manweights of fruit to the ground. Every stranger eating means less fruit left to rot. We are welcome.'

Louis *felt* welcome. But rishathra was not sex. His body knew. His body wanted Roxanny.

And Claus wanted his blood.

Night on the Ringworld was rarely too dark to see. The Hinsh didn't want sleep; they conversed. The ARMs mostly listened.

Louis asked about the horned beasts. 'The grass eaters? They don't bother us, we don't bother them,' a man said. Of the sky he said, 'The stars used to hold their course. We could use them to tell time, if we wished. Now they're loose, wandering across the sky. Only the Vashneesht know why.' They spoke of the crops they'd left behind, and of the weather. Dull people, really.

They talked about the sudden wild winds.

'The climate will change,' Louis told his lady companion, whose name he'd memorized as Szeblinda. His translator would fish out all eight syllables. 'You may have to follow the pufftop forests as they die off to anti-spin. Carry melons and drop the seeds where you want more. Other folk may be running away from the disaster. You'll have to deal with them when they get here.'

'Will you stay with us, to advise?'

'We have to move faster than that. We're trying to solve it *all*,' Louis told her.

CHAPTER 13

Gray Nurse

In the morning Louis found himself on a grassy hill. He stood to look about him.

The flycycles hadn't been moved from their place on the river's shore. Acolyte slept between them. Hanuman and the Earth folk were nowhere visible. The Hinsh had departed. Downslope toward the river were melon trees and broken melon shells. A puddle of orange-and-chocolate fur beside the pool had to be Acolyte.

He walked on down.

He expected the Kzin to wake as he approached, but Acolyte didn't move. His sides moved. Good: the Kzin was breathing. Now, what mischief were the ARMs up to?

Louis took a flycycle aloft.

Claus and Roxanny were on the other side of the creek, behind a hill. They were working with the heavy

oblong brick she'd stowed in Louis's baggage compart-
ment. It unfolded into something like a holoscreen
keypad: the library from their little spacecraft.

Wembleth and Hanuman were peering past them
into the hologram display. Roxanny saw Louis and
waved. He waved back.

That didn't look like they were keeping secrets. Louis
returned to the pool.

Acolyte was sitting up, stretching. He looked around
him. 'Where is everyone?'

'Across the river. Are you all right?'

'Well fed and well slept out. I found a small deer or
something. Louis, nobody told me not to gorge. We
should have arranged to stand watch.'

Louis stretched. 'I wondered if they'd stunned you.
Hey, I slept as well as you did. The ARMs are doing
something tricky, I think, but Hanuman's watching
them. Shall we see?'

They took a flycycle across.

Claus awaited their descent. He said, 'Luis, Acolyte, I
want to interview both of you as to what you saw at
the puncture. Any objection?'

Louis thought of objections, but none that Luis could
back up. 'Show us how it works,' he said.

'Just the Kzin first,' Claus said.

'We'll help each other,' Louis said, and Acolyte

rumbled agreement. Then Wembleth too wanted to participate. That allowed the three to play off each other in an interview that became an animated conversation.

Louis gambled that the ARMs didn't have equipment to detect lies in the tremor of a voice. *Gray Nurse* or another in the ARM fleet might.

As to what 'Luis' had seen, Louis stuck close to the truth. They had been indoors: they'd missed the explosion (and Luis knew nothing of industrial antimatter). As he and Acolyte arrived from . . . somewhere . . . a great light had appeared, not much brighter than the sun, but huge. Then a glare-yellow doughnut the size of a mountain range lay blocking the region they had come to see.

He was asked about his background. He invented, but kept it terse. A twenty-year-old wouldn't have centuries of memories; he wouldn't tell stories well, and he'd be a bit shy around elders. Acolyte, who really was only twelve, was able to stick to his own memories, because Chiron (Luis said) had never confronted the half-grown Kzin. Luis speculated aloud whether the puppeteer was afraid.

And the library fascinated all three interviewees.

Protector – 1 Adult stage of the Pak species, where the line runs from child to breeder to adult. **2** Hominids in general are descended from Pak. They too have a breeder stage, at which they usually spend their lives, and an adult stage rarely achieved. **3** Archaic—

If Claus or Roxanny looked up a reference, Wembleth, Luis, and Acolyte crowded in to look. So did Hanuman, though he was generally ignored. Roxanny didn't like to be near him; he favored Claus, and Claus treated him as a pet.

There were hot buttons everywhere in the text.

Pierson's puppeteers – A species of great industrial power and sophistication, once common through *known space* and beyond, now thought to be fleeing the galactic *core explosion*. See *General Products company*. Physiology . . .

Core explosion – Thought to be a rash of supernovae . . . due to reach Earth in twenty thousand years. Inadequately studied.

General Products – A company once owned and run by Pierson's puppeteers. In human space they sold almost nothing but spacecraft hulls.

Known space – Those regions of the galaxy's Major Arm thought to be explored and understood by known sapient species.

Ringworld life forms are little understood. Ecologies tend to familiar patterns, but no trained biologist has had opportunity to investigate.

Mammals –

Hominids – Related to the genus Hominidae on Earth. Probably all such species derive from Pak breeders imported from the galactic core, subsequently evolved in many directions.

Louis Wu – {rotating hologram}

'Now give us some privacy,' Roxanny said without looking up.

Louis and Acolyte backed away. Hanuman climbed into Claus's lap. Claus scratched the anthropoid's head, and didn't seem to notice its high cranial capacity or the ridge on top. The interview had lasted nearly two hours.

Louis and Acolyte settled beside the flycycle. Louis deployed the kitchen. Acolyte said, 'Hanuman wants the library.'

'Tunesmith will too.' Louis passed the Kzin a squeeze of broth.

'One flycycle would hold all three of us if Hanuman rides my lap or yours,' Acolyte said. 'Hanuman learns fast. He might already know all he needs to run the library. Then we go, unless you truly want the ARM woman as mate.'

'Good plan. We go when Hanuman's ready,' Louis said. He sucked at a squeeze of green tea. He was not nearly so sure as he sounded.

The library codes might not be easy to crack.

The ARM might not let them go easily.

Anything could happen. The ARMs were in a shouting match, though Louis and Acolyte were too far away to make it out. Then Claus was back at work with the library, Wembleth and Hanuman were peering over his shoulder, and Roxanny strode briskly toward the flycycles. 'Luis!' she said with a whip in her voice.

Louis offered her a squeezebulb. Roxanny looked startled. 'Oh! Thank you. We've been in touch with *Gray Nurse*.'

'And?'

She glanced at Acolyte. 'Let's go somewhere,' she said.

She led them across the river on stepping stones, then behind some low bushes. Sitting, they were hidden. Louis kissed her. She accepted the kiss without response, then asked, 'Do you still want rescue? Do you want to visit Earth?'

'Last time I didn't have a choice.'

Shrug. 'You'd be very valuable. I could try to get you citizenship—'

'Roxanny, my father was an illegal birth.' He wanted

that established, *Luis Tamasan isn't registered*, before she tried to look up an imaginary man. 'Citizenship in what? What does it mean?'

He listened carefully to her answers. There would be changes in civilization since his departure. It sounded like there were more laws, more restrictions. Maybe only in Sol system.

Luis wouldn't know – 'Birthright? Roxanny, what is a birthright?'

'I'll find it for you in the library. Basically, you're born with one or two birthrights depending on – tanj – mostly on your genetic pattern. If you're healthy, you probably have two birthrights. You can lose it, or get more. Two birthrights make a child.'

Louis Wu had used up his birthrights. Faking his ID would involve faking *that*, and the penalties were draconian. He said, 'It doesn't sound like I want to settle on Earth.'

'No, given a bastard father. It's the most interesting world, though.'

It was just possible, he thought, that Luis Tamasan could become a whole new person. If he settled We Made It or Home, why would anyone ever try to connect his gene pattern to a Louis Wu? He could pay taxes. Learn a new profession. Marry— 'What are our odds of getting to space?'

'We know where a puncture is, if the whoever – the wizard – hasn't closed it.'

'The Phantom Weaver.'

She shrugged. 'Whatever you like. *Gray Nurse* can fire projectiles at a puncture from underneath. That'll tell us if it's been closed. Beyond that, who knows? Will Acolyte go along with this?'

'I suppose.'

'Would he come?'

'You can't get *him* citizenship. He's a Kzin. You're fighting Kzinti, aren't you?'

'There hasn't been a formal war in, oh, four hundred years.' She tapped her sleeve and read what appeared. 'In sixteen hundred falans. He'd be all right. There are hundreds of thousands of Kzinti citizens in human space.'

'I wouldn't tell him to come. He's younger than me, you know.'

'Let's get back.'

Louis didn't move. 'What about Wembleth? Do we want him?'

'Yah. He's a real native, after all. He must know wonderful things, and there are people who would kill to read his genetic pattern.' Roxanny stood and semaphored her arms at Claus. 'Let's get back.'

A shadow square had blocked all but a sliver of sun. Acolyte was squatting before the library, Claus standing behind him. Nearby, Hanuman picked imaginary parasites, looking solemn. The little protector looked up at Louis and made an urgent twirling motion.

Claus raised his hand, holding something L-shaped.

Close behind him Roxanny snapped, 'Luis, don't!' Hanuman *eeked* at the sound. She had one too: a slender flat object like the butt of a handgun, clearly a weapon. Old yogatsu training told Louis she was outside his extreme reach.

Behind Roxanny, sunrise glowed on the edge of a ridge.

The light should have grabbed his attention. But Louis was facing Roxanny and Claus and two guns. His mind caught up too slowly. Hidden or not, the sun is always at noon. That *couldn't* be the sun.

The ground trembled.

Acolyte hadn't moved; he must have been warned not to.

'I think we'll do better alone,' Claus told them, smiling, victorious. 'We only need one flycycle, but we need you to tell us how to fly it. You both know how. We only need one of you.'

Louis turned away from the fireball rising above the ridge.

The flare must have half-blinded Claus. The ground lurched, Louis lurched, Claus lurched, and Hanuman jumped into Claus's arms. Claus tried to move him aside. Acolyte turned as he rose. His claw swept across Claus and hooked him under the throat.

Louis whipped around and ran two steps. His fist took Roxanny under the jaw. He gave it plenty of follow through. She went down, rolling, and Louis leapt after her, afraid he'd hit her too hard, but he had to have that gun. In his peripheral vision, Acolyte hurled Claus into the ground in a spray of blood.

Louis's foot landed on her gun hand, and he had the gun. 'Don't,' he said.

She did. Her foot lashed out and caught him in the gut. Louis moved his hand: the gun missed her when it went off. Dust blasted out of the turf. A sonic weapon. He was still on his feet, trying to back away. Her other foot hooked his knee. He disengaged. She was up. The heel of her hand caught his cheek, and he was sprawling, still trying to avoid firing. Then she had his gun hand, and twisted, and had his gun. She aimed at a rising flycycle. He kicked her off balance. She fired as she fell.

He was on the ground, screaming. It felt like all the bones of his left hip and leg had shattered. Roxanny fired into the sky, lowered her arm and cursed.

When his eyes could focus, she was pointing the gun straight at him from four feet away.

The fireball was dying above the ridge. A spacecraft came out of the glare and began to settle.

One flycycle was still on the ground. The other wasn't in sight. Hanuman and Acolyte and Wembleth weren't either. Claus lay on his back, his head torn nearly off, his entrails displayed.

Roxanny had him under the gun. 'Why don't I just shoot you?' she asked.

'Roxanny, don't,' said Louis Wu, master of sarcasm. He dared not move and he couldn't think. Just as well. A twenty-year-old would break under the fury in her eyes. 'Don't shoot me,' Luis said. 'I'll fly you anywhere you like. Only I can't move.'

Wembleth appeared from behind a tree, saw the gun in Roxanny's hand, and ducked back.

'I don't need your flycycle,' Roxanny said. 'We've got a ship. Wembleth! Get aboard and take a seat. Luis, can you stand up?'

'Futz, no!' Louis said.

She stooped above him and picked him up in her arms. His leg and hip sagged as if boneless. She nearly dropped him when he screamed. The pain blasted his mind away and he missed the rest.

Louis was on his back. Some kind of talk show was running on the ceiling, but the voices didn't match. Aha: the sound was turned off. The voices had been speaking for some time, against a noisy background Louis took for a ship of war.

'I had brothers once.' Wembleth sounded drugged. Wembleth's translator device sounded crisp and alert. 'Stayed with their home turf when Father and I moved to . . .'

'. . . Move often?' A male voice of command, one Louis had never heard.

Wembleth: 'Yes.'

Roxanny had shot him.

Louis couldn't believe it. How badly was he hurt? His mind was muzzy; he'd have trouble keeping a story straight. If they questioned Luis Tamasan, they'd hear far too much. Louis tried to move.

He couldn't feel much. There was a tickle behind the back of his neck. His eyes could move, and his head, a little. He could just see that he was naked, on his back, immobilized in something like a stretch rack . . . or the Intensive Care Cavity of a military autodoc. The noisy background suggested a ship of war. He listened to the voices, trying to make them out.

Male officer: '. . . brothers?'

'Chosen brothers. Grew up faster than me . . . stayed with their own, to find mates.'

'Seen many kinds of human . . . ?'

Wembleth: 'Twenty, thirty species . . . reshed with . . .'

He thought he could guess what had happened up there.

A ship beneath the Ringworld floor had fired anti-matter bullets upward. No need to find an eyestorm already in place. One bullet to tear away the foamed scrith meteor insulation. The next to blast a hole through the scrith floor and the landscape above, big enough for a small troop transport to pass through.

It was crazy, vicious, simple, and direct. He should have seen it coming instead of making elaborate long-range travel plans.

Wembleth: 'Can't get anywhere if you don't know . . . reshtra . . . don't try to guess—'

Roxanny's voice. 'War? Do you ever fight—'

'Seen carnivores fight plant eaters . . . eaten me too. That what you mean?'

'Ook.'

Mmm? Turning his head wasn't easy: Louis was restrained in a nest of attachments, and he'd lost all sensation below his neck. But there was Hanuman, in a cage big enough to hold a Kzin. They locked eyes in mutual sympathy. Then something blocked Louis's view.

Roxanny Gauthier hung back behind a burly man, maybe a Jinxian, both wearing falling jumpers with ARM insignia. The man loomed over Louis, judging. He said, 'You'd be Luis Tamasan.'

'Yah,' said Louis Wu.

'You attacked one of my people.'

I lived to regret it. 'Sorry.'

'I'm 'Tec-Major Schmidt. You're a civilian prisoner. That gives you certain rights, but you're in futzy poor shape to exercise them. These stunners only stun if you're far enough away, but you were right up against

'Tec-First Gauthier. You've got bones broken into shrapnel from your hip to your knee. The 'doc can heal you if you don't move for a while. Five days.'

'Tanj.' Better make nice— 'Thank you, sir. I suppose I'd be crippled for life without your help.'

The officer grinned. '*Oh* yah. Now, can I free your arms? It would mean you can eat. Otherwise you're on tubes.'

'I won't try to pull loose,' Louis said.

'You could hurt yourself pretty bad if you did. Stet.' The tickle behind his neck moved down his spine – his arms came back to life, the left very tender, bruised from elbow to fingertips – and further, until – 'Hiii!' – and back up an inch. Louis could still feel bruises along his ribs, but not that awful shattered shriek of agony that started with his left hip.

Schmidt's hands manipulated a video remote in Louis's peripheral vision. The talk show disappeared; Ringworld jumped into being, spilling off the ceiling, and down the rectangular walls. Schmidt asked, 'Where do you come from?'

'Rotate it. More. Stet. Sir, that's the Great Ocean. Look along the spinward edge. . . .' Louis began describing the Weaver village he'd lived in last year. People, houses, the river, visiting Fishers, the webeye camera the Hindmost ('Chiron') had sprayed across the stone face of a gorge. These ARMs had no way of checking. If they could, Weavers would tell stories of

Louis Wu and the Hindmost as Vashneesht having some kind of quarrel.

But his mind was turning foggy. Louis hadn't been drunk in a long time, but it was like this.

Schmidt zoomed on the Great Ocean region. 'You live there? And your parents? Who else? A Kzin family? This puppeteer you told us about?'

'No, not Chiron. Finagle knows where Chiron lives,' with a laugh he wished he could suppress. His tongue was curling out of control. 'Kzinti don't live in the village, they're from somewhere on the Great Ocean.' If they pushed him, he'd reveal another partial truth: that Chmeee lived among Kzinti who had taken over the Map of Earth, natives and all.

'Tec-Major Schmidt said, 'A lot of Kzintosh call themselves Chmeee. He was some kind of legendary hero. What do you mean, Map of Earth?'

Louis realized he'd been babbling, thinking out loud.

Schmidt repeated, 'Map of Earth?' with steel in his voice.

'Sir. There.' Louis pointed into the ceiling, into the Great Ocean, where the continents of Earth were arrayed around its north pole, a hundred thousand miles spinward of the Map of Mars. He knew now that he couldn't keep secrets. Maybe they'd drugged him, maybe it was just painkillers. He'd last as long as he could, and then tell them his name and watch Roxanny explode in his face.

Roxanny said, 'Futz. They keep human slaves?'

Luis: 'Homo habilis. Pak breeders.'

Schmidt: 'Unchanged? Like the skeletons in the Olduvai Gorge?'

Luis: 'I never saw one. Like to see their noses.'

'Maybe they're a little skewed?' Schmidt said, clearly speaking for a recorder. 'From what we already know, a trillion Pak breeders had a quarter million years to evolve without protectors to cull the mutants. The Kzinti would have done some selective breeding. Anyway, these animals wouldn't have evolved into actual human beings, right, Luis?'

Louis's words came slowly. 'They could have evolved intelligence. We did. Did you want to invade?' He laughed. 'Rescue? These archaic Kzinti built the bigges' sea ship in history, and that was a thousand years ago. They're not using jus' spears and clubs.'

'We can beat seagoing ships. Now, what kind of tech has the puppeteer got? Anything weird?'

Whump.

Louis said, as Luis, 'How do I know what's weird?'

But he heard himself continue, 'Cameras like copper spiderwebs? Out of a spray gun?' his voice lost in a recorded bellow. The ceiling was flashing an unfamiliar distress symbol. *Hull breach*in*aft portside consumables tank. Power*lost in*sections two*and*three.* Schmidt and Roxanny drew weapons and turned away, stooping to get through a small oval doorway. Louis spoke to nobody: 'He's got stepping disks too. What was that sound?'

Gray Nurse shook herself. Gravity went away.

Hanuman said, 'Invaders. We'll either be rescued or killed. Expect surprises. No protector would leave us in alien hands.'

'Why not?' Louis heard the whine in his voice. 'Why the futz can't they jus' leave us alone?'

He didn't hear Hanuman's answer. It had become too noisy. A spacecraft being boarded made a fearful echo chamber.

Roxanny Gauthier ducked back through the oval door and around out of Louis's sight. A moment later Wembleth drifted loose, too drugged to act. Roxanny touched points on Hanuman's cage, and it opened.

She was talking in a hysterical whisper. 'I don't know what they are. Not Kzinti. Nightmares.' She looked at Louis, immobile in his medical cage, and said, 'Sorry.'

'Wha's happening?' Louis asked. She touched his lips with a forefinger. She braced herself behind Louis's medical cage. Only her projectile weapon showed, aimed at the doorway.

A voice spoke from somewhere, 'Tec Schmidt's voice sounding much too calm. 'All hands, we're fighting from the radiation refuge. I can see invaders on the hull and in four, five, six, and ten. Our motors are burned out, but we're under acceleration anyway. We don't know where it's coming from. We're also facing friendly fire, ARM missiles incoming, sixty and counting, no alien attackers yet. 'Tec-Admiral Wrayne doesn't want us captured, I guess.'

'Why didn't we see it coming?' she whispered. 'They've got an invisible ship! Shh.'

Schmidt's voice – 'The missiles are veering away!' – died in a roar of static.

A shadow blinked past the little door. Roxanny fired, and cursed. What came through then looked like a small man filmed fast-forward. It was behind Roxanny before she could turn, and Louis couldn't see the rest.

Three bulkier man-shapes zipped through the door, moving more slowly. They sealed it behind them. They were wearing skintight pressure suits. They deployed a balloon with inflatable tubes around it: a big nonstandard rescue pod. They didn't wait for it to inflate.

Spill mountain people come in a variety of species, but they all look more or less alike: burly bodies and short thick arms and legs, large lung capacity, thick fur for insulation, hairless faces. These three had been spill mountain people. Now they weren't. They wore pressure suits and big globular helmets, but their faces gave them away: mouths hard and toothless, like flattened beaks; big Roman noses; hairless skin wrinkled into leather armor. A mummified look, and an uncanny grace. They'd eaten tree-of-life. They were protectors.

The fourth came around into view towing an unconscious Roxanny. It was a protector, but not of the spill mountain people. Smaller, more slender. A dead-looking face with no more nose than an ape. Louis didn't recognize the species, but it wasn't a Hanging Person. Louis had thought Tunesmith was involved in this. He was less sure now.

They pushed Wembleth into the rescue pod, then Roxanny. Hanuman crawled in without a struggle. Then the protectors turned to Louis.

'I'm injured,' he said. No reaction.

They studied the machinery around him, talking tersely in a language Louis's translator didn't have. Then they switched things off. When one reached behind Louis's back, pain came as if he'd been hit by a truck.

He fought to keep from fainting, holding his attention on his breathing. Later he remembered a good deal. The feel of their hands, large, with blunt fingers and knobby knuckles. Brown eyes with epicanthic folds. The slender odd-man-out protector gave orders in monosyllables. The others detached Louis from the ICC, pushed him into the rescue pod, and sealed it. A framework still held his leg and hip immobile. Two studied the machinery that had held him while another cut a wide hole in the hull.

Air puffed the rescue pod into space.

CHAPTER 14

The Spill Mountain People

Gray Nurse was an ARM warcraft, built more like a spear than a ship, with a few smaller ships along its length. An intruder had attached itself like a remora near the fore end. It was lighter than *Gray Nurse*, built like the skeleton of a sunfish: a cabin, then an extensive grid of crosshatching girders like those found on a Belt mining ship meant to carry rocks and ore. Louis couldn't immediately see anything like a motor.

The protectors followed the rescue bubble into space. Others, all spill mountain protectors, emerged from further aft in *Gray Nurse*. Some towed the rescue bubble to the sunfish ship and moored it to the grid. Then they spurted away on rocket plumes, leaving their prisoners exposed to open space.

Maybe it was the drugs, maybe it was his body's

defenses: the pain had gone out like a tide. Louis looked around him at the universe.

A dusting of light motes, motionless a moment ago, were swept away in an eyeblink. Spy probes dismissed as by a sweep of God's hand, but how?

Roxanny was stirring, trying to wake up. Hanuman was just watching. Wembleth was very jittery. He spoke; saw that he was not understood; switched languages. His translator said, 'I don't understand.'

Louis said, 'Talk to me, Wembleth.'

'Where am I, Looeess?'

'Under the Ringworld.'

Wembleth looked up at the black wall that blocked half the sky. 'We are falling.'

'There's nothing to hit. You get used to this—'

The protectors were back. Two were pushing a fair-sized mass: the medical cage. They moored it to the cargo grid next to the rescue bubble. There was other cargo to be attached. Then they swarmed away to the cabin, leaving one still on the grid.

Gray Nurse was whipped away.

Louis felt no acceleration beyond a kind of flutter, but he felt his hair writhe about him. They must be doing hundreds of gravities. *Gray Nurse* was just *gone*. He'd seen nothing like a rocket motor, nor even a thruster.

Wembleth had his arms over his face.

The sunfish ship followed the thread of a spillpipe

beneath the Ringworld's black underside. A slow hour later, by the watch face in the back of Louis's hand, the spillpipe led them around the rim and up into a glare of sunlight.

Louis looked down along the inside of the rim wall, a thousand miles down toward a few tiny cones along its base. Beyond was a wide shore – twenty to thirty thousand miles of shore, it must be, given how high they were – and then an infinity of blue water seen from high enough to show the texture of sea bottom, and a few sparse clusters of big flat islands.

The clustered islands were peculiar. They all looked alike, and there was something else too. Louis had never seen anything like it, and that alone meant that he was looking at the Other Ocean.

They were dropping toward the rim wall. They'd been in flight for less than an hour.

'Wembleth?'

'Roxanny! Can you talk?'

She blinked. 'Luis? They took you too. Where are we? Who are these—?'

'Spill mountain people,' Louis said. 'There are lots of species. Do you ARMs know about—?'

'Down there below us, *those* are spill mountains,' she said. 'They're bigger than they look. Do you know what they are?'

'They're just the mountains,' Louis said, secretly amused.

The spill mountains had grown larger. Each of the little cones had a few silver threads of river running from its base.

'Pipes run under the Ringworld floor. They pump sea-bottom slush up over the rim. Otherwise all the fertile soil would wind up in the sea bottoms and nothing would grow.'

They were dropping toward one of the peaks. Roxanny said, 'Those mountains are waste heaps leaning against the rim wall, forty to fifty klicks high. People live on them. We've seen balloons going between the peaks. But, Luis, I think the ones who attacked us were protectors. Do you know about protectors?'

'Same thing as Vashneesht? Magicians. Very smart, very fierce, and they're born in armor. We wondered if they were myths. There are some artifacts.'

'Oh, they're real. One of those looked different from the rest,' Roxanny said. 'A primitive protector got as far as Sol system, seven hundred years ago, all the way from the galactic core. Its face looked like that one's.'

'The joker. That's the one in charge,' Louis said.

'How do you know that?'

Bram and Anne, both Vampire protectors, had found it easy to enslave spill mountain protectors. Spill mountain people couldn't live on the flats. In every case their entire species was isolated on some single mountain, held hostage with nowhere to flee. A spill mountain protector was born trapped.

Luis wouldn't know that, so Louis said, 'I heard him giving orders.'

They were crawling down the sky toward one of the spill mountains. Louis could hear a thin whining and feel a tremor in the rescue bubble. The sunfish ship had no kind of streamlining. They sank past an icy peak. Green showed much lower down. The sunfish ship moved close and slid sideways along a staircase of ledges, and now Louis could see trees and tiered fields and glimpse snow heaped in regular cones. Miles below was a breathtaking view of an endlessly rolling land, intricately detailed in tiny seas, rivers, ridges of hills.

There was a thump. Louis drifted against the bubble wall. Then the gravity generator went off and he slumped against the curve of wall in full gravity. Pain lashed up his leg and hip.

He didn't quite pass out. Roxanny whispered to him, 'Things happen in war, Luis. Don't hold it against me,' while the protectors moved around on the ice and rock, detaching treasure from *Gray Nurse* and carrying it away. Several were working on *Gray Nurse*'s 'doc.

The joker protector opened the rescue balloon. Warm air puffed out; thin cold air blew in. The joker stepped in, sniffed, looked at each of the occupants in turn. Roxanny was wary; Wembleth cringed in terror. Hanuman's eyes met the other protector's. They didn't try to speak, but they knew each other for what they were.

The joker touched Louis's leg and its brace, using great care.

Wembleth bolted for the opening. The joker swiped at him and missed . . . or else changed his mind. Wembleth bolted along the ledge, past conical houses, and was out of sight.

Wembleth was suffocating again. There wasn't enough air. The folk around him didn't seem to be having trouble. A few children watched him curiously.

He'd snatched up the translator device Roxanny had given him. Learning their language would be easier now . . . but it would still take hours. Strangers were always well treated, but the Vashneesht was a stranger too. Wembleth knew he'd have to hide *now*, and without help.

The houses were tall heaps of snow with a single small hole for a door. He'd be found quick in one of those, and only one way out. He considered hiding in a snowdrift, but only for an instant. He'd freeze. He wasn't wearing enough clothing. And he was leaving footprints!

A ridge of naked rock gave him the chance to backtrack. He followed it to where he could jump across snow onto the angled trunk of a huge elbow tree. His knees betrayed him as he jumped; he landed on the slope, slid, caught himself, and clawed his way up sixty feet of naked trunk. The top was a dense green tuft. Wembleth burrowed into it.

He could see out, a little.

Four spill mountain protectors, naked in the cold and their own thick white fur, wedged *Gray Nurse*'s 'doc through the opening into the rescue bubble.

Louis moaned when they moved him. The protectors were fiercely strong and surprisingly gentle, but it hurt. They lowered him into the Intensive Care Cavity and one reached around behind him. All sensation went away below the small of his back.

Though the military 'doc was severed from *Gray Nurse*, somehow they'd got it running.

The joker turned when Roxanny spoke. 'You are in violation of several dozen laws enforced by the ARM and related governments.'

The joker answered in unknown speech.

Roxanny's translator would pick up the language. Good, and Louis's would catch it too. Immobilized as he was, there was no more he could accomplish here. Louis went to sleep.

Through the greenery Wembleth watched the protector leave the rescue bubble. Roxanny followed. A dozen children followed her. The protector tracked his footprints for a time, then jumped across to the ridge of rock, examined it with her nose to the ground, then came straight toward him. She ran lightly up the trunk. She reached into the tuft and pulled Wembleth out into empty air.

She let him dangle from one hand as she climbed down. He was frozen with fear and cold.

A dozen children crowded the rescue bubble, and more swarmed outside. Hanuman was clowning for them. They shied back when Louis stirred and woke.

He smiled at a wall of white fur and two dozen eyes. 'Hello,' he said. A few voices answered. His translator did not.

Most of the pain above his waist – left arm, ribs – had eased off. He wondered how long he was going to be like this. If Roxanny and the joker had taught each other their speech, then the joker hadn't been speaking local dialect, and that meant Louis couldn't even talk to these kids.

But Roxanny and the joker were coming back, and Roxanny was holding Wembleth's hand.

They couldn't get through the crowd to reach the rescue bubble. They didn't try. The joker began to lecture, pointing occasionally at the humans and Wembleth. The kids inside couldn't hear, so they went out. Presently the joker sent Wembleth and Roxanny in, and gestured four remaining kids out, and closed the bubble.

Roxanny glared after the joker, who was hopping away on the struts of the cargo grid. 'She won't talk,' Roxanny said bitterly.

'Translator won't work?'

'The translator's fine, but it doesn't have anything to say.'

Louis asked, 'Are you keeping ARM secrets?'

'So's she! Yes, *she*, she told me that much. She said her name was Proserpina.'

Wembleth's teeth chattered as he spoke. His translator said, 'We're going for another ride.'

Louis asked, 'Are you up for that?'

The man shivered violently. 'I pissed my clothing last time. Thank you for not noticing.'

Louis sniffed. The air in the bubble had never ceased to smell clean and fresh. 'Protectors build good machines,' he said. 'We'll be fine.' He saw the joker enter the ship's cabin.

Gravity went away. 'We'll be fine,' he repeated.

The sunfish ship floated away from the cliff, then straight up. Blue sky darkened to black.

Louis said, 'I've figured out this ship. Gravity control—'

'Magnetic,' Roxanny said crisply. 'They must use the grid. Luis, there's a superconductor grid in the Ringworld floor. If this ship is using a magnetic drive, then it can thrust against the Ringworld. It's like leaving your motor at home. I felt my hair stand up. Didn't you?'

'Stet, but I meant the cabin gravity. Powerful, but it flutters. Why wouldn't Vashneesht fix that? I think they're too arrogant to test what they build. They do it all in one shot.'

'Got it all figured out, do you, kid?'

Louis flushed. He said, 'Stet, it's magnetic. You'd have near infinite range and huge acceleration as long as you stay near the superconductor net. You could use it as a weapon too. Push away missiles and ships. It could even be seen as a message.'

'Message?'

'"I can't invade you. I'm purely defensive." Like a fort.'

'Mmm. Or just "Keep out."'

'We're falling again!' Wembleth burst out. 'Roxanny, where are we going?'

Roxanny shook her head.

They crossed a wonderfully fractal shoreline, all curliques of bay and beach, and were over the ocean. Ocean and sprinklings of islands. If you thought of them as islands, you didn't see that much speed, but they'd be one-to-one maps of a world.

Near the shore of the Other Ocean the clusters were a bit foreshortened. Otherwise they were all maps of the same world. One sprawling continent with a spine of mountain; four smaller bodies and an archipelago of scattered tiny islands, all to antispin of the mainland; all showed a grainy texture. If you had to tell someone where you were – say, Tunesmith, if you could get hold of any kind of communicator – how would you?

But the shadows were different. Bands and flecks and patches of shadow on only a few of the islands.

Roxanny said, 'This is Ocean Two! Do you suppose we're going to one of the maps?'

'Sure. What do you make of the shadows, Roxanny?'

'We're too high to tell.'

Louis didn't answer. What should 'Luis Tamasan' know about this? But shadows just didn't happen in a place where it was always noon, and Louis Wu found it freaky.

Roxanny said, 'Luis, Wembleth, there's two oceans on the Ringworld, you know? There are all those *billions* of little shallow seas with corrugated shorelines to give the locals lots of convenient bays and harbors, and all the trillions of klicks of twisty rivers. But then there are two big counterbalanced oceans, the one with all the inhabited worlds in known space on it – that's yours, Luis – and this, this endlessly repeated map. It's probably one-to-one scale of *something*, but it's no world known to the ARM.'

Louis started to laugh.

Roxanny glared at him. She said, 'There are thirty-two

of these maps, all of the same world! So after we land, we *still* won't know where we are. Is that what has you amused?'

'Yah. Does the ARM have any idea what the Pak homeworld looked like?'

'A permanent war zone. Every Pak protector wants his gene line to rule the world. I'm just repeating the briefings,' Roxanny said, 'and we got all that from a stray Pak protector via Jack Brennan, and *he* was a Belter turned protector who couldn't be trusted worth tanj. So, no, we don't know the shapes of the Pak continents. Maybe they change. These creatures are *powerful*.

'The joker – she looks like Pak breeder skeletons we're still finding in Asia and Africa. So where's the joker from? The Pak homeworld? But maybe it's the Map of Earth. Luis, you said the Map of Earth was originally held by Pak breeders.'

The sunfish ship was descending toward an island cluster near the Other Ocean's antispinward shore . . . fifty thousand miles near, maybe. Any distortion was lost in detail as the land rose up to meet them. There were crescents and pools of shadow on the land . . . but how could they be shadows, with the sun just overhead? They looked almost like pictograms, or writing. A lone mountain near the continent's midpoint glittered. Dwellings? With windows?

The grainy look of the land became interlocking dots
of all sizes, circular features, as if the land had been
battered by meteors. They skimmed a forest, slowing
now. Louis recognized chains of elbow trees and other
familiar vegetation.

He said, 'Most of what's on the Ringworld must have
evolved as Pak plants and animals.'

'Good, Luis.' A verbal pat on the head.

Something about these patterns—

'It's a garden,' Roxanny said.

'Roxanny? This *big*?' They were still miles high.

Still, she was right. The landscape wasn't croplands,
but it was just as certainly *shaped*. Variety and color:
rainbow ripples that must be thousands of square miles
of flower beds; varied stands of trees in all the colors
of autumn and more, still seeming no larger than hairs
in a dandy's beard. A veldt shadowed with black arcs.
Ponds, lakes, seas like silver plates with little central
dots of island.

Roxanny said, 'Formal gardens are all rectangles,
unless they're supposed to look like wilderness. What
kind of garden is all circles, and no two the same size?
This is like . . . right.'

Like the Moon, Louis thought. 'Like a war?' All circles,
all craters. The Pak homeworld.

'Vashneesht,' Wembleth said positively.

'Yah, the joker is trying to impress us,' Roxanny
said. Louis laughed.

He glimpsed rectilinear outlines peeping through the wild colors. They dropped. There was a thump. Gravity ceased its flutter.

CHAPTER 15

Proserpina

She brought the mag ship down in the garden, six miles downhill from the Penultimate's mainland habitat. As soon as she'd safed the motors, Proserpina rolled out of the cabin and ran aft. A sense of order might help the aliens adjust, but she'd learn less if she gave them too much time.

Isolated, shorn of her senses, imprisoned in the Isolation Zone for all of these millions of falans – Proserpina had still been able to infer general details of Ringworld history: infighting, dominance games, reshaping of world-sized stretches of topography, shifting alliances, changing genetic patterns . . .

There was only one Repair Center, set halfway around the Ringworld from this, the Isolation Zone. The Repair Center could be seen as the Ringworld's natural throne room. A Ghoul was in power now, and that was good.

He was short of experience, and reckless (not good), and probably male. Males wandered further. Where tree-of-life was scarce, a male would find it first.

Control was what this was all about. In earlier ages she had seen conspiracy after conspiracy, and had always found a way to stay neutral without being destroyed. There was always a master of creation, and – after one awful early experiment – it was never Proserpina.

She hop-stepped over the struts of the cargo grid and slid into the rescue bubble.

The woman spoke. 'We need to talk.'

Proserpina perceived 'Tec-First Gauthier's impatience and was amused. The woman was young, though not young for a breeder. Her stance suggested a different gravity; her speech was a bit altered from what Proserpina had heard while eavesdropping on the Ghoul's retinue. Gauthier was one of the invaders. She'd have much to tell, once she stopped refusing to tell it.

Proserpina's silence made the woman uneasy. 'We need to talk to make the translators work,' she added.

Proserpina didn't smile. She couldn't. They'd talked while they hunted Wembleth in the spill mountain village, but they'd said nothing. Nouns, verbs: not enough to cue 'Tec Gauthier's speaking device. Gauthier was keeping secrets.

So was Proserpina. When she needed to talk, she would.

The brachiator watched her and did nothing. She'd

been expecting subservience. The little protector must serve another, perhaps the Ghoul.

One of the males made a soft-voiced request. Proserpina didn't know his speech. She'd work it out presently. He stood like a local, a little stooped, but at home with Ringworld spin gravity. He wouldn't have much to tell. What he wanted was clear: he was hungry.

The other male was injured and immobilized, naked and helpless. He watched. Proserpina was struck by his patience. Though no protector, he was an elder, of the same species as the woman. This would be the Ghoul's breeder servant, Louis Wu of the Ball Worlds.

'You're all hungry,' Proserpina said in Interworld. The men were unsurprised, but Gauthier jumped. 'You can all tolerate fruit. We'll work out details of your diet presently. We're all omnivores, I think, except you,' looking at the little one. 'How are you called?'

The woman recovered her aplomb. She gestured: 'Luis Tamasan. Wembleth. Roxanny Gauthier. Proserpina? How did you learn our language?'

'I've hacked into a library,' Proserpina said. She saw the woman bristle: *Gray Nurse's computer! Stolen!* 'I chose my name from your literature,' speaking now to Luis/Louis. Wu and the little protector were keeping secrets too.

She clapped her hands. 'Let's feed you. There's fruit outside, and a stream.'

'I'll have to feed Luis,' Roxanny said.

'You must learn what's edible. Come. Luis, we'll be back soon. Your device is giving you nutrient, but it's best if your digestive systems are exercised.'

'Thank you,' he said.

Roxanny looked dubious, but she went.

Roxanny followed the protector. Wembleth followed Roxanny, holding Hanuman's hand. The ape scrambled along faster than his little legs were up to.

From the back the joker looked like a small, scrawny, bald woman. She stood a meter and a half tall. All of her joints were swollen; her back was a column of pebbles. Roxanny knew that she should be afraid of the creature, but she couldn't *feel* intimidated.

Proserpina was talking to Wembleth in Interspeak. Wembleth chattered in his own language, and Roxanny listened to his translator with half her attention.

'Mother abandoned us. I never asked Father about it; he was touchy there, but I listened. They both used to go exploring. One day she was just gone. Some species do that, turn vicious and solitary, like the Swamp Folk. Friendly and curious when they're young, *great* rishathra, then something triggers, and they bulk up and change attitude and go off into the swamp. I was afraid I'd do the same. Interbreeding is rare, and you don't know what you'll get.'

'Have you rished with Swamp People?'

'With a Swamp Girl until she mated, and afterward we were friends. Then she got pregnant, and she went off alone to raise the children.'

There were low buildings in the forest. Trees masked them. Trees grew from the roofs, or up the side of a minaret. A huge tree grew through the hollow core of a ring two stories high.

Shadows ticked at the corners of her vision. Tree shadows wouldn't move in this weird place where it was always noon or night. Roxanny became sure that there were animals in the forest, watching them.

Proserpina was fast, darting among the trees, plucking and gathering plants in varied colors and shapes. 'Try this,' she said to Luis's long-armed pet, setting a purple blob in his hands. It resembled an eggplant, but it sprayed red juice when Hanuman bit into it. Hanuman buried his face in it.

'Here. Here.' Proserpina distributed other fruits, and watched for reactions. Roxanny's yellow globe was bitter. She dropped it. A handful of green cherries was edible, but sour around the seeds. Wembleth liked the inner rim of a mottled yellow ring – he had to fit his head inside it – and Hanuman's purple blob.

'Roxanny, is this place very different from your Ball Worlds?'

'Very.'

'How?'

'I haven't been here long. I'm still looking.' Roxanny

was reluctant to speak. Sooner or later the protector would be asking questions she shouldn't answer. Still – weren't there things she could learn from a protector?

So she temporized. 'We learned a lot before any ship landed. It's always noon here. I expect that could drive a person nuts. If you ever saw a sunset, it would be the end of the world.'

'And a mining system would hit vacuum. That's not all bad. Industries can sometimes use vacuum.'

'A year ago you were shooting down every ship that came near the Ringworld. Why did you do that? Why did you stop?'

'There was a protector Vampire in the Repair Center. He did the shooting. Another replaced him.'

'And now it's a kinder, gentler time?'

'Not while you're playing with antimatter, dear one! That will have to stop! You could destroy us all, and yourselves too. I think you must be schitz. Roxanny, you flinched.'

'Did I?'

'Are you schitz? Were you schitz? Were. How were you cured?'

Roxanny snarled, 'I stopped taking the stuff!'

'Stuff?'

'The Amalgamated Regional Militia used to draft schitzes for the lower echelons. We've tried to breed that trait out of ourselves, so it's hard to find a real schitz, but there are biochemicals that can imitate the schitz state. You see things, think thoughts, hear voices that a citizen never dreams. I took the stuff during training. I can get a shot during a mission, it makes things easier, but I try to stay off it. I'm not schitz, Proserpina. My genes are clean.' Roxanny clamped her lips closed. This was far more personal than anything she'd intended to reveal.

'Lower echelons? Do any of the top ranks go schitz? No, never mind. Do warriors such as yourselves have children, Roxanny?'

'No. I can't. I've had my shot.'

Proserpina stared at her. Then she turned away to gather more fruit. 'I'll feed your injured one,' she said. 'Eat. Explore. Enjoy,' waving vaguely at the forest and its hidden buildings. 'The stream is that way. Follow it back. We'll talk soon.'

Roxanny watched her go. Had she really been left to explore unsupervised? The prospect was terrifying and irresistible. She was in the Garden of Eden. God walked here. Nothing was otherwise harmful.

The building –

It was a toroid. One door, no windows. A sequoia-sized tree in the center lifted it two meters off its foundations. While Roxanny hesitated, Wembleth jumped to reach a doorsill, lifted himself, and was in. Roxanny waited a beat, then followed. She wished she had better armaments than the needler in the small of her back.

Roxanny jogged around the perimeter. It was all one

big tubular room, a few degrees tilted. She found nothing worth seeing or stealing. The floor was deep in dirt and rotting leaves. No obvious lighting, barring the transparent roof. No offices. No toilets.

She asked Wembleth, 'Do you know this style of building?'

'Vashneesht work. Very old. These walls cannot be harmed, but many lifetimes of wind made these corners round. I think servants of the Vashneesht lived here. Look, this was bed.'

The vegetable trash? Roxanny was used to float plates.

The next building over looked like a pump house nested in a forest of pipes. It was, but it also held toilets, a huge tub for bathing, and dust heaps that must have been towels. Wembleth understood: he knew more primitive means for using wastes for fertilizer. Sewage and wash water flowed into a sprinkler system. It was all powered from the roof, from converted sunlight. Roxanny and Wembleth spent an hour bathing and then investigating the system. The remarkable thing was that it still worked.

Roxanny led them along the river, in the direction of flow of the shadow squares, antispinward. They came to a wide, white sand beach. Huge combers rolled in from an endless ocean.

Roxanny tried her mag specs. She knew what she ought to see, but the horizon was a line of haze; the specs only magnified it, or picked out currents of heat. She'd be peering through hundreds of miles of that, to see subcontinents belonging to this same little map. How long would it take to get used to the Ringworld's scale?

She'd get a better view from the roof of the arcology; but that was not walking distance.

Proserpina paused at the edge of the garden long enough to instruct her servants. Aliens were not to see them. Aliens were not to be interfered with. Aliens were not barred from the Penultimate's long-abandoned buildings.

Hanuman was eating and watching her from far up a tall tree. Proserpina gestured him down.

'Who do you serve?' she asked.

The brachiator spoke a musical phrase, then translated into Interworld. 'Tunesmith. He derives from one of the Night People varieties. His secrets are not mine to give.'

'Why do you conceal your nature from the ARM? Why should I?'

'A ship of the ARM exploded three days ago. It tore a hole in the world's floor that would have destroyed us all.' Hanuman described the location quickly and precisely. 'Tunesmith repaired it—'

'How?'

'Secret, but his means are limited. Another such event would end everything. You and Tunesmith and I have this in common. To hold ARM ships away from the world is our only hope. Kzinti also must be kept distant. Puppeteers would rule us to make us dependable. They would make the Ringworld safe to a point beyond habitability. Who knows what Outsiders might do? There are other factions. Question 'Tec Gauthier or scan any ARM ship's library. Giving information to any of these invaders would only lure them all here to learn more. To tell them of protectors might scare them witless. Rewarding invaders with valuable data—'

'Enough of your chatter, I understand you. What of Luis Tamasan?'

'What sources have you been scanning?'

'Scan is too large a word. I've barely had time to browse in the libraries of *Gray Nurse* and *Hot Needle of Inquiry*.'

'Seek "Louis Wu".'

'*Gray Nurse* has the report he made to the United Nations following the *Lying Bastard* expedition. Should I hide his identity too?'

'Please yourself. He plays a frivolous game of mate-and-dominate with the ARM woman.'

'Stet, we will leave all as it is for this little time.'

Hanuman asked, 'What is this place? Are my charges endangered?'

'No, but guard them if you will. This was the domain

of the last rebel but one, the Penultimate,' Proserpina said. 'Will you serve me?'

'No.' No ambiguity, no hesitation.

'I want to talk to Tunesmith. How may I do this?'

'Tell me what you want said. Give me a vehicle.'

'I have all of the history of this structure and its regents, all for barter. The Repair Center is not the Ringworld's only secret. Do you dare withhold my knowledge from Tunesmith?'

'No. Tunesmith is more intelligent than you or me, but he cannot act without data.'

'Where is he?'

'Some distance up the arc.'

'You came to investigate the antimatter explosion. You left your vehicle behind when the ARM ship took you.' Hanuman didn't react. Proserpina said, 'You have no transport. I have only this one mag ship. To make another would delay us for days. Can we spare the time?'

'I must guide you to Tunesmith.'

Proserpina thought about this. Could she find a way to guard herself? Or was it time to die, if Tunesmith chose to make it so?

'I'll make things secure here first,' she said. 'Wait until tomorrow night.'

Louis Wu was not unhappy. He was getting a long rest, prone in the Intensive Care Cavity. Nobody expected anything of him. Let others deal with the Fringe War, antimatter fuel tanks, the dance of protectors. He dozed, and thought, and dozed. . . .

And he fell asleep, or was put to sleep. He woke under high, dark trees. His massive ARM autodoc was no longer attached to the sunfish ship. The joker stood above him.

He tried not to be dismayed that she'd come back alone. Hanuman must be with the others: he'd protect them.

She asked, 'Are you well?'

'Check the readouts,' Louis said.

She took him at his word. 'You're healing. You're getting nourishment and something to calm you.' She tapped at a screen. 'You wouldn't be getting *these* inputs if you didn't have internal injuries. They're still healing. This other concoction seems to be brewed from tree-of-life root, or some synthetic analogue, but the machine isn't feeding that to you either.'

'Really? Tree-of-life? The stuff that—'

'Here, this tube.'

Louis tried to sit up. 'I can't see it.'

She sketched a mark in the air. Louis knew that symbol, a trademark half a thousand years old. 'Boosterspice.'

'Intended to restore a breeder's age-raddled body? And you don't need it. You're an old man made young. Is boosterspice one of Tunesmith's secrets?'

Louis blinked. 'No. It might be an ARM secret.' He'd been told as a child that boosterspice had been made via genetic engineering done on ragweed. It now struck him that the longevity treatment had been introduced, and allegedly changed human nature forever, about two hundred years after an alien ramship reached Sol system. It could fit.

'You are fertile. I can smell it. Roxanny spoke of shots to make a person sterile.'

Louis smiled. How would a genderless protector ever understand that?

He said, 'I was chasing a woman named Paula Cherenkov. I knew she wanted children. I had the habit of bugging out of human space from time to time. I always thought I'd smuggle something some day . . . never did. This time I went to Jinx.

'Some worlds think just like flatlanders when it comes to the population explosion. Some worlds don't have much habitable territory. Not Jinx! When they need more room, they expand the terraformed regions. I got them to reconnect my vas deferens.

'Then Paula left Earth because she wanted a *large* family.

'A few years later I brought a new intelligent species into known space. The UN wanted to give me a birthright for finding the Trinocs and serving as their first ambassador. Now the doctors were waiting to fix what shouldn't have been already fixed. When Nessus made *his* offer, I went to the Ringworld.'

Proserpina set her hands on Louis's belly and moved them around. Pressure above his left hip. 'Old damage to the gut?'

'Yah.'

'There's barely a trace. This floating rib is newly cracked—'

'Agh!'

Hands like a score of walnuts palpated his numb hips, then ran down his legs. 'Six breaks, maybe more, all on the left. It doesn't matter, they can all heal at the same time. In four days you'll walk, in seven you'll run. Would you try solid food?'

Louis pointed: 'That one's good. The Hinsh gave it to us.' She broke a canteloupe-sized yellow fruit for him, and fed him, and ate some herself.

He asked, 'Who are you?'

'I'm the oldest protector, the last of the rebels,' she said. 'Tell me who you are. The woman doesn't know. She didn't perceive Hanuman either. What does she think *he* is?'

'We let her think Hanuman is a tame monkey. She thinks I'm the son of an ARM who got himself stranded. Can we keep it that way? Roxanny is an ARM detective. There are things they shouldn't know.'

'ARM is one of the factions—'

'Amalgamated Regional Militia. From Earth, the United Nations police since eight hundred years ago. There are a few hundred ARM ships in the Fringe War.

How much do you know, Proserpina? Have you been hacking into *Needle*?'

'Yah. Puppeteer civilization is too fascinating. I could become lost in it. Still, this Hindmost has extensive records of human civilization. Do you know the name "Proserpina"?'

'Pluto's wife, the Lady who rules Hell. Greek myth, Elizabethan pronunciation. Is this Hell to you?'

'In a loose sense. Tell me about Tunesmith.'

'Not yet. I want to know about you. Who you are.'

He had the impression she was grinning. She said, 'Your muscle cues aren't easy to read, flat on your back, hips and legs inert, and the rest hooked to all these pumps and sensors. Still, I sense something proprietary. Do you own Tunesmith?'

Louis laughed. 'He thinks he owns me.'

'You don't agree, but you don't hate him. You'd free yourself if you could. Will you serve me? No. For a time, then? Perhaps if you knew me better? I'm not prone to rages or bouts of frantic activity or megalomania, Louis. I don't suck blood, though you served a bloodsucker. I've been passive for millions of falans while the rest of my kind burned themselves out. Of course you must know me first, if we have time. My tale is complicated. I helped build the Ringworld.'

'I've heard that before,' Louis said.

'From some braggart breeder? They've become hugely various, haven't they? My telescopes won't penetrate atmosphere well enough, and I dare not travel to see more, but I've dealt with spill mountain species. Louis or Luis, I'm the real one. I broke promises before the work was finished, so it was finished without me, but I believe I'm the last builder. Would you like your legs back?'

What did she mean? She bent over him, reached around behind him. Pain surged.

'Can you tolerate it? It's better if you can feel what's going on.'

'That's pretty fierce,' he gasped.

'I'll cut the input by half –' (The pain receded.) '– and change your chemical balance a little.' The pain fuzzed. 'There. Will you try to urinate and evacuate? The 'doc system is equipped to handle that.'

'In privacy, please.'

'Stet.' She turned away. 'Then you can tell me about the people of the Ringworld. Who have you met? What are they like? I have the right. Our children became their ancestors.'

Louis considered keeping silence. It was not his nature. He couldn't hide anything from a protector anyway. He did wonder if Proserpina had set ARM truth drugs dripping into him.

But the vampire nest wasn't a secret to be kept. It was a futzy good story. Breeders – Ringworld hominids – had evolved into an ecological slot elsewhere occupied by vampire bats. Louis Wu had interfered with the weather over a world-sized area. His intentions had been good — he'd ruined the environment for some dangerous plants — but over the next few years, vampires moved under the permanent cloud deck established by Louis Wu, and took over a floating industrial park.

That happened far around the Ringworld's arc from where Louis was dwelling with a Weaver species. He'd watched through the Hindmost's webeye camera. Louis described it for Proserpina, and the Weaver village, and that led him back and back. Floating buildings gathered to form a city, and the shadow farm beneath, that grew a hundred kinds of fungus. The Ringworld slid off center, near to brushing against its sun. Back and back, until he was telling her how he'd come to the Ringworld, lured into an expedition to explore something strange beyond the worlds he knew.

She knew what questions to ask, when to keep silent, when to break and feed him fruit. 'Here, this machine makes a nutrient fluid too. Would you eat that?'

He tried it. It was basic stuff to feed an injured soldier. 'Not bad.'

'You eat meat too, don't you? Fresh killed? I'll hunt you up a sampling tomorrow. I'm more of a scavenger than you are, I think. How did you return to the stars? Through an eyestorm?'

'Something like that.'

He spoke of Halrloprillalar, the City Builder who claimed that her kind had built the Ringworld. 'She was joking with me, but she had it backward. She and her species nearly destroyed it.'

'How?'

'They dismounted the attitude jets on the rim wall and built them into their spacecraft. Proserpina, why did you let that happen?'

Poker face. 'We made attitude jets to be easily dismounted so that they can be easily replaced. We expected them to wear out in time. Was this a part of the Fringe War?'

'No. Earlier.'

'We'll speak of this again. When did the Fringe War start?'

'Tanj, I don't know. The first ships may have got here ahead of the Hindmost, a hundred falans ago. You stole *Gray Nurse*'s library, didn't you? Have you got it running? See if it's got footage of *Needle* coming in.'

'I'll do that,' said the protector.

Louis called after her. 'Check on the others, will you?'

'They're safe here, but I will. Sleep.'

It was night, and he'd talked himself hoarse. He slept.

*   *   *

He woke to find Roxanny and Wembleth asleep on the plastic sheeting. He didn't disturb them. In an hour they woke, found the store of fruit, and ate.

Roxanny fed him delicately. Perhaps she'd raised a child once.

She and Wembleth had spent yesterday exploring while Louis lay in his ICC. 'These elbow trees are easy to climb. It's even somewhat safe, once I found some rope. We got a wonderful view. It's all flat, the horizon never curves out of sight, and I had these.' Mag specs. 'Luis, did you notice one big central mountain, coming in?'

'Yah, inland.'

'It's windows top to bottom, but there are only a few picture windows. The rest looks like a spray of glitter everywhere. I'd call that structure an arcology, but *big*, and built by military, or maybe paranoid crazies. Straight highways with towers at the end, wonderful fields of fire. Big helipads. I didn't see any guns; I just saw where they should be mounted.

'There's only that one huge palace. Over the rest of the island – I keep saying island, just because I can see so much of it, even though most of it dwindles into what looks like fog. *Continent*. The buildings nearby are all very basic, and there's nothing big further out. Wembleth thinks it's all housing for breeders, *Homo habilis*. We didn't see any, they could all have died off, but Luis, if this was a protector's home, there'd be defenses and research labs and libraries, wouldn't there?'

'Well, there's the arcology,' Louis said.

She grinned at him. 'Do you even know what *arcology* means?'

'Big building.'

'Well . . . yah. I don't think she's using it. It was left by the previous tenant. I think Proserpina has a base, maybe on the little continents, maybe on another Map. She wouldn't have turned us loose where she works. This place is . . . remember I said "garden"? Suppose you had to turn the whole Earth into a garden? Earth *is* a closed ecology, but it changes. It drifts.' She looked deep into his eyes, seeking understanding. 'Gardeners don't like weeds. They'd do something about deserts . . . wouldn't have to worry about tundra because there's no winter . . . but a gardener might have to control the weather.'

'Weather's chaotic. It can't be controlled,' Louis said.

'What if you had *huge* air masses to work with? An area of a thousand Earths, and no hurricane patterns to foul you up because you're not on a spinning ball. Air masses wouldn't move *fast*—'

Louis laughed. 'Stet. Maybe.'

'We won't actually see other maps,' she said, suddenly depressed. 'No boats for guests. What do you think, Luis? One whole supercontinent for a garden, and breeders are an integral part of the garden. Defenses on the islands. Telescopes and research facilities. Mines . . . you don't get mines on the Ringworld, do you?'

'If you could reach the spill mountains,' Louis said.

'Materials might layer out according to density. Otherwise, no mining rights. You dig for oil, you hit scrith, then vacuum.'

'Proserpina *can* reach the spill mountains.'

Louis shrugged. 'I can't help you explore. Be cautious. Every culture has fairy tales about someone finding something he shouldn't.'

'Even so,' Roxanny said, 'I'd like to get into that building.'

Wembleth and Roxanny went out again after breakfast.

Proserpina was back at midday. She asked, 'What are stepping disks?'

'Where did you find those?'

'Your own report to the ARM, Louis Wu. You didn't tell enough. What if I had to *make* stepping disks? Is the Ghoul protector doing that?'

'You first. How are my companions?'

'Exploring. Hanuman went off alone, Wembleth and Roxanny are together. They'll learn little in this place. The last rebel to die lived here. I took charge of his habitat, but the Penultimate's palace is trapped. I leave it alone.'

She hoisted a miniature deer nearly her own weight. It dangled, its neck broken. Big insects buzzed it. 'I use this animal for food myself. Can you eat it?'

'Maybe—'

'Treat it with heat?'

'Yah. Clean out the body cavity. Shall I—?'

'You may exercise your upper body, but otherwise rest. Your bones are pinned together, but let them knit. I will cook. I can research this.'

Barbecue smells made him hungry. In an hour she was back with a roasted carcass. She stripped off pieces of meat for him. He found it pleasant to be waited on.

'"But always at my back I hear Time's winged chariot hurrying near",' she said. 'No, eat. I need to know how urgent this matter of the Fringe War is. Does Tunesmith have it under control?'

'More or less,' he said.

'Eat. Is it more, or less?' She scowled at what she saw in his face. 'Less. Hanuman tells me of the blast that tore a hole into space. I saw it from a distance, and knew I must act. Antimatter. Could it have killed all life? Did Tunesmith really prevent that?'

'Yes.'

'What did you see?'

'Wembleth and Roxanny would eat some of that,' Louis said.

The protector met his eyes for a long heartbeat. 'I'll fetch them,' she said. She set a great slab of meat in his reach, and departed.

*   *   *

Daylight was fading when they returned. Proserpina and the others cooked dinner outside. Louis smelled wood smoke and roasting meat. What Roxanny brought to Louis included vegetables: green-and-yellow leafy plants, and roasted yams.

Proserpina was becoming a skilled chef. She ate with them, but what she ate was raw meat and raw yams. When they had finished eating, she said, 'I want your trust.'

The ancient protector's eyes locked with theirs, skipping past Hanuman as if he were a dumb animal. 'Wembleth, Roxanny, Luis, you'd be demented to trust me knowing no more than you do.'

'Tell us a story,' Louis said. Proserpina was keeping Hanuman's secrets, and Louis's, and perhaps Roxanny's too. There was no reason to trust her, and every reason to listen.

'These events all took place near the galactic core. We who held our world were ten to a hundred million protectors of the Pak species,' the protector said. 'The number varied wildly in the endless war.

'Something more than four million falans ago – I've lost track of time to some extent – ten thousand of us built a carrier ship and some fighter scouts. Eighty years later, six hundred were left to ride them.' Proserpina spoke slowly, reaching far back into her memory. Interworld was a flexible language, but it wasn't built for these concepts.

'This land is a good map of the Pak world. Did you see its shape? Circles everywhere,' Proserpina said. 'Blast craters, new and ancient, from an endless variety of weapons. These maps were identical when we built them, but they've changed since. On the Pak world and here, we fought for any advantage for our blood line. Luis, *what*?'

'Well, it's strange,' Louis Wu said. 'One world, over and over? The Pak world was in the galactic core. Suns are packed close together there. You came *here*, thirty thousand light years in one leap. Why didn't you use worlds closer in?'

'Yes, our worlds were much closer together than yours. Endless room, endlessly coveted. We saw no way to reach them in a spacecraft carrying breeders, because we would fight for advantage of the breeders. If we solved that, we'd face another problem. Any world would require reshaping for periods of thousands of years. Before the work was complete, each would be snatched away by armies of other protectors. We could see that this had happened. Worlds near Pak were shaped to a Pak ideal, then blasted back to barren waste long before I was born. We saw no way to take other worlds unless we could change the circumstances that shaped us.

'This is what we did, we six hundred. First, we gave up nearby worlds. If another ship could reach us, that world was too close. We found records of a voyage into the galactic arms, a route already tested by an earlier colony ship. The colony failed, but we knew no intervening danger had stopped it from reaching its target world.

'Second, we segregated ourselves from our breeders. We housed them in a cylinder topographed like a rolled-up landscape. Their food would grow there too, water and air and wastes recycled, a locked ecology. No pheromones from breeder housing would reach the flight control complex. The breeders were not to love us; they would not be aware of us at all. Any protector violating the ban must die.

'Of course there was natural selection at work. Many breeders would die, did die without the company of protectors.' Proserpina's eyes sought theirs. 'Even now, four million falans evolved, don't you Ball Worlders sometimes need the companionship of something greater than yourselves?'

Roxanny said, 'No.'

'I find records of scores of religions.'

'We've outgrown them,' Roxanny said.

After a moment's pause, Proserpina said, 'Stet. Many breeders died for lack of our company, but less every generation. Again, many protectors found we *must* smell or touch our own kind. Many found ways to enter breeder housing, and died when they were caught. Others stopped eating. In the first thousand years we lost half our number. Replacing them from breeder stock was a chancy thing. Natural selection took its toll.

'What emerged at the end of three hundred and fifty thousand falans of travel, was a race that can live without the smell of our own blood line constantly in our nostrils.

'We veered away from the target world. A colony there had failed, but we could not know how badly. We might find protectors already in place, and our ship was a fragile bubble. We believed — Yes, Roxanny?'

'Earth?'

'Yes, your world, Earth. We could have had Earth. Your tree-of-life plants weren't growing right. Your protectors died. Their descendants were mutating in many directions. We didn't know that. I learned too little of the Earth colony before your evolved breeders began blasting radio waves at the stars. By then—'

Proserpina blinked at them; started over. 'We arrived in the local neighborhood. We found worlds we might take, but our ambitions were greater than that. We chose a system with a gas giant planet huddled close up against its star. We surmise it formed far out in the disk that became the planets. Then it was drawn in over the billions of years, eating lesser worlds as it came. Thus we found a planetary system already cleared out for our convenience, and most of the mass gathered in a single body, a mass of almost twenty Jupiters, Roxanny.

'So we built. We met difficulties working that close to a sun, but we could use the sun's magnetic fields to confine the masses we worked with, particularly the hydrogen we needed for fusion motors to spin up the ring.

'Stars that can generate extensive planetary systems form in clusters. There were stars with planets around us where we stopped, and some were Pak-like or close to it. We identified those that might evolve dangerous enemies. We collected local ecologies and settled them on maps of their worlds.

'We never approached Earth, Roxanny. We were afraid. We studied the system intensively at long range. The Map of Earth became home to our own breeders. We needed fifty thousand falans to build an ecology into the Ringworld's inner surface, but we started there, with the Map of Earth as a test bed.'

'Whales,' Louis said. 'There are whales in the Great Ocean. *Some* protector must have gone to Earth.'

'It may have happened after I was isolated,' Proserpina said. 'Wembleth, are you keeping up with this?' Proserpina changed languages and spoke rapidly. She switched back: 'Later I'll show Wembleth maps of the sky, and diagrams. You two should try to tell him what a Ball World is. Roxanny, these maps of our world are prisons. We knew some of us would break the one law. We built the prisons first, to warn each other. Any felon would be isolated with a world to rule and a population all of her own kind, just as if they'd each conquered the Pak homeworld, but all made hostage to the majority.

'I was one of those.'

'Why?'

'Oh, Roxanny.' Proserpina's body language suggested impatience and bitter laughter. 'We thought we would win! Eleven of us thought we could take the Repair Center. We'd breed our descendants to all of the lines, and cull to keep our traits dominant. In a thousand years we'd be safe, even if the power balance changed, even if an insurgence should kill us. We planned it all in an afternoon, and collected our resources as fast as ever we could. Even so, we were a little slow.

'They confined me on one of the Maps, not this one. They collected a hundred of my line and scattered them in pairs through this land. I must build a land they could live in. I must guide the breeders myself so that ultimately they meet and interbreed, or else inbreeding would destroy them. While I did all that, time passed me by. I was out of the loop. Others of my descendants lived among the Ringworld's expanding population, and their genes were hostage too.'

Proserpina fell silent. Louis asked, 'How long did it last? What stopped it?'

'A few hundred thousand falans – I'm guessing, Luis. Wembleth, Roxanny, you don't understand? On the Ringworld we built, a breeder population expanded to

a trillion. At some point they became a chaos of mutations. Mutations are of no use to a protector; they don't
smell right. Luis asks me when the protectors stopped
culling their tribes, and why. I witnessed too little. I
don't know why. I'm guessing even at when.

'I was a prisoner. I spent long periods in depression, noticing nothing. I never quite starved myself.
When I was myself, I made telescopes but not probes.
We were barred from intrusive investigations. With
telescopes I could see nothing nearby, but I could
study what was happening far up the arc. Meteors
continued to be intercepted. An eyestorm formed; I
guessed at the dynamics; I saw the storm dissipate. It
meant that protectors were still doing repairs. Luis,
what?'

'Depression. Sorry, I don't mean to interrupt—'

'How can I not notice when you want to speak?'

'These bouts of depression, do they make you miss
things? I'm wondering about the rim-wall attitude jets,
and Fist-of-God Mountain.'

'Where is it?'

'Near the far ocean. It was a giant meteoroid impact,
from underneath. It didn't leak much because the land
was pushed up.'

'I would not have acted. This is work for the resident protector.'

'There was a *fight* for who would be resident
protector.'

Roxanny and Proserpina stared at Louis. Then Proserpina moaned. 'I've been remiss.'

Louis asked, 'Did your jailers give you tree-of-life?'

'Yes, but neutered. A virus causes the gene flip that makes a breeder a protector. The virus lives in tree-of-life root. Neutered tree-of-life will still feed me, will feed any protector, but it won't change a breeder. What made you ask that, Luis?'

'Just a thought.' Tree-of-life only grew in the Repair Center, as far as Louis knew. Apparently it had died out elsewhere. 'Is it easy to get rid of the protector virus?'

'Yes.'

'But you got more?'

'How did you know that? Yes, I filtered it from the air when it grew thick enough and scattered far enough, four hundred thousand falans after creation. I cultured the virus and grew it in my plants. I made a few servants then, not enough to be noticed, and sent them on errands. But they revolted, and I had to kill them, Luis, and the next time I tried it, it didn't work. My plants had been neutered again. I know not by what means, and the virus wasn't in the air any more. You ate tree-of-life tonight.'

Roxanny gasped. Louis gulped. He said, 'Tasted like a yam. I think it probably is a yam, Roxanny. Proserpina, when did it happen?'

'Something more than a million falans after creation. You know what happened, don't you, Luis? Tell me.'

Louis shook his head. 'The protectors are gone. That's all we know.'

Proserpina said, 'I understand now. Species differentiation has been extreme in the past two million falans. I can see how far *your* species has veered, Roxanny, under pressures that favor intelligence, hairlessness, swimming talent, and a two-legged run. My telescopes can observe the spill mountains. I went to visit them when I dared, when I was sure I was the last protector in these lands.

'Their people fission into incompatible species under nearly identical conditions. I've tapped the heliograph communication network formed by the Night People. Eaters of the dead, aren't they? And that intelligent, and as breeders! Some half-intelligent protector ruled the Repair Center for a very long time. I can't guess how many other variations there are.'

Roxanny said, 'Thousands.'

'But on the Map of Earth there isn't room for mutations to settle in and compete and shape each other to strangeness. My servants settled my breeders among the Pak of the Map of Earth. My line may thrive there. Luis, *what are you hiding?*'

'I'm sorry.'

She loomed over him, small and dangerous. 'Talk to me.'

Prone in his casket, he said, 'I have a friend on the Map of Earth. I want him protected.'

'Tunesmith wouldn't let another protector near the Map of Earth. *I* haven't survived by challenging the resident. What are you hiding?'

Roxanny spoke. 'There are Kzinti on the Map of Earth. He said so. His friend Acolyte comes from there.'

'Archaic Kzinti,' Louis said. 'Not the same as the armies of the Fringe War. They sailed across the Great Ocean and formed a colony on the Map of Earth, not that long ago.'

'While I was in depression,' Proserpina said. 'I left too much to the resident. Stet. I'll research Kzinti, archaic and modern. Maybe we can deal. But I must confront the resident.

'Tonight I must go away. Tunesmith must be dealt with one way or another. I may be gone for days. 'Tec Gauthier, you must care for Luis. Luis, shall I give you back your sensation?'

'Try it.'

When pain came, Louis wondered if Proserpina was taking revenge on a bearer of bad news. But there was no more than an ache, though it ran from hip to heel.

'Wriggle around if you feel like it, but carefully. Don't detach anything.' Proserpina stroked the tree swinger's head. 'Little Hanuman, would you like to come with me?'

Hanuman considered, then jumped into her arms. She looked around at them. 'I make one proscription. All of what you can reach is open to you, save only the big building to spin and starboard, and the continent nearest to antispinward. I'm sure the big building is trapped. I haven't dared it myself. The little continent is where the Penultimate kept the dangerous species from Pak. Analogues of wolves, tigers, lice, mosquitoes, needle cactus, and poison mushrooms, the plants and creatures we never wanted among our breeders. Most of them were extinct when we left the core stars, but we saved a few. We might have released them, had we known that our breeders would evolve into their ecological slots.'

She turned and was gone so quietly and easily that it was as if a ghost had evaporated.

CHAPTER 16

Meeting of Minds

She would let him fly!

Hanuman prepared. The chair was wrong for him; he reshaped it. Proserpina watched.

They stepped into the forest to collect a store of fruit. Sudden as lightning, Proserpina snatched a weasel-like animal out of a bush and broke its neck. She tossed it aboard with the fruit and the water.

She took her place on a horseshoe of couch and improvised a crash web. Hanuman studied the ring of tell-tales and controls for some seconds before he dared touch them. They had a half-random look: fitted in whenever there was something new to be monitored.

The vehicle was nothing like an airplane.

Relaxed as if poured into her couch, Proserpina watched him lift and swoop and spin and dip almost low enough to shatter a tree and minaret, lift too fast, slow until the wind-induced tremor went away, then rise sedately into the vacuum where he could build up some *speed*.

The mag ship was as much a wonder as any of Tunesmith's ships. Its brute strength was startling: it could easily have torn itself into shreds of foil. Its motor was the Ringworld floor itself, powered by sunlight falling on trillions of square miles of shadow squares. Sailing lines of magnetic force, it moved less like an airplane than like an undersea vessel.

These controls weren't all involved with flying. Hanuman was aloft for some time before he tried anything esoteric. Proserpina watched but did not interfere as he manipulated magnetic fields beneath the landscape. Soil lifted and shifted. In his wake, a stream began to change its course.

He'd seen Tunesmith manipulating such forces in a command post in the Repair Center. This wasn't just a spacecraft. It was an entire Ringworld defense system.

Under guidance from the mag ship, the superconductor cables below the landscape could attract, repel, or shift anything metallic: incoming meteoroids, alien ships and missiles, even the occasional solar storm or lethal surge of cosmic rays. Hanuman might be good enough to orchestrate such a defense. He had watched Tunesmith at work.

The land below Hanuman was only a mask over vacuum. Knowing that in his gut, *seeing* it in the

Ringworld's underside, ridges that were canyons and riverbeds, creases that were mountain ranges, had almost destroyed the newly created protector. Hanuman had never grown used to it. Only now did he begin to feel that he was its master.

Its master, barring the presence of a greater protector. Proserpina was greater than Hanuman. As a breeder, she'd evolved closer to intelligence; the tree-of-life virus had done its work on a bigger brain. She had more experience too. But Tunesmith was brighter than she.

It was a bribe, letting him fly. Hanuman understood that well. He understood, too, that he was telling secrets with every move he made. *Hanuman is a master pilot, and expendable. What has he flown?* How much did she see? How much did she already know? She reclined, and watched.

He circled above land scoured bare and half-hidden beneath tiers of cloud. The hole had closed, but even now the atmosphere had not flowed in to fill the partial vacuum. He told Proserpina, 'This would have spewed all the Ringworld's air to the stars. Tunesmith stopped it.'

'How?'

'I may not tell.'

'Good enough that he has a way. How did you come here? I saw no ship large enough for my sensing devices.'

'I may not tell.'

'Stepping disk. Louis Wu described them for the ARM. We must find one. Show me that wreckage.'

Hanuman skimmed over the vast deflated balloon that had been Tunesmith's meteor plug — she'd have found it without his help, of course — then hovered above the ruin of an ARM pressure tent. 'Set down?'

'Yes.'

They donned pressure suits and walked through the wreckage. He saw no reason not to answer her questions. What she asked told him a little of her thoughts and purposes, though Proserpina was learning more than Hanuman was.

They moored the heavy ARM kitchen 'doc to the cargo grid, and lifted again.

The battlefield had been disturbed. Proserpina walked through it, observing first, then asking questions. Hanuman tried to see what she saw. The sonic hadn't left splashed projectiles or scorch marks. There was the ant-covered splash where Claus had died. Hoof prints: small herdbeasts had run through this place afterward. Prints of big hands and feet: scavengers had come to the smell of blood, and found nothing. The ARM lander had taken Claus's corpse.

The flycycle was upside down, resting on its rack and seat backs. There were more scavenger prints around it and on it. Ghouls had tried to fly it;

Tunesmith's locks had held; they'd turned it into a joke.

Hanuman said, 'Tunesmith is smarter than you. Why not let him play? You've done that for ages.'

'I must still be satisfied as to his fitness. I must speak to him.'

The flycycle was too heavy for the strength of two protectors. Hanuman crawled under it. The vehicle lifted and righted itself. He turned the holoscreen on. Louis must have turned reception off and left the sender going. Now, how to hide the lightspeed delay, to conceal Tunesmith's location?

Hanuman saw no way. He said openly, 'Now you may speak to Tunesmith. He cannot see us yet. Expect a delay of half an hour.'

'He's on the far side of the Arch? Conversation will be painful. Stet, I'll begin. Tunesmith!' and she howled what Hanuman had given as his true name. 'You have been meddling with the basic design of the Ringworld. You must have surmised my existence. Call me—' followed by a decidedly unmusical sound. 'I reside in the Isolation Zone. Louis Wu and your pilot are both safe. Louis Wu is injured and healing. We hold 'Tec Roxanny Gauthier, an ARM, of the Ball People. The Kzin Acolyte is missing. I presume he's with you.

'I want to trade secrets and promises with you. What I have to offer is some knowledge of the Ringworld's construction and history plus whatever I can get from

Roxanny Gauthier. We all want to protect the structure from what Louis calls the Fringe War. Haste seems called for. I beg you to reassure me that you can plug a hole if another antimatter explosion happens. Reassure me that you can outfly these intruders. Hanuman seems skilled and apt, but he is no better than his vehicles. Also my direct lineal descent—'

Proserpina paused, then said, 'I must inquire as to the state of the Map of Earth. Tell me what you can. I give speech over to Hanuman.'

Hanuman chattered at length. Meticulous descriptions of Proserpina, Roxanny, *Gray Nurse*, and ARM warriors, the sunfish ship, the flight from the rim wall, the continent on the Map of Pak, local vegetation probably imported from Pak, Proserpina's not-quite-hidden servants . . . Concise as the Ghoulish language was, he spoke for a long time.

When he stopped, it was not because Proserpina forced him to. He had given away every secret he knew, and Proserpina had not killed him to stop his mouth.

Proserpina climbed from the flycycle saddle. 'How shall we occupy our time?'

'Lunch.'

'Good.'

They spread fruit on the grass and added a weasel carcass. Proserpina asked, 'How do you suppose our guests are getting on?'

Hanuman ate a dwarf apple. He quoted something

he'd found in *Needle*'s library. '"When the cat's away, the mice will play." Did you leave them a boat? Anything that flies? No? Then they'll try to reach the Penultimate's palace.'

'There's no access,' Proserpina said.

'Not even for you?'

'I have mapped hypothetical routes, but I deem the risk unacceptable. The Penultimate's inventions are nothing I can't evolve for myself. Hanuman, they are only breeders.'

'They will search.'

'Hello. Bored?'

'Yah.'

'How are you entertaining yourself?'

'Counting up mistakes,' Louis said. *There's another one. Youths don't remember enough mistakes.* Did they? He didn't really recall. It had been too long.

'Are we still friends?'

'Sure, why not?'

She cocked her head, studying him for signs of sarcasm. 'Luis, I want you to forgive me for shooting you.'

'Okay.'

'Tanj, you're easy. You could ask me to forgive you for Claus.'

'Claus pretty much killed himself,' Louis said.

'Your friend killed him.'

'First chance he got. Stet, why not? It's a prisoner's duty to escape. Why in the name of sanity would Claus hold a Kzin at gunpoint?'

'That's war.'

'Who declared war? Roxanny, who decided to imprison me? I could have been conned into going for a ride. Done that way, maybe you could have had Acolyte too.'

'What if you said no?'

He asked, genuinely curious, 'Are you schitz?'

'What? . . . Not right now.'

The ARM was manned by schizophrenics and paranoids. Everyone knew it. In real life, any 'doc could provide chemicals that would keep a schitz sane, but in the ARM, they did without chemicals at least some of the time.

Louis didn't comment. Roxanny glared at him. 'This is pretty personal, isn't it, Luis? I've been diagnosed not schitz. I didn't join the ARM because I was schitz, I did it for the adventure.'

'Ah.'

'But I can fly on psychomimetics. I'm not getting them any more, but they were used in training.' She shrugged it off. 'Want to go for a walk?'

'I don't climb out of this thing for another two days.'

'You're going to love it. This place is the Garden of Eden. There's nothing harmful, and God walks. She's just gone away for a bit.'

'Any idea where she went?'

'Nope. Why did she take the little ape? I thought it might be a pet. Then I thought, maybe it smells like a relative. What do you think?'

'Not a relative. No more than you or me.'

There was silence. Then, 'Luis, are we lovers?'

He smiled. 'In this condition?'

'I saw her turn off the nerve block. Does it hurt much?'

'Not much. Aches.' He watched her take her clothes off. His own must be back aboard *Gray Nurse*. Suddenly he felt helpless. He wondered what she would do if he said 'No.'

She ran her hands over his feet. 'Feel that?'

'Yah.'

Her hands moved upward, part massage, part caress. Where he winced in pain, her touch grew lighter.

The thrill never went away. Among the Giraffe People he'd been too flustered and in too much of a hurry. When she climbed onto the ICC, he said, 'You drop all your weight on me, I'll scream my head off.'

'Nobody'll hear, my poor boy. I sent Wembleth to look for anything that flies. Let's see if I can get you interested. Luis, how old are you?'

'Two hundred and—'

'Seriously.' She squeezed him intimately. 'Sometimes you seem older. You know things you shouldn't.' Breast tips brushed against his chest hairs as she hovered above him. 'How do you know there are whales in the Great Ocean?'

'My father told me. You can see huge levels of detail underwater from high enough up.'

'Oh.'

'You've been treating me like a kid, Roxanny. I'm not sure I like it. I'm not sure I don't. But hey, you're definitely in charge now.'

'Oh, yah. So let's see how agile I am.' With a certain dexterity, she fitted them together. 'I'm over fifty, Luis. This 'doc is my boosterspice supply for the foreseeable future.'

'Well, don't bounce too hard or you'll wreck it.'

She laughed. He felt the ripple in her powerful belly muscles.

'Roxanny. Did you know . . . boosterspice is made from tree-of-life?'

'What? No! Who told you that?'

'Proserpina. Look at the . . . implications. If the United Nations was playing with tree-of-life . . . half a thousand years ago . . . what else have they done with it? Maybe there's a protector running the ARM.'

Her eyes got big. 'I don't believe it. Luis, the ARM's top rank is all paranoid schizophrenics! And they don't take their shots! Can't you—'

'Keep moving. I thought that was just rumor.'

'Well, everybody says so. They'd never let a protector rule them. It might take over the Earth!'

'But if they did let a protector get loose, he'd run the ARM. And he'd think like a paranoid schizophrenic, wouldn't he? Roxanny, I should stop distracting you.'

'Tanj right you should. Thinking about the ARM is no fun at all. This feel good?'

'Yah.'

'You're not ticklish?'

'Used to be.'

'Not at all?'

He giggled. 'No. Nope.' He'd got his tickle reflex under control, long ago.

Wrong.

The holoscreen view of Tunesmith matched Proserpina's imagination: elongated jaws, a face bare of beard, knobs at the jaw hinges, flat nostrils, sharp-edged cheekbones: a Ghoul turned protector.

Tunesmith spoke the Ghoul tongue. Proserpina was only confused for a moment. The heliographs had spread a common language. She knew written Ghoulish, and a version spoken near the spill mountains. She had listened to Hanuman while he spoke into the holoscreen. It was only a matter of pronunciation. 'Omnivore plains runner? I have long wondered about you. Your species survives on the Map of Earth, but not unaltered—'

Proserpina yowled. Hanuman was up a tree and

hidden in its puffball top, before his mind quite caught up. But Proserpina was still at the holoscreen, and Tunesmith was still speaking—

'Local carnivores, transplanted Kzinti, have been selecting among the local hominids for such traits as please them. The exception is an invader who came with the first expedition. Chmeee tends hominids in his little sector of the Map, lets them run wild, and does not eat their meat or allow his servants to harm them. We might solve your problem most easily by giving the Map of Earth to Chmeee. We could deal with him through his son or through his ally Louis Wu.

'The Fringe War is a more difficult problem. I believe we must meet. You must view the Repair Center, and I must not leave you unwatched.

'What I know of you leads me to believe that you have learned not to act. Such a degree of self-control is rare in one of our kind. I believe I would be safe in your presence if I can offer reasonable guarantees for your own safety.

'A guarantee you might accept is your knowledge of what I am. We evolved as intelligent breeders. My own several species survive as eaters of the dead. Thus we normally see harm to any race as bad. Where other hominids survive well, so do we. Wars are not good for us; a battle is a glut followed by famine. Drought is not good, so we guide locals in water and canal management. Deserts are not good; we guide locals in replanting. We teach flood control and farming. We keep local religions, but we guide them away from messy practices, jihads and human sacrifice and cremation. We keep track through heliographs managed by the people of the rim walls. We control our numbers.

'If I see no reason to harm you, I will not. If I desire your good will, I will act to your benefit. Learn what you can of me, and decide whether you will come to meet me. I will send a service stack to rendezvous with Hanuman's flycycle.'

The face of Tunesmith went away. The picture remained: a background of interstellar space, skeletal black structures in the foreground. Proserpina shouted, 'Hanuman!'

Hanuman climbed down.

Proserpina's grip had bent the armrests of the skycycle's forward chair. She said, 'My descendants are being eaten by large orange carnivores.'

'Did you know before last night?'

'I knew that most of the Ringworld was out of my control and barred to me. This was not nearly the worst of what I imagined, but I knew with my forebrain, Hanuman, not with my glands. Well, what is a "service stack"?'

'Float plates topped by a stepping disk. I can guide us through the stepping-disk system.'

'We should look to our guests first. You take the flycycle. I'll take the mag ship home. I have an errand.'

Evening.

'It isn't the same as rishathra,' Louis said. 'Can't you feel the difference?'

'Kid, you've had more experience than I have at that,' Roxanny said, 'so you say. What are we doing for dinner?'

'You could go hunting.'

'I feel lazy.'

'Will this system make dole bricks?'

Roxanny looked it over. 'Just soup.'

'Draw me a mug.'

She dialed for two. 'Luis, how would you get into the mountain?'

'I haven't even seen it. My daydreams have mostly involved walking erect, not climbing around in an artificial mountain. What are you thinking?'

Roxanny said, 'We'd need transportation. Even on Earth, arcologies are too big to explore on foot. Then I'd worry about security. Protectors were very territorial, it's said.'

'This is good stuff.'

Roxanny sipped. It was a heavy, grainy soup. 'You get tired of it fast.'

'Think about breeders.'

'What?'

'Breeders. Pak who haven't turned protector. Plains apes, adults, and children. They can run alongside an antelope whacking it on the head with a knobbed bone, and not fall over. Keeping their balance may be what got them the big, complicated brain. But they can still climb. If there are booby traps in that futzy great building, they'll be set to leave breeders alone.'

'Well, unless the breeders are kept out by something like, I don't know, a *fence*?'

'We should look for a fence,' he agreed. 'Roxanny? Don't go alone, stet?'

'What's that?' Light outside.

'Flycycle riding lights.'

Roxanny went out to look. She came back holding hands with Hanuman. 'That protector sent the flycycle home on automatic.'

'It's got an autopilot. She might have fiddled with it. Where is she?'

Roxanny shrugged. 'Nobody was aboard but the Beast.'

CHAPTER 17

The Penultimate's Citadel

On the fourth day Roxanny told him to walk.

'It'll be another day yet,' he told her.

'I know, but the diagnostics say you're nearly cured. Benefits of youth, I guess. Luis, soldiers turn out of the 'doc when they have to fight, and futz the diagnostics. It doesn't hurt them.'

Louis was tempted, but— 'What's the hurry, Roxanny?'

'Wembleth says he's found a way in.'

'Ah.'

'We've got a flycycle. It won't fly without you. Proserpina seems to have got it to fly itself, but I can't. Proserpina hasn't come back—'

'Where's Hanuman?'

'Somewhere in the forest gorging on fruit, I think. Why?'

'He needs taking care of.'

'No, he doesn't. Luis, I don't know what she's doing, but the joker won't stay away forever!'

So Louis climbed out of the ICC. He limped with one hand on Roxanny's muscular shoulder, out to the flycycle where Wembleth was waiting. There were little sharp pains all through his left leg, hip, ribs.

Roxanny asked, 'Will this thing hold three?'

'Sure, Wembleth can perch in the middle. Give me the front seat.' Louis took his seat, wriggled carefully into a position of minimum pain. Wembleth crawled up between him and Roxanny. It was crowded, and the native's wild pelt brushed Louis's neck and ears.

He asked, 'What did you find, Wembleth?'

'A path into the fortress,' the wrinkled man said.

'Stet. Point me.' Louis took off.

It wasn't symmetrical, or self-consciously artistic. It looked like a mountain – like the Matterhorn, all tilted planes done in dark stone, with a pervasive glitter from thousands of windows. A broad veldt surrounded the base, ending in a vertical cliff.

The veldt was a tilted plain of gold and black: lines and arcs of black grass on a field of gold. Louis asked, 'What do you make of that?'

Wembleth said, 'The black is dying back.'

'Black isn't unreasonable for a plant,' Roxanny said. 'Chlorophyll throws away all the green light. What if a plant could use it all? There are some that do, in known space.'

'Yah, but Wembleth's right too. This looks like . . . writing that's been eroded, partly erased. How about this? Genetic engineering. The Penultimate planted it for decoration. It's just not as hardy as the hay, wheat, whatever.'

From a height, the cliff did look artificial. Louis steered the flycycle close, then skimmed along the edge.

'This would stop plains apes,' Roxanny said. 'Not a flycycle.'

'Nope. Do you feel lucky? Protectors are—'

'Territorial, yes, Luis. Wembleth, are we close?'

'Go more slow. Go up.'

Louis took them up. 'Here,' Wembleth said when they were flying along the rim of the cliff. 'Go left, starboard.'

The tilted plain of grass might have been a lawn if it weren't so big. Patterns shifted restlessly on its vast expanse. Wind? Louis borrowed Roxanny's mag specs. With their aid he could make out thousands of creatures resembling yellow sheep.

Ahead, the rock barrier had fallen. Soil above had spilled after it. 'Quake? Wembleth, what makes quakes on the Ringworld?'

Wembleth shrugged. Roxanny said, 'Meteors?'

'I don't see a crater.'

'Then try this, Junior. We have here a protector stronghold. What if some other protector wanted in?'

'Long, long ago,' Louis said. A whole ecology, several varieties of grass and a puffball forest, had invaded the fallen rock and earth. 'But that track is new.'

It began as a series of scorched craters in the trees below the overgrown slope that had been a wall. The scattered dots became a dashed line of freshly chewed, carbonized earth as it rose up across the lawn and higher, into the curved walls of the Citadel itself.

'We weren't wrong about defenses,' Louis said. 'Something climbed this slope, and weaponry fired on it all the way. Wembleth, how did you find this?'

'Roxanny sent me out to look around. The slope looked dangerous. *Something* must have done all this damage. I climbed a tree for a better look. Look, it goes all the way through those holes in the wall.'

Roxanny said, 'Follow that path and we'll be safe. All the booby traps are already triggered.'

'You sure? Good, then I won't turn on the sonic shield.'

'You've got a shield of some kind? Stet, turn it on!'

'I was being sarcastic. Roxanny, it's crazy to go in there. That's a protector's castle. There's no telling what games he's — what did she call him?'

'Penultimate. The next-to-last protector on this sea

of maps. There could be a million years of miracles in there. Louis, we can't turn back now.'

It's easy to be a coward when you can't fight and can't run. Louis looked behind him, seeking an ally. Wembleth's posture urged him forward, as eager and impatient as Roxanny.

Louis flipped the sonic fold on. He couldn't see it working; they weren't moving at anywhere near sonic speed.

Dark animals had been circling the yellow sheep, hidden beneath the grass. Now they streamed straight toward the flycycle, snarling crazily. They looked like dire wolves.

They'd certainly stop Homo habilis who got this far. Louis skimmed above them, through cratered grass, following the path.

It was a time of surprises after ages of predictability. Proserpina brought the mag ship down at her base, and found:

No flycycle.

Everybody gone.

She found Hanuman among the fruit trees. He hadn't known that the flycycle was missing, but his guess was the same as Proserpina's. They ran for the mag ship and set it floating toward the Penultimate's Citadel.

*   *   *

On the path of destruction Louis was following, they found places where the Penultimate's own defenses had blasted away thick rock wall and left windows standing or fallen intact. The windows were hexagons about the size of a man. They were stronger than the stone. Diamond?

Louis could feel mechanical senses watching him.

He took the flycycle through a gap the size of a sailing yacht.

Sound struck at them. It was almost speech, a million angry voices yelling incomprehensibly, all muffled by the sonic fold. Light blazed at them, dimmed by the mag specs Louis had forgotten to take off. Behind him Wembleth and Roxanny both had heads bowed, tears running from their eyes. Louis looked for the nearest cover: a melted hole in a second wall. It looked too small for the sonic fold. He turned it off, screamed against the sound, went through, flipped it back on.

The roar eased, the light eased.

They were in a jumble of machinery, in a corridor twenty meters across and much higher. Some of the machines were tall and skeletal, like construction machinery. Many looked half-finished. The place looked like Tunesmith's workshop, or Bram's, but more crowded.

Roxanny said, 'I was hoping whatever went through here shot out the defenses.' She was rubbing her eyes. Wembleth seemed okay. But—

'That *stench*!' Roxanny said. 'Like a circus!'

She was right, though 'Luis' would never have seen a circus. Wembleth said, 'It smells like Blond Carnivores running a troll drive. I don't understand.'

It was bad enough with the sonic fold keeping some of it out. Louis asked, 'Pak planet panthers? That might drive away breeders, that and the lights and noise. I wonder what this smells like to a protector? That unwashed crowd stench could be someone else's children, millions of them. Maybe a thousand angry protectors smell like this. That's it, it's a warning for protectors.'

Roxanny said, 'Us too. Time to q—'

Wembleth jumped from the flycycle, dropped a meter, and landed with bent knees. He ran, weaving between machines and parts of machines, following the dashed line of melted floor. He looked back at the flycycle and happily waved them on.

'I was about to say, "Time to quit",' Roxanny said. 'But let's follow Wembleth. *Right* behind him, Luis. No short cuts. I think he's right; we shouldn't get high enough to be shot at either. And don't get too close.'

'Stet,' Louis muttered. 'No point in being right there when something cremates the poor bastard.'

The scars of blasting led Wembleth around the curve of the corridor, then rose up a wall. He couldn't follow on foot. He waved the flycycle down and climbed up between them. He pointed past Louis's ear. 'There, high up.'

The blast trail had broken through, high up. Louis looked around Wembleth at Roxanny. She shrugged.

There wasn't any cover. Louis took the flycycle straight up and through and let it fall. A beam – not a laser, a jet of plasma – fired at the hole after they'd dropped below it, and followed them all the way down to cower in a maze of ramps. The wall collapsed under its fury, a dozen meters too high to harm the flycycle.

They were deep inside the faux mountain. This interior cavity was mostly empty space laced with a maze of ramps of Brobdingnagian size. Louis wondered if it had been intended as a training ground for warriors. If that, it was other things too. As Roxanny had guessed, there were wonders. Here was a line of crude machines floating by magnetic or gravitic levitation. There, light rays in a haze of dust bent through a scintillating focus. There were guns or instrument packages mounted where ramps crossed. They all looked ruined by heat.

Louis was tempted to stray off the path of destruction. Roxanny was right, a lot of guns had been shot to pieces here . . . but he could still feel sensors seeking him. *Later?*

He floated across a broken ramp to a blackened flight of steps. It was fatuous to suppose that a death trap wouldn't repeat, yet Roxanny's optimism seemed to be working. A projectile weapon rained bits of metal on them, but the sonic shield diverted them all until Louis could drift the flycycle under a ramp. He left the path to veer around a fallen wall. Something exploded in a glare of light; the sound barely reached them.

'Wait,' Wembleth said. 'What's that?'

It was a war zone lit up like a holoflick ad. Rubble like a stack of pancakes slumped in the glare, soggy but not quite molten. It had been one of Tunesmith's service stacks. An attack laser on a wall high above them bathed the rubble in pearl-white light. As they approached, it burned out.

The stack still glowed white hot, and black at the top. Those float plates wouldn't fly after treatment like that. The stepping disk at its tip—

Hold that thought. 'End of the trail,' Louis said.

Roxanny said, 'Yah. I'd say this is what we've been following, and I'd say it was armed. Down there—' She pointed at the foot of the stack. 'What do you see?'

'More melted machinery.' A glitter of lenses. 'Laser cannon?'

'A weapons and shield package. It sat like a cap on that, that tower. It must have shot up everything that attacked it—'

'All but one, Roxanny. That last weapon got it.'

'That last weapon just burned out ten seconds ago! Everything that's tried to hurt us is *damaged*. Luis,

Wembleth, we have here a perfect chance to go exploring!'

That seemed a little too fortuitous to be credible. 'You say burned out. What if it's just sputtering?'

'Your point?'

'Go home now. Stick to the path, but photograph everything. Work our way back. Study what we've got. Show it to Proserpina if we can't solve it ourselves—'

'Luis, what does any of that get us?'

'Might get us another way in,' Louis said. 'Roxanny, have you got a better idea?'

'Get out and look around. Luis, if we're on foot, we'll look like breeders. We *are* breeders. I don't think the defenses will fire at a breeder on foot,' Roxanny Gauthier said.

'Breeders are naked. Get naked?'

'You're already naked.'

'And you're already schitz.' Louis turned the flycycle and started back. That last plasma beam had burned a nice big hole in the wall. It ran to floor level. They'd be safer leaving than they'd been coming in.

Wembleth gripped his shoulder. 'Look. Plants.'

Far above their heads, greenery dripped over the edges of a ramp. It did seem a funny place for a garden.

'We know a way out,' Louis insisted. 'One.'

Roxanny too was gripping his arm. Her voice was soothing. 'What's biting you, Luis? Look, this ramp is as wide as a racing freeway. Just take us straight up. If something attacks, we fall back to here, and that's back on the safe path. Stet? Go straight up.'

The ramps had no railings. Louis didn't say so. Roxanny saw him as a coward, and somehow he couldn't stand that. He lifted the flycycle straight up.

Nothing fired on them.

A green jungle spilled over both sides of the upper ramp.

Roxanny said, 'The guns won't fire on crops either. This was the Penultimate's food supply.'

'You don't know any of that. You're betting three lives!'

'ARM detectives do that, Luis. This is our last chance to learn anything without Proserpina learning it too. And Proserpina is not my superior officer! Take us there, Luis.'

'The jungle?'

'Yah.'

He started to turn, and something found them.

The sonic fold rang like a great bell, and kept ringing. Louis shouted against the sound. He turned off the lift motor, and Roxanny had better be right! The flycycle dropped. In midair he passed out.

From the moment it came in view of the Citadel, the mag ship was observed. Proserpina worked to muffle the wavelengths reflecting from the ship. As they neared the mountain, something got through: projectiles stuttered toward the mag ship, then veered away. Light blasted up at them and also veered. Hanuman kept flying. It was all he could do while Proserpina fought the ship.

His path wasn't in doubt. He hoped 'Tec Gauthier had followed the chain of chewed landscape. Even if she had, she could still be dead in a hundred ways, and her companions too.

He asked. 'Do they live?'

Proserpina didn't answer. Her fields delicately plucked a section of wall away. There was an inner wall, and she plucked that away too. Light flared and was gone. Hanuman was looking at something like a beehive. Proserpina took them in.

There were strong arms around Louis, easing him down to a flat surface. Everything hurt.

He was familiar with this pain: the injuries he'd been healing from, plus a whack on his jaw and a ringing in his ears. He opened his eyes. Roxanny was lifting Wembleth into the forward seat. Blood ran from Wembleth's nose and ears.

She shouted. 'You awake?' He could barely hear her. 'Here, help me with this.' She lifted him into position. She was trying to hook Wembleth into the medical systems. 'We had crash fields,' she said, 'but he didn't.

He might have broken his back or his neck. Look, he's got a nosebleed.'

'So do you,' he shouted.

She looked at him. 'So do you. I guess that's the sonics. Tanj, is he dead?'

Louis, with Roxanny supporting him, finished mating Wembleth to the medical system. Readouts flickered on. 'He's alive,' Louis said. 'Trauma all the futz over his body. He'll feel like me when he wakes up.'

'It's feeding him boosterspice, isn't it?'

That ancient trademark— 'Yah. He's never had boosterspice before. I think he's old, Roxanny. He'll eat up the whole supply.'

'Tanj. That would have been *my* boosterspice supply. All right, Luis, put your hands on the controls.'

'We can't fly in this position. We should get into seats.'

'I know.' She set his hands on the flight stick and the keypad. She turned on the lift. Then she pushed him hard in the chest. He flew backward into space.

He fell two meters onto rock. A sea of pain washed over him. He couldn't breathe. He saw the flycycle lift, and pause.

'You're Louis Wu,' Roxanny said, leaning over from the aft seat to meet his eyes. 'You're a quarter of a thousand years old. You were the servant of a Pierson's puppeteer until you changed masters, and what you serve now I wouldn't care to describe—'

Groaning, Louis rolled to his knees, then managed to stand. He stretched up, but the flycycle was floating out of reach. The controls shouldn't have served other hands than his. Maybe Proserpina had hacked the security system so she could use it herself.

Louis asked again. 'What *is* this?'

'I made Proserpina tell me, but I guessed first, Louis. There's just too much wrong with the way you act. You played me for a fool—'

'No, Roxanny, no. I liked being treated like a kid, being young again. No responsibility! Roxanny—' Louis Wu was fleeing from the ARM. He couldn't tell her that. There were other things she couldn't know and still run loose. He said, 'I love you.'

She pointed at a mass that was still red hot. 'What is that?'

'A service stack. Float plates from . . . elsewhere on the Ring.'

'What about the weapons? Those.'

'Don't know.' He could guess. Tunesmith must have lost a service stack exploring the Citadel. He'd armed the next one and invaded again, and got this far.

'And that silver cap?'

He couldn't answer.

'That's a puppeteer stepping disk, isn't it? And it's pumping light and bullets and whatever else falls on it into some other space. That means it's still working, and that's *why* it's still working—'

'Dangerous! Roxanny, you have no idea where it leads!'

'All the things you lied about! I am not a child.' Roxanny studied him. 'I didn't believe her. You didn't make love like an older man. So I tried you out, and you *do*.'

'How could you—'

'There was a teacher.'

'Roxanny—'

'Well, we seem to be a target here. I think I'll just try it.' The flycycle lifted, slid sideways.

The pile of ruined lift plates glowed dull red. The plate at the top was dull silver. Roxanny dropped the flycycle onto it and was gone.

She was upside down and falling. Roxanny's breath streamed out in a long silent scream. She fell along smooth, vertical, red rock toward ochre sand a long way down. Past her feet was navy blue sky touched with pink.

Then the flycycle righted itself and began to rise again – but her scream remained. The flycycle had emerged on Mars with the sonic fold off. In a vacuum you scream, or else your lungs rupture.

Mars. Ridiculous. Insane. But she knew this place, she'd trained on Mars. Her spinning senses found the Arch, the Ringworld rising over itself. So she wasn't quite crazy, it was the Map of Mars on the Great Ocean halfway round the Ringworld. Even so, she and Wembleth would be dead in minutes, in an atmosphere that would be poison if it weren't too thin to matter.

The blood that still streamed from her nose was foaming. Wembleth's mouth was open in a long scream; he clutched the flycycle controls as if throttling them.

The flycycle eased up above a single silver plate like the one they'd come through: an inverted stepping disk.

Wembleth reached out, pulling at the umbilicals that attached him to the flycycle's 'doc. He swung a fist at the edge of the stepping disk. The rim popped up on a hardware keyboard. His fist pounded the buttons. He twisted flycycle controls, and the vehicle dropped, twisted, and rose to touch the stepping disk's undersurface.

There was air and baby blue sky.

Roxanny sucked air, gasped, gasped. She said, 'Perfect,' her throat a raw whisper. She hugged Wembleth. 'Perfect. You saved us. That *thing* would have come after us. Proserpina. And Luis. Louis Wu.' After a long moment she lifted her head. 'You just slammed touch points at random, didn't you? I wonder where we are.'

She could see everything there was of it. They were on a tiny island in the midst of a flat, calm sea. Nothing but scrub was growing here. It seemed a safe place to leave a stepping disk and its stack of lift plates.

Roxanny popped the cover and tapped touch points. 'There,' she said. 'Let's see them find us now.'

Louis tottered toward the service stack. He'd do better with a walking stick or a crutch. He stopped where the heat was too much. He *had* to follow her . . . but he couldn't get close. He sat down to think.

Jump to the stepping disk from a higher ramp? Yah, stet.

The service stack wouldn't be red hot forever . . . but it would take a long time to cool down. A day, two? He'd have to feed himself while he waited.

In a minute he'd start climbing toward the hanging garden.

Sputtering light woke him. He'd dozed, or fainted. He watched without surprise as Proserpina's ship descended. Lasers stuttered from a dozen directions. The sunfish ship flickered. Then all the lasers died in fiery puffballs, and the big sunfish ship hovered above him.

Hanuman, in full pressure gear, emerged from the opening hatch.

'They went through there,' Louis called. 'I have to catch them, but it's too hot. *Wait*!'

Hanuman jumped. He landed on the stepping disk and was gone.

What had turned it on, anyway? Plasma heat? A random bullet? Must have been something like that.

Why would Tunesmith send a service stack in here with the stepping disk running? Louis saw Proserpina in the hatch, wearing a pressure suit. He called, 'Watch out, it's still going!'

She dropped onto the stepping disk and was gone.

The sunfish ship turned, questing blindly. It lifted toward the hole in the wall, outside and gone.

Louis wondered how much trouble he was in.

Everyone had left him. He hadn't felt this alone since . . . he couldn't remember. Roxanny had left him. How would he ever explain . . . or did she understand too well?

He'd thought of her as his woman, decreed by fate, the only Homo sapiens woman in a vastness of three million worlds.

She'd taken the flycycle. Proserpina had programmed the sunfish ship to take itself home. Louis was on foot. That was good news and bad. It was a futz of a long way to a food source, but it was all downhill. Hunger wouldn't kill him. The Penultimate's defenses wouldn't kill him, if he believed Roxanny's analysis: he would be seen as a wandering Homo habilis. He was nearly naked already.

But he had to find water sooner than that.

There'd be water to feed that vast green veldt. Even so, there was water closer: not far above his head. His eye could follow ramps around and up and over to the hanging gardens.

Louis began to walk. Nothing shot at him. Maybe Proserpina had shut down the rest of the Penultimate's defenses.

He rested more and more frequently. Presently he was crawling. A walking stick sounded really good. Maybe he'd find a sapling in the hanging garden. Then, walk home to Proserpina's base. Climb into the ARM 'doc and finish healing. Figure out what to do next.

He knew that smell.

He'd found the Penultimate's tree-of-life supply!

It was a futzy good thing, he thought dizzily, that he hadn't landed the flycycle in the garden. Roxanny would have eaten. She was . . . maybe past the age, maybe not, given decades of boosterspice. She'd be a protector, or dead. Wembleth might have eaten too, he thought. The native's elegant black-and-white hair could be a sign of age.

Water welled up, pooled on the ramp, and ran into the plants. Louis waded into it on hands and knees. It rose to his belly. He only stopped once, when he realized he was kneeling on bright cloth: on a woman's skirt with a hologram running round it. Wild horses ran below Wyoming buttes, around and around.

No telling how long it had been here at the bottom of the pool. Good cloth didn't rot. Teela had owned a skirt like this, bought at a shop in Phoenix. And Louis was crawling again.

He crawled into the garden, dripping, pulling the skirt behind him. There were trees: he could pull himself to his feet. There was more than tree-of-life here. He saw fruit, snap beans, fist-sized ears of corn. . . . He knelt and began to dig.

He pulled up a yellow root, shook off some dirt, and bit into it. It was like chewing wood.

This was twice insane. He was too young. Carlos Wu's nanotech 'doc had made him too young. There was no reason for him to be interested in tree-of-life. It might kill him. He went on eating.

CHAPTER 18

The Ringworld Floor

Hanuman caught the rim of the stepping disk with a hand and a foot. Rocks like rust-colored teeth waited far below him. For millions of falans his kind had known what to do about *falling*.

Proserpina flicked through. Hanuman caught her belt, but he wasn't needed: she had the rim of the stepping disk. 'Trap,' she said. She pulled herself onto an ochre rock. 'Crude. Aliens?'

Hanuman said, 'Tunesmith is careful. Anything might come through from the Penultimate's home. Proserpina, we were told to wait. He's sent us a service stack.'

'Follow,' said Proserpina. She swung around from the rim and thumped soundly against the stepping disk. Nothing happened. 'Gauthier's changed the link.'

'I know the protocols.' Hanuman popped the controls

open, freed a hand, and tapped rapidly. 'We'll lose Gauthier's link. Do you care where the detective and the native went?'

'She'll change the settings again. They're lost in the network. Go.'

Hanuman swung himself down and was elsewhere.

Under a hemisphere of artificial sky, a sun burned low, red, and flattened. Veldt stretched out around Hanuman, with a lake and a low forest in the distance.

Proserpina flicked in behind him. She gaped at the lowering sun. 'Was there a planet-born protector?'

'Yes. I don't know details,' Hanuman said.

'I am suddenly very hungry.' Proserpina loped toward the trees.

'I surmise,' Hanuman said, 'that protectors lose their hunger when they have too little to protect. Were you idle for a very long time?'

They were running through yellow grain, and Hanuman was falling behind. He recognized the trees ahead.

His memories as a breeder were murky. He was old, slowing down, joints starting to hurt. The troop had fought an intruder. Hanuman, fiercest of the males, got close enough to inhale a scent that sparked a rage of hunger. He'd eaten himself stupid, then estivated, then . . . woke like this, in a pocket of forest transplanted deep underground, with its own wandering sun. His own forest to keep him sane, and puzzles to train his newly expanded mind.

The trees were fruit trees. Lower plants grew at the edges. Ringworld life was Pak life, and all these were edible crops. Proserpina's hands plunged into the dark soil. She tore a yellow root out of the ground and ate, and gave another to Hanuman.

Presently she asked, 'Where's Tunesmith?'

'I can't call him.' The pressure suit Proserpina had worked up for him was a quick fix. It didn't fit well, and it didn't have a communication link to Tunesmith. 'He'll find us,' Hanuman said.

'I was trapped on a single map for more than a million falans,' she said. 'When my Pak brethren ceased to supervise the Ringworld landscape, I continued to test for protectors in the Repair Center. The Repair Center has remained active, and I have remained passive. I'm the last defense. One day I will be needed. Even now that day may not have come, but we must see. I should explore. Where can you take me?'

'Your interest is in the massing of alien craft near our sun, isn't it?'

'Yes.'

Hanuman rewrote settings. 'Come.'

*　　*　　*

They were in a vast, dark, ellipsoidal space.

Stars glared unimpeded, light-enhanced, in walls and floor and ceiling. Spacecraft were harder to see. Tunesmith had set blinking circles round the ones he'd found; he might have missed others. Thousands of ships. Hundreds of thousands of tiny blinking points: probes.

Only Proserpina's head turned.

Three long swinging booms ended in chairs equipped with lap keyboards. All three were empty. Hanuman asked, 'Would you like—?'

'Shush,' she said, and continued to take it all in. Stepping disks: one visible. She couldn't see the one she was standing on. Weapons and cameras: she couldn't see those either. The star projections could mask anything.

If Tunesmith attacked, it would be from above, and Hanuman would attack too. She was ready – but that was instinct speaking. Practically speaking, if Tunesmith wanted her life, it was his. She asked, 'Do you know these ships?'

'Some of them.' Hanuman pointed out a few: Puppeteer, Trinoc, Outsider, Kzinti, ARM, Sheath-claws.

'Some are only observers,' Proserpina said. 'Some are arrayed for war. Badly. The ARM would win if they struck there and there . . .' Her voice wandered off. 'And wreckage from this ship or this one might strike the Ringworld. That tail design confines antimatter fuel, doesn't it? Has Tunesmith considered destroying all of these fleets?'

'Tunesmith considers everything.'

'But I don't know his tools. He must be at work on something! Something besides mere defensive meteor control. I won't know anything until I know what we can fight with. Or run with.'

Hanuman said, 'Run?'

'I speculate.' Proserpina walked around the curve of the glowing wall. Under a glare of light were the bones of an ancient protector, laid out with some of his tools. The joints were swollen into knobs. Vertebrae in the back were fused.

'They had already begun to mutate,' she said. 'Do you know that we kill mutants? Do you still do that?'

'Of course, if they smell wrong, or behave wrong.'

'This one was very good at what he did. Look at the state of the bones, the scarring from mere age. He must have survived tens of thousands of falans. Hanuman, should we have loosed our predators?'

'No.'

'But these who were our own shape have occupied every ecological niche we didn't fill.' She looked hard at Hanuman. She'd almost managed to ignore his mutant smell. 'I see your point. Not just scavengers like this one, but brachiators like you. Mutations and evolution are good, if only you can stop it *now*, always *now*, so that your own kind need not change.'

Hanuman didn't answer. She was only stating the obvious.

But Tunesmith spoke. 'Your kind, your original Pak, *did not* survive. That's what mutations and evolution are for, Proserpina. Something almost of your shape has multiplied into the tens of trillions. You don't like some of us? When did you ever like all of your neighbors?'

He was standing atop a chair on a boom just above her head. He could have nailed her in an instant. Too clever, too quick.

Proserpina said, 'Bet. Even odds we'll be dead in nineteen falans, if I read these patterns right. You've studied them longer. Hello, Tunesmith.'

Tunesmith leapt down. 'Hello, Proserpina, revered ancestor. Are your guests safe?'

'I see this as more urgent than their lives. You have been meddling with our basic design!'

'Yes, but not quickly enough. I need all the help I can get.'

'What design changes have you made? What changes do you contemplate?'

'What would be your approach to dealing with the Fringe War?'

'I might have tried . . . can you give me a way to make pictures?'

Tunesmith set his chair swinging near the elliptical wall. Now the starscape was gone, and the wall was deep blue. Tunesmith waved at the wall: white lines appeared.

Proserpina jumped to another chair. She waved shapes to life. Sun. Shadow squares. Ringworld. They were white lines and curves, and then they were photographically realistic views. Proserpina's arms moved like a concert master's. The sun took on detail: magnetic fields cradled the interior. The fields changed: *squeezed*. The sun's south magnetic pole curdled, churned, then sprayed light.

'I might have tried this,' Proserpina said. 'When we built the Ringworld, we set a superconductor network within the foundation structure. We can manipulate magnetic fields.' The sun's south pole jetted X-ray-colored flame. Slowly the sun moved north, leaving the Ringworld behind. Its gravity pulled, faint lines on the blue wall, and the Ringworld followed.

'We use the sun for thrust, up to a few meters per second squared by Interworld measurement. Beyond that—' Streamlines formed. The Ringworld moved on alone, the sun lost. 'Flux of interstellar matter through the Ringworld can be steered to the axis to undergo fusion. The jet from the sun gives more fuel. A fusion exhaust confined by magnetic fields replaces the sun, bathes the Ringworld in light, and serves as a ramjet too. The Ringworld survives. We can continue to accelerate.'

'Drawbacks?'

'Deceleration would be difficult but not impossible. Fields could be adjusted to thrust forward. Tides would shift.'

Tunesmith waited.

'When we stopped, there would be no sun.' Proserpina shrugged; the picture distorted. 'It doesn't matter. We can't even begin. The sun grows too hot if we try to accelerate it. The shadow-square ring can be pulled almost closed, for shielding, but if the shadow squares fell behind or were pulled ahead, landscape would be charred.

'Worst, it's too slow,' Proserpina said. 'The sun's gravitational pull isn't enough. I can manipulate the sun's magnetic fields to pull harder on the Ringworld, and it still isn't enough. Alien intruders still follow. I can't think of a way to leave them behind.'

'It's the wrong principle,' Tunesmith said. 'You didn't know. You lack information. Did Louis Wu speak of Carlos Wu's medical system? Or the spacecraft we stole from the Kzinti?'

'No.'

'I'll give you details when I need to. Meanwhile — those protectors vicious enough to hold the Repair Center have not always been diligent. They've allowed meteor impacts, eyestorms, erosion, and sometimes an exposed sea bottom. That fool bloodsucker left thousands of places where the Ringworld's foundation shows through. I need you and your allies and servants to find these places and shake a dust into them. I have been working with others of my own kind, with the Ringworld-wide network of Ghoul species; but I haven't been able to reach enough of these breaches. We move too slowly.'

'What is this dust? What does it do?'

'You need only know—'

'I must judge for myself!'

'I don't want an equal partner, Proserpina! The dust spreads itself through scrith, but first the scrith must touch it. How can we put more of it in contact with the Ringworld floor?'

'My servants in the spill mountains,' Proserpina said, 'are useless on the flats. They suffocate. They'll spread dust along the spill mountain edges, on the rim wall, if you can get the dust to them. They'll travel by balloon from peak to peak.'

'Good. My own spill mountain protectors have been doing that. What else?'

'Water folk,' Proserpina said. 'We'll use them. We need to reach the spill pipe system that circulates sea bottom sediment—'

'Flup.'

'Yes, flup. We use that word too. Flup accumulates in the bottoms of the seas. Without our tending, it would stay there. Topsoil all through the Ringworld would be lost under the seas in a few thousand years. We've set in place a circulation system of spillpipes that runs under the scrith floor and up the outside of the rim wall, to fall over the edge. It becomes spill mountains. Ultimately it replenishes the earth. If your dust can be introduced into the seabottoms, can it spread into the scrith from there?'

'Yes.'

'How long will it take?'

'If we begin now, less than two falans.'

CHAPTER 19

Wakening

He ate, and he hid.

Louis crawled among the plants, working his way deep into the jungle. He lived on his belly, reaching out of the shadows to dig for the yellow roots. The hanging garden was too exposed. He couldn't do anything about that; he couldn't leave his food source. Every hominid species on Earth and the Ringworld must have kept at least this one trait: a breeder turning into a protector would hide lest other protectors find him.

Shadow and light: days flickered by.

Nothing seemed to be looking for him. He wondered about that. A loose protector ought to be a matter of concern. It suggested that the Ringworld's protectors had other concerns: they were all involved in the Fringe War problem, ignoring the usual lethal dominance games. It must be bad. He should be helping.

Changing body, restless mind. Why was he eating tree-of-life at an effective age of twenty or so? That had an obvious answer, but the implications were serious.

The 'doc had given him the symptoms, but hadn't really made him an adolescent. Why not?

Tunesmith had opened Carlos Wu's experimental autodoc and spread it out like an autopsy patient, to solve all its puzzles. He'd kept Louis Wu in there much longer than Louis needed, to test his notions, and for another reason. The 'doc's nanotechnology had rewritten Louis Wu's genetics, possibly over and over, until he was ready to become a protector at any time Tunesmith chose.

If Tunesmith had studied nanotechnology in such detail, by now he'd know that subject better than any mind in known space. What was he doing with it?

And that too was obvious, given the theft of *Long Shot*.

Louis's mind wandered away, fizzing with inspiration, seeking other puzzles.

Where was the Hindmost? Aboard *Hot Needle of Inquiry*. A ship built like a glass bottle could still be furnished with hidden control rooms. Where was *Hot Needle of Inquiry*? It didn't matter. Louis could reach the ship by stepping disk, and that was all that mattered, unless — was it flightworthy? He'd have to learn.

Why was Tunesmith's nose so large, when Proserpina's was almost flat?

Did Louis Wu have children or N-children among the ships of the Fringe War?

Where was *Long Shot*? Tunesmith might be studying the ship where he'd worked on *Needle* and the autodoc, in the Launch Room beneath the Map of Mons Olympus. The Launch Room was roomy enough. It was the first place Louis would look, if he ever got over this . . . torpor. It felt like he was thinking very fast, but his mind was like ten thousand butterflies in a field, lighting everywhere, going nowhere. His body . . . he couldn't tell.

He hid, and he ate.

Where had Roxanny taken Wembleth? She'd fled from Louis Wu and his protector allies. Of course she must have burned her bridges behind her: changed settings on the stepping disks, maybe burned out the last one before hiding herself. How would he ever find them?

One hundred and fifty-one days flickered past. Then it was as if he'd wakened from a doze.

He stayed where he was, half buried in dirt and plant stalks. His hands moved over his face and his body, finding a new shape. Swollen joints. Vanished testicles, penis shrunken to nothing. His skull had softened, expanded, hardened again, leaving a minor crest of bone. His face was a hard mask, lips fused to gums and ossified. His nose was enlarged. He'd look like a clown. And his sense of smell had become almost magical.

Hah! He'd solved it, the problem of the noses.

A human nose forms a kind of hood: it will hold a bubble of air for a swimmer. Apes don't have the hooded nostrils because they don't swim. Humans have evolved halfway in every direction, including the aquatic: most of their skin is bare, like the smooth skin of a dolphin.

Fate really did intend mankind to swim.

Breeders lose most of their sense of smell because it would drive them crazy. They would kill any stranger who came near their children, even doctors and teachers. They would protect their children from *everything*, driving *them* crazy.

Louis's nose told him that the Penultimate's arcology-sized refuge was empty of enemies. The only life here was burrowers and insect analogues, and an old scent that went straight to his hindbrain.

He looked at the watch tattooed on the back of his hand. Swollen knuckles and wrist bones distorted the digital display. It was telling Canyon time. He did the math and found that he'd been dawdling for two falans. Far too long. But it was right, he'd counted one hundred fifty-one thirty-hour days. An old ARM record said that Jack Brennan had changed to a protector much faster than that.

Something had slowed his metamorphosis.

He tried to stand up, already guessing the answer.

He couldn't stand straight. He'd been half-healed when he began to eat yellow root. The injuries were embedded in the regrowth pattern. He'd become a protector, but crippled. His knee, leg, hip, and ribs on the left side were twisted out of true. His body was nearly fat free, the fat burned out of him during too long an estivation.

He limped through the hanging garden, learning how to move all over again. A protector who couldn't fight. He reached for something badger-like and caught its leg only because it was so slow. He ate it in haste, and judged it was enough.

A few ramps below was the scorched and half-melted service stack. He limped down and had a look. It had cooled, of course. He tried to pop the controls open, but melted metal had fused it shut.

He climbed painfully onto the stepping disk. Nothing happened.

His fist slapped the rim hard.

Mars! He twisted and reached up to slap both hands against the inverted stepping disk before he could fall away. A moment later he was in a handstand in a field of high grass. He rolled to his feet *quick* (where was Tunesmith?) and found himself under a blue hemisphere, in the tree-of-life garden where he'd killed Teela Brown.

Tunesmith?

Nowhere.

He popped the stepping-disk controls open and began to play. First things first.

There was a mile-long craft on the Great Ocean. *Hidden Patriarch* had brought Kzinti to conquer the Map of Earth, centuries ago, and on that ship was a stepping disk. Louis didn't remember its code, but he found it.

Hidden Patriarch. He flicked in wire-tense, ready to fight or die.

Nothing came at him. He could see a bronze fractal spider web looking at him from a rusted iron wall: one of the Hindmost's webeyes. Otherwise the location didn't seem to be guarded.

He'd left *Hidden Patriarch* almost beneath the Ringworld's starboard rim wall. Such a view could reduce a man to the size of a proton. Mountains as big as Everest lined its base, green with riotous life. Spill mountains were all seabottom muck, all fertilizer.

The librarians hadn't moved the ship. The Hindmost said they'd been returned home. *Hidden Patriarch* might well be empty.

Louis popped the controls, taking this disk out of the network. Now he was unreachable.

For a few moments now, Louis only thought. His memories were muzzy – a long lifetime of breeder memories. His memories of this last hour were diamond clear.

Long ago, it seemed, he'd studied a map of the Hindmost's stepping-disk system. Now he reached back into those memories to find settings and placements for various locations. They were mostly lost . . . but what he needed was a disk only recently put into service. Thought and memory gave him the code by which the Hindmost designated stepping disks. Wouldn't Tunesmith keep that system? It would give Louis a handful of settings to try.

He'd better have a pressure suit.

He popped aboard *Hot Needle of Inquiry* and yelled, 'Hindmost's Voice! It's Louis!' Despite changes in his throat structure he made himself *sound* like Louis Wu.

'Don't move. You are not Louis Wu,' said a flat voice like the Hindmost's.

Louis didn't move. He was in the crew cabin. For an instant he considered familiar food, a shower, and a change of clothes, but it just didn't matter. He said, 'Tell the Hindmost Louis Wu has become a protector. I need to talk to him.'

'Louis? I warned you!' said the same voice.

'I knew. Don't tell me where you are. I've come for a pressure suit. Have you been watching the Fringe War? Has anything happened?'

'An antimatter missile destroyed one of the ramjets on the rim wall,' the puppeteer's voice said. 'Twenty-eight Ringworld days ago. The explosion was tremendous, not just antimatter but kilotonnes of confined plasma under fusion. Spill mountains melted. I couldn't learn what faction did that. I thought chaos would follow. I made ready to depart, but nothing happened.'

'Those attitude jets always were too vulnerable. Tunesmith must have set up something else by now.' Louis's mind ranged ahead of his words. 'The Ringworld builders never did want rim wall ramjets as anything more than a temporary fix and a safety feature. They built the superconductor grid to move the system magnetically, push against the sun. Tunesmith controls that.'

'You're guessing.'

'I guess good. I'm a protector. Free me, Hindmost, and I'll get off your property.'

'What's it like?' the Hindmost asked.

'I feel confined. I'm crippled,' Louis said. 'I can't fight and can't run. I can think faster than I ever did before. I see more answers. That's confining too, in a way. If I see the right answer every time, there're no choices.

'Tunesmith has a plan. I won't interfere unless he threatens my N-children, but I should talk to him. It's just that there are things I have to do first. What about you? Do you have a plan?'

'Run away when I see a chance.'

'Good. Do you remember where Tunesmith worked on *Needle*? Do you have webeye cameras in there?'

'Beneath Mons Olympus.'

'Is *Long Shot* there? Is it functional?'

'He took the ship apart and put it back together. He hasn't tested it since.'

'What about Carlos Wu's autodoc?'

'It hasn't been touched.'

'It's still spread out across the floor?'

'Yes.'

'Watch for me to cause a distraction. Then get the autodoc aboard *Long Shot* in working condition. Can you do it?'

The scream of a demented orchestra. 'Why would I even consider committing burglary on a protector's turf!'

'But you'll have a protector on your side. Hindmost, we are under a deadline. Tunesmith will not consider your convenience. He will act as soon as he can, because he can't predict when the Fringe War will go to hell. If we can't get off the Ringworld soon, you'll lose your home forever, and so will I, and worse.'

Into the silence that followed, Louis said, 'You're thinking you could hold me prisoner until you turn me over to Tunesmith. Buy something with that. Shall I tell you why you can't do that? Do you remember three chairs in the Meteor Defense Room, on booms?'

'I remember.'

'Tunesmith only needs one.'

The Hindmost understood. He was as quick as some protectors. 'Triumvirate.'

'He let me see that on purpose. It's a message, a promise. Tunesmith, Proserpina, and me. He extrapolated a surviving Pak protector, and he knew he could feed me tree-of-life. He didn't expect me to be running loose. He probably won't mind finding me crippled like an ancient Greek slave. He needs my input. He can't guess what the Fringe War will do as well as I can.

'See, you can sell me to Tunesmith, but you'll have to deal with me afterward.'

'You're free to move about the ship,' the Hindmost said.

Louis let himself slump into his more natural twisted pose. 'Give me access to the stepping-disk master controls. I need to rewrite some instructions.'

'To make yourself hard to find? I can help.'

'Me and a couple of others. I don't need help.'

After he had finished reprogramming the stepping-disk system, Louis flicked into *Needle*'s cargo bay. He extruded a pressure suit. It didn't fit him well in his twisted condition, but it would do. He took some gear: a rope, mag specs, a flashlight-laser.

He tapped at stepping-disk controls and flicked out.

He was in orbit. He'd thought that might happen. The settings he wanted were the most recently deployed, and some of those would match orbiting service stacks.

He spent a few moments looking down at the Ringworld's face. This was a region he'd never seen in detail, partway between the Great Oceans. There were ochre deserts, and tiny pockmarks of impact craters, and three little knots of cloud: eyestorms.

Tunesmith wasn't making repairs unless he had to. Given what he was doing, Tunesmith might be glad to find places where the landscape was ripped down to the scrith.

Aircraft and spacecraft he saw none. That was better than his predictions. By now the Fringe War might have worked its way down to the surface. Louis still had time.

But he would have made this side jaunt despite the Fringe War. A protector didn't often have choices. He tapped in another setting.

Still in orbit, but elsewhere. An ARM camera the size of a gnat was looking at him from two meters away.

That tore it! Now they had a verified protector sighting. Or would the pressure suit and his twisted shape hide his nature for long enough? He tapped and flicked out quick.

Night wasn't particularly dark on the Ringworld. Nothing was here but sand and scrub and Tunesmith's service stack, and the calm surface of a sea. Louis prowled about for a bit, but the sand wouldn't hold footprints.

But it held a trace of a scent.

They'd flicked in here, but they hadn't stayed long. They had a flycycle to play with. Louis walked around the island, using mag specs to study the distant shore. A flycycle ought to stand out.

Nothing. Try again.

Nowhere. He flicked in and was trapped in branches and thorns.

He looked about him, he felt about him, before he tried to move. The thorns didn't do much harm to his leathery skin. Behind his hardshelled face his mind grinned.

Tunesmith had sent a service stack to rendezvous with Louis's flycycle.

Half a year ago. Roxanny, riding the flycycle, might have moved several times before she gave up. Tunesmith's programming would hold: the service stack would follow the flycycle. For all Roxanny knew, it might be covered in sensors and cameras! Finally she must have run it into a jungle and let thorn plants grow over the flycycle and service stack both.

Louis did some careful cutting with the flashlight-laser. The brush started to burn around him. Not a good thing. He crawled down through the thorns, around the edge of the stepping disk, picking up scratches, cutting more brush as he went. Popped the rim and turned off the stepping disk, and lofted the stack of float plates before the fire could roast him.

The forest ran a fair distance, following a river, and he'd been in the middle of it. Now he was above it, with a fine view. Where would a pair of strangers go after abandoning their transportation?

Not far. Wembleth would lead Roxanny to the nearest center of civilization: *he* knew strangers were welcome everywhere. Follow the river downstream and they'd find *something*.

What Louis found was a convergence of two rivers and a small village. He drifted toward the conical houses. Somewhere a voice shouted, 'Vasneesit!' and Louis thought, 'Stet.'

A fire was growing in the forest. A pillar of smoke to gather attention, right where Roxanny and Wembleth had left their vehicles. Looking toward the fire, they'd see a stack of float plates limned against smoke. And what then? Would they hide, or flee?

Hide. They couldn't run faster than a service stack.

Louis sniffed. Population of a thousand to fifteen hundred, smelling like meat eaters, not many elders, lots of parasites but little disease. And—

There.

He set the stack down in the village square. Locals

gathered. They were short, brawny, wolfish-looking men and women. Eyes faced front from deep sockets. Small sharp jaws protruded a little.

An elder tried to speak to him. Louis couldn't understand the language, but he tried to placate the man with body language. When that didn't work, he nipped the elder's nose, then knocked him down. A brief shoving match and the man was groveling.

Fair enough. Louis followed the scent. The source had changed houses, but it would have been stronger if they'd moved through open air. Were there tunnels under the village?

A young man popped out of a doorway with Roxanny's sonic in his hand.

The buzz just brushed him before Louis's laser beam touched the metal butt. *Carefully!* The man dropped the sonic and ran inside. He wasn't one of the Wolf People. He was only a few centimeters shorter than Louis, curly brown hair around the face and head, bare skin elsewhere. He was clearly human. Louis's nose knew him.

'Wembleth!' Louis limped after him. 'I just want to talk.' He moved inside, afraid they'd outrun him, but he was limping faster than they could move. His hand caught metal swinging toward his head, turned and had a wrist and metal bar. 'Roxanny.'

The fight went out of her. She stared at him in fathomless terror. 'What are you?'

'Don't you believe in Vashneesht?' She didn't react. Not funny? 'I'm Louis Wu,' he said. 'Your sonic left me twisted, but otherwise I'm a protector. You were lucky. You would have eaten tree-of-life if we'd gone where you pointed me.'

'Louis.'

He sniffed: she was carrying a child of his own blood. She could kill him before he harmed her now. He said, 'Do you know—?'

'I'm pregnant. It happens.' Roxanny looked him in the eye. 'You said you were fertile.'

'It's Wembleth's child. I can smell.'

'Stet. *Why* were you fertile? Most men use up their birthrights. Didn't Louis Wu?'

'Roxanny, *every* life is unlikely.'

Her smile was a mere flicker. 'And why am *I* fertile? You sure didn't arrange *that*.'

Louis said, 'Someone jiggered your med specs. You all used the same 'doc aboard *Gray Nurse*, didn't you? Someone wanted to get you pregnant so he turned off your sterility patch.' It was the most rational answer.

Roxanny said, 'Coroner-First Zinna Hendersdatter. She thinks I took Oliver away from her.' She had her aplomb back. 'So protectors make mistakes?'

'There's never enough data. It's why protectors second-guess each other. Roxanny, I just want to talk and then I'll be gone. Wembleth?'

'Don't hurt her.'

Wembleth's head and arms poked out of a hole in the earthen floor. He'd been there for some time. His beard was brown and somewhat curly, tipped with white. Boosterspice had made him young, and in that state he looked something like Teela Brown and quite a lot like a young Louis Wu. He had a crossbow.

'You don't have to come closer,' Louis said. He let go of Roxanny, who backed away. He held still, wondering if Wembleth would fire, wondering if he could catch a crossbow bolt. 'You've been practicing Interworld speech?'

'Yah, Roxanny wants to join the ARM fleet.'

How? Louis wondered. If he'd seen a way, he'd have had to block it.

'Roxanny,' he asked, 'where did you leave *Snail Darter*'s library?'

'I took it aboard *Gray Nurse*,' she said. 'Why?'

'My children, their N-children, one or two might have joined the ARM fleet. I have to see the roster. There'd be a current copy in every ship in the fleet.'

She laughed. 'There are tens of thousands of men and women in the ARM ships! Are you going to scan them all?'

'Yah.'

She shrugged. 'Maybe Proserpina picked it up.'

'You'll have to leave here,' Louis said. 'I brought the service stack. I'll reprogram it so it'll stop following the flycycle. It's very important that you can't be found.

I got this close to you by just following the programming in the stepping disks. I followed your scent from
the forest, Wembleth.'

'With a nose like that, I'm not surprised,' Wembleth
said rudely.

Louis touched his enlarged nose. 'Do you know that
you're my son?'

Wembleth snorted in disbelief. 'I would have
thought you might be mine! But you're older than you
looked.'

'You're younger. I never saw a human being who
hadn't used modern medical techniques. No depilators,
no tannin pills, never a dental program. I thought you
were another species. But Teela Brown was your
mother,' Louis said.

Roxanny shook her head. 'She'd have had a five-year
patch.'

'She must have decided she wanted my child. She'd
have to have had her sterility treatment reversed before
we left Earth. It would have taken both of her
birthrights. She never told *me*.'

Wembleth said, 'Wait. You mean it? *You're* my
father?' He seemed horrified.

'Yah—'

'Why did you leave us?'

'Teela left *me*. I thought then that she left me for
Seeker—'

'But what did you *do*?'

'I didn't protect her.' How could he, against her own luck? 'She went into an eyestorm and we lost her. When we found her again, she was with Seeker. She'd have been carrying you when I left them near the Great Ocean, and as for what she did after that, I'd be guessing.'

'You are Vashneesht,' Wembleth said. 'You're good at guessing. I've never understood. Why did mother leave us?'

Louis knew he should be going. Every second might be precious. Once upon a time Proserpina's people had cleaned the Ringworld system of every menacing rock. Now it was infested with ships . . .

But in the presence of his son and growing grand-child, Louis was inclined to stay; and Wembleth needed reassurance.

He said, 'I left Teela near the Great Ocean. There weren't any stepping disks on the Ringworld then. Seeker – the man she left me for – he might have known how to use the transport that runs along the rim wall. It's a magnetic levitation system, Roxanny. They found something to get them there; there's enough Builder technology lying around. They took the maglev system all the way around to the Other Ocean.

'You'd call that crazy unless they were running from something fearsome. Not from me, I think, but maybe it was what she thought I'd bring. The Fringe War. Teela might have been afraid of puppeteers. Nessus meddled in her life, pretty well destroyed it, and she didn't want that to happen again. She knew any of us would look where we last saw her.

'So they found a place halfway around the arc, and she settled down and made a life with Seeker and you. I hope she was happy.'

'Mother was happy,' Wembleth said, 'but restless too. She never had any more children—'

'Course not. Seeker wasn't her species.'

'She and – Seeker – my father,' with a bit of a glare, 'took turns exploring. I never knew what they were looking for. One of them had to stay with me. They did more of that after I was older. I was near eighty falans when she disappeared.'

'And never came back?'

'Never did,' Wembleth said.

'She found tree-of-life.' *Teela's luck*, Louis thought. *Poor Teela. If anything, it was her genes that were lucky*. He said, 'I don't know just how it happened, but that tuber grows on every one of these maps of the Pak world, and most maps once held a protector prisoner. A few prisoners must have found some way to infect roots with tree-of-life virus, just as Proserpina did. I think Teela found the Penultimate's garden. It would have got Seeker too if he hadn't been exploring alone. She woke up as a protector. Wembleth, she wouldn't ever leave you unless it was to protect you from some greater danger.'

Wembleth scowled.

'No, really. She saw what we all saw. She must have guessed what was under the Map of Mars. Roxanny, it's a huge volume, an area to match all the land masses of Earth, and forty miles high. You can't miss it. It's the Repair Center for the whole Ringworld. Teela could see that most of the rim-wall ramjets were missing. Somebody had to get into the Repair Center to try to stabilize the Ringworld before it brushed its sun.'

She'd wanted power too, Louis thought. *Futz, she was a protector*. He said, 'She rode the rim-wall maglev system, and then anything that could reach the Map of Mars on the Great Ocean,' his mind running ahead of his mouth. 'Maybe she went to the Map of Earth first, to see how the archaic Pak were faring, and picked up *Hidden Patriarch* there. That's how the ship got to Mars—'

Roxanny said, 'Say what?'

'It doesn't matter. What happened next was that Teela tried to murder Bram.'

Roxanny said, 'Bram?' and Wembleth said, 'Murder? My mother?'

Louis said, 'There was a protector already inside the Repair Center. Teela didn't *know* about Bram, but she knew that *if* there was anyone on site, he wasn't doing his job. He was letting the rim-wall attitude jets be stolen. He'd have to be replaced.

'Wembleth, I talked to Bram. I got his version of what happened. Bram wasn't the brightest of protectors. He never figured out this next part.'

'Teela was a protector. She did what she had to do. She took an older man off one of the other maps, probably, and disguised herself. She went with him into the Map of Mars as a pair of breeders. They went exploring through the Repair Center. By the time they found the tree-of-life garden, Teela must have seen enough, or smelled him. Somewhere there was a protector. She let the man eat tree-of-life, and she ate too.

'The man died. Teela pretended to go into a coma. She might have lain motionless for several turns. Bram was supposed to come and examine her to find out what she was, then kill her before she could wake up as a protector. She would have taken him by surprise and killed *him*.

'But Bram didn't come. He must have decided to let her wake. She had to go to Plan B. She left the Map of Mars without ever letting Bram know she knew about him. She set about repairing the rim-wall jets, and then . . . she contrived to get herself killed.'

'How? Louis, how?' Wembleth demanded. He was still holding the crossbow.

She had attacked Louis and his companions, and contrived to lose the fight. Louis had killed her himself.

He said, 'Bram had us at his mercy. We were hostages for as long as Teela was alive. She'd have been his servant, and he was incompetent. She had to die to save the Ringworld, and she did.'

'But—'

Louis rode him down. 'What matters now is that I would do anything for you. In practice, what I have to do is lose you again. It's indescribably important that the ruling protectors, Tunesmith and Proserpina, be unable to find you.'

'What would they do, kill us? Question us?'

'They'd protect you.'

Wembleth set the crossbow down. His hands were shaking. 'Vashneesht! Stet. I like these people, but we can move again. Must you know where?'

'I must not,' Louis said firmly.

He went outside. Wolf-people youths were clambering over the service stack. Louis shooed them away. He reprogrammed the stepping-disk controls and the float controls too.

Wembleth and Roxanny had followed him out. 'I'm going to flick through,' he told them. 'After I'm gone, change this setting, then *tap the crosshatch button*, here, and flick through. Then go wherever you like.'

'Can't we be traced?'

'I fixed that, Roxanny. You're ghosts as long as you tap the crosshatch before you flick out. Even so, Tunesmith will solve that pretty quick, so bounce around for no more than . . . half a day, give me that much . . . then stop flicking around and get away from the service stack.' Louis flicked out.

CHAPTER 20

Telling a Tale

Launch Room. Louis only needed an instant here. He wanted to see the workspace, *Long Shot*, and the nanotech autodoc.

Carlos Wu's rebuilt autodoc was spread around the stepping disk he'd flicked onto. Tools lay about. He could guess their intent, most of them. Cables and rainbow threads of laser light led to a score of instrument stacks. This maze would take minutes to disentangle . . . an hour or more for the Hindmost.

Long Shot loomed, a bubble a mile tall. At first sight it looked partly disassembled. A curved hatch as big as a fairgrounds gaped near the bottom. Equipment was piled about, and there was lightweight packing stuff everywhere.

Look again: that stuff wasn't intrinsic to any likely hyperdrive system. Here was a General Products #2 ship, a lifeboat. Those were tanks. Those, inflatable habitats for ground and orbit, and a deuterium refinery fitted to suck up seawater. Some of it was mere misdirection. Distorted hull fittings turned out to be a holoprojector left running.

Tunesmith had cleaned out cargo and packaging to get at the works, done his investigations, and rebuilt the ship. Close that hatch and – Louis couldn't instantly see how it would exit the cavern. Hmm?

The linear cannon roared like the end of a world. Lightning ran through the hole in the floor, up and out through Mons Olympus. In the silence that followed, Louis heard Proserpina's shout.

'They'll notice!' In Ghoulish.

They were over by the hole, looking down along the linear cannon: Proserpina, Tunesmith, and two little protectors either of whom might be Hanuman. Tunesmith bellowed, 'They know I'm here. They'll guess I'm active. The ones with brains must have deduced what's under the Map of Mars by now. Some may even rest easier because I'm closing holes in the Ringworld floor.'

'. . . Risk?'

'The missiles most of these factions have been using, one antimatter explosion wouldn't tear up much of the Repair Center. An enemy couldn't *know* he'd hurt me, and he'd anger me, and I might find him. I admit there's risk. I'm stalling. I don't want the ARM and the rest of them wondering what the Mars protector is up to. So this is what I'm up to, closing holes. Keeps me out of mischief.'

They wouldn't scent him: Louis was in a pressure suit. Louis couldn't smell anything either, so he kept looking around. He saw a few Hanging People protectors. They weren't near him. He saw a webeye camera sprayed on the 'doc's Intensive Care Cavity. He waved at it, *Hi, Hindmost!* and wondered if Tunesmith was linked into the same cameras.

'. . . need the holes?'

'I'm through with them. We're almost . . .' Their voices dropped as their hearing came back. Louis wasn't going to learn more this way.

He saw them cover their ears, so Louis covered his. As lightning roared up the linear cannon, Louis picked up a grippy and flung it at Proserpina's head, sixty meters away.

Proserpina caught it and sent it whizzing back at him . . . almost: it would hit the service wall, shatter, and shower him with slivers. Louis danced around the service wall, caught the grippy as it struck, and flung it slantwise at the floor, to ricochet at Proserpina, who caught and returned it. Suddenly other objects were in motion, tools and a random chunk of concrete and a long dead animal as big as Louis. The animal disintegrated in his hand. Louis caught the rest and returned them. He turned a spigot on a tank and was behind the service wall again, popped *up* and returned the grippy and a block of lava tuff, then threw himself behind the puff of featherweight packing plastic that had emerged from the tank. He kicked it upward and was behind the tank while they looked for him there. The grippy burst through the foam plastic, shattering it—

But there were too many things moving now, and elements in his torso and hip were trying to tear themselves apart. He caught what missiles he could, juggled them, and presently set them down. He limped toward the protectors.

Proserpina said, 'Funny man—'

'What makes you feel so safe?' Tunesmith demanded.

'You left me a chair. You fiddled with my metabolism.'

Tunesmith said, 'Louis, everything has happened out of sequence. You ate early and finished your change late. An ARM ship exploded early. We could have taken our sweet time extrapolating the behavior of all these factions in the Fringe War. Now – talk to me. What will they do?'

'A sanity check first?'

'Whose?'

'Have you solved how *Long Shot* works?'

'Yes.'

'And embedded the principle in a quintillion nanotech devices? Made from a much-altered experimental autodoc?'

'The numbers—'

'And run nanodust into the superconducting network under the Ringworld, so that its structure can be altered?'

'Yes, with help from Proserpina and our associates.'

'Proserpina, are you with this?'

'Yes, Louis. There weren't enough holes in the landscape, so we had to drill in spots—'

'Is it *working*?'

Tunesmith said, 'I think so.'

'Stet, I'm sane and so are you, or else we're all crazy. Is the system ready to go?'

'It may be, if my power storage holds. I can't include the shadow squares or the sun. At best I can only run for a little more than two days. But, Louis, I'm not sure the nanosystems have finished infecting the entire grid. I need to know how much time we've got. What will the Fringe War do?'

Louis's mind was dancing down a new path. 'You can build a new day-and-night system. Tunesmith, why not build a real Dyson sphere? Ten million miles diameter with a sun at the center and the Ringworld around it. Make it thin like a solar sail so light pressure will inflate it. Give it windows to let daylight through to the Ringworld. The rest of the material is a photoelectric transformer. You'll be collecting most of the power of a sun.'

Proserpina said, 'You're fresh, Louis.' In Ghoulish

speech that implied meat not ready to eat: unacceptable immaturity. 'Protectors can be scatterbrains. You must solve one problem at a time. We're still looking at the Fringe War fleet. When will they strike?'

'There's another matter—'

Tunesmith bellowed, 'No! Already some faction has destroyed one of my attitude jets. Who? What motive? Was it a deliberate provocation?'

'Show me the event. Meteor Defense Room.'

They flicked out.

He absolutely couldn't signal the Hindmost. The puppeteer would have to move *now*.

Meteor Defense. Proserpina and Tunesmith took their chairs in a jump. Twisted Louis had to climb to reach the third chair. He looked for where stepping disks ought to be. The one he'd come through was clearly marked. A Hanging People protector, Hanuman, flicked through an unmarked site and awaited orders. Others might be concealed *there* or *there*. Bet on three or four, no more. Why were the chairs on these booms so massive?

The wall displayed the Ringworld system as if viewed from the sun. The Ringworld was a mere outline, white threads against starscape. 'I need a pointer,' Louis said, and found touchpoints on a knob. 'Stet. These are Outsider ships, right? Two. Do you see more?'

'No.'

'We're not really of interest to anything that different. These,' he highlighted lenses and spheres, 'are Kzinti, and these are ARM,' long levers studded with lesser ships. 'I don't see the Sheathclaws' ship.'

'It went away.'

'Probably ordered off, or they might have run from Kzinti. Kzinti use telepaths as slaves. What are you wondering about?'

'Interactions,' Proserpina said.

He needed a way to use up some time, then send the protectors off on some sort of distraction. Louis drew a net of lines linking various ships, and added vector arrows. 'See? Distance and velocity and gravity, you need to take it all into consideration, so it's complicated—'

Proserpina snapped, 'It is not! It's only different. We did this all the way from the galactic core to the Ringworld site! They've arranged a standoff, but it's unstable *here*—'

'Yah. And this balance won't hold if – if some dissident faction, say the One Race contingent, is actually running *this* ship or—'

'I don't see how it held this long. I don't see how it could hold much longer,' Tunesmith said. 'But you know them all, Louis.'

'It won't hold. You're missing the effect of the Outsiders. They're more powerful than the other factions and everybody knows it. Just being here, they've made it all more stable until now. Everybody's been wondering what the Outsiders will do. What the Outsiders will do is nothing, and the whole Fringe War is gradually coming to know that.'

He was seeing it now, the disintegrating patterns, strength built up here, bluff here. Two bar-shaped ARM ships poised to destroy one great Kzin lens. Thirty-one ships edged up around one Outsider ship in hope of protection that would vanish like dawn frost on the Moon. Futz, the balance just wasn't there.

'Tunesmith, this whole house of cards could come down at any second. Don't wait. How fast can you get us moving?'

'Half a day, with luck.'

Louis turned, shocked. 'Why so long?'

'I need to run all the power in the shadow square system into the superconductor grid. If I did that too early, it would leak—'

'Can't you get magnetohydrodynamic power from the rim ramjets?'

'What a good idea. It would have required a certain amount of redesigning, say twenty to thirty days and a thousand spill mountain protectors. I need half a day, then *go*, and no more Fringe War.'

'Start now,' Louis said.

Patiently Tunesmith said, 'You've only just arrived. We don't even know, *you* don't even know who attacked us twenty-eight days ago. Where's the danger coming from? Can I just kill it? The superconductor net has been rewiring itself for only two falans, crystallizing into its new configuration. Even if the change is complete, I need to test it.'

Sometimes you just have to gamble, Louis thought. But Tunesmith wouldn't act fast enough without more pressure. 'Show me how it happened,' he said.

The sky changed: ships moved, stars didn't. The Ringworld went solid. A frame zoomed on one of the attitude jets, a gauzy glittering net molded magnetically into a hyperboloid of rotation with a line of white fire running down the axis. Suddenly it was bright, bright, dimming – the motor was gone, and a piece was bitten out of the rim wall. Along its foot, spill mountains were burning.

'Is *this* all you've got?'

'Various frequencies.'

Replay, hydrogen alpha light. Louis waved it off. 'It's too overt for puppeteers, too restrained for Kzinti. Maybe a Kzinti dissident. There are ARM dissidents too; we could ask Roxanny. Or anyone who'd like to see both sides reduced a little. I've never been sure about Trinocs, or puppeteers.'

'Not much help,' Tunesmith agreed.

'Tell me what you know about Teela Brown.'

Proserpina asked, 'Who?'

'An insane puppeteer scheme,' Tunesmith said. 'She

was a victim. General Products, the merchant arm of Pierson's puppeteers in human space, set up a birthright lottery on Earth. The attempt was to breed for lucky humans. In practice what they got was a few statistical flukes, like Teela Brown. She . . . Louis! *Did you have a child with Teela Brown?*'

Louis said nothing.

'*Where is your child?*'

Louis said nothing. Among protectors, a poker face is easy; body language is hard.

He waited until he saw motion. Proserpina left her chair in a long jump. Tunesmith jumped in a different direction. Hanuman looked uncertain; he remained at the visible stepping disk, the far one. As soon as the protectors were committed, Louis jumped toward Tunesmith's chair.

One of these chairs *had* to be a stepping disk. It was a natural hiding place. Two would be redundant, though all three had been made too thick and too wide – and Tunesmith would have claimed the right one. But other stepping disks in this room had to be guarded. If Louis was right – and he was, because Hanuman instantly launched himself toward the same chair.

Hanuman got there first. The chair started to swing aside, but Louis was there. Hanuman caught Louis with a powerful kick, but Louis had the mass. He slammed Hanuman into the stepping disk and reached around the dazed hominid to pop the rim and turn the disk on. They both flicked out.

Heel of the hand, a blow to Hanuman's head. Hanuman went limp. Louis pushed, sent him flying. Grinding pain in his hip: Hanuman's kick had broken something.

They were underground, somewhere beneath Mars. He popped the disk's rim and tapped controls, *fast*.

Louis flicked in, popped the rim. If Tunesmith tracked him to this sandy, barren island – or Hanuman signaled him a minute or two from now – he'd find Louis's footprints, hours old. He might even find scent traces of Wembleth and Roxanny.

And if Teela's genes were lucky, Wembleth and Roxanny and their child would be well out of Tunesmith's reach by now. But *every* surviving gene pattern is *insanely* lucky, and Teela's luck didn't matter a tanj to Tunesmith. What mattered was this:

Louis Wu could never give a dispassionate, trustworthy answer to Tunesmith's questions while he could shade his answers to favor his bloodline.

One more move. Louis tapped controls, then hit #, and flicked out.

* * *

In the crew quarters aboard *Hot Needle of Inquiry*, Louis rapidly typed up a bleu cheese and mushroom omelet and a salad. He stripped off his pressure suit, then his clothes. He dialed up a falling jumper and put it on. He turned on the shower just long enough to wet the bag. He half-expected to hear the Puppeteer's Voice, but it didn't come.

He flicked into the cargo bay. A flycycle would have been too big, but he typed up a flying belt modified for magnetic lift. He ate most of his salad and omelet while he waited, a hairy four minutes, for the flying belt to be built. Put it on, flicked back to crew quarters.

Now, where would a puppeteer hide a stepping disk? An escape hatch had to be here: the Hindmost might find himself trapped in crew quarters by a man and a Kzin. The toilet seat? Too small. The shower?

The shower *ceiling*. It was the right size. The code would be puppeteer music: Louis could never sing it. Maybe he could hack it, but first—

He set his hands against the shower ceiling and said, 'Hindmost's Voice, put me through.'

He was in the control room. He used the stepping disk there.

Neither Hanuman nor Louis were where the first flick had taken them. The second flick put Tunesmith and

Proserpina on a barren island. They found Hanuman groggy, trying to sit up. Proserpina examined him. He didn't seem badly hurt.

Tunesmith asked, 'How are you?'

'Injured, not badly. He held my life and released it,' Hanuman said.

'That shows good self-control. Proserpina, see if you can find traces of your escaped guests. Hanuman, rest.' Tunesmith went to work on the stepping-disk controls.

'I find their scent,' Proserpina called. 'Falans old. In rut.'

'This changes all,' Hanuman said. 'I must warn my people.'

'Your people are tree dwellers! How can they hide from what must come?'

'Stet. I know what to do.'

'Do it after we're gone,' Tunesmith said. 'Then rejoin us in Meteor Defense.' He and Proserpina flicked out.

Launch Room. Little Hanging People protectors were all lying prone about the cavern below Mons Olympus. The Hindmost was working on a laser projector. 'How are you doing?' Louis called.

'I'm still disconnecting instruments. It's hard to tell where it's safe.'

Louis began disconnecting laser and cable attachments,

pacifying Tunesmith's instruments where necessary. He wished he could move faster. Something with sharp edges was loose in his hip; the flesh was badly swollen. 'You're not safe on the Ringworld,' he said. 'How are you going to move the 'doc components?'

'I hadn't decided.'

'I was hoping you'd think of something. Stet. This next part is risky.' Louis finished disconnecting sensors. The 'doc's components were still connected to each other. Louis left them that way. 'I'll be gone at least an hour. Get this stuff ready to be lifted with magnetic fields. Leave the roof open.'

'Wait. What are you about to do?'

'No time.'

'Where are the protectors we're robbing? What can I accomplish when death may find me in a moment? Tell me what you've *done*!'

Better if he knew, and Louis had already cost himself an hour at least. Give the Hindmost a minute. He said, 'I tried to tell Tunesmith that the Fringe War is about to blow up—'

'Eee!' A raucous chord of dismay.

'—Just as I'm telling you. If you tuck your heads under you, you will die in that position. Do you believe me?'

'Yah.'

'I let Tunesmith guess I had a child – yes, a boy with Teela's genes. Congratulations, they survived. Your breeding program is still in force—'

'What of later inbreeding?'

'Oh, Hindmost, there must have been other ships crashed on the Ringworld. Wembleth's children will find mates.'

'Stet.'

'I flicked out to a few places, ended where Tunesmith can find traces of Wembleth. Then I used my block on the stepping disk and went to *Needle*. It won't take Tunesmith long to get around the block. When he does, he'll find out I went to *Hot Needle of Inquiry*, took my sweet time there, and didn't leave.

'I must be still aboard. I went to get Wembleth, right? It follows that we're trying to leave the Ringworld. The Fringe War balance must be ready to fall apart *right now.* No protector would otherwise risk his child's life this way, in a ship that can be shot down by Fringe War ships or blocked as easily as Tunesmith can block *Needle.*

'If Tunesmith and Proserpina followed that line of logic, then they're getting ready to end the Fringe War, and they will not disturb us here, as long as you keep these protectors asleep and take care to shut down these cameras. Can do?'

'Trust me,' the Hindmost said.

Louis took a moment to think that over. The Hindmost knew how to open the roof into Mons Olympus. *Long Shot* was too big to launch using the linear cannon, so the ship would rise slowly, on fusion jets, making too good a target. The Hindmost wouldn't have the nerve, and it was far too dangerous anyway.

So he wouldn't launch without Louis, Louis could trust him, and that settled *that*. Louis flicked out.

Meteor Defense. '*We* never did *locate* the ship,' Tunesmith said. 'Can you block his takeoff?'

'Yes. And I can search near space for any ARM ship coming for him. He can't possibly escape me. He must be mad. A failed transition to protector can warp a breeder's brain.'

'Sudden understanding can do that too. Mad with fear?'

'But is he afraid of the Fringe War, or of what we'll do?'

Proserpina's eyes half-closed. She looked a little like Hanuman in that pose. She said, 'He didn't expect to delay us long. He'd have just enough time to get clear, if we begin now and ignore Louis Wu and his freemother child.'

Tunesmith looked up at the crowded sky. 'Begin,' he commanded.

Hanuman flicked in on a ridge of bare scrith. He looked down across miles and miles of forest, reviewing his options.

Louis Wu was the protector who had no children on the Ringworld – *unless* he'd had a child by Teela Brown. Louis-protector could have no interest in Teela, who was dead, *unless* she'd left a child; and that child would be Louis Wu's. The chain of logic was so straightforward that even a Hanging People protector could follow it.

Tunesmith had seen it in a moment. And in that moment, Louis Wu had gone to rescue his child and get him to safety.

It followed that the Ringworld's death was likely and immediate. Tunesmith would act.

And what now? Hanuman's people were tree dwellers! They didn't have minds; they couldn't follow instructions even if he had any to give. How was he to hide them from the sky?

Wish for a rainstorm?

Find and fetch Teela Brown's lucky child, bring the creature here, *then* wish for a rainstorm?

Hanuman decided.

He detached a float plate from the depleted service stack. He stayed above the forest, enjoying the scents of thousands of his people below the canopy. Brothers, sisters, N-children. He did not dip down to see them. There wouldn't be time.

Tunesmith would move immediately. Where a treetop blocked the sun, already Hanuman could see a glitter to the shadow squares. Power was being beamed down.

He settled his disk on raddled earth. A few Burrowing People emerged. He spoke to them.

'You must stay underground for two days. For you this is easy. Do not watch the sky. Spread the word as far as you can, but be underground before shadow hides the sun.

'There will be lights beyond your experience. Do not look at the sky until the light fades. Afterward the sky will be very dark. Go spin-and-port to where you will find Hanging People. Help them. They are mine, and they will have gone mad.'

CHAPTER 21

In Flight

Penultimate's Palace. Louis flicked in and rolled off the burnt stack of float plates. Nothing fired on him.

The flying belt took him out and down. He skimmed above the yellow lawn, wondering at the black markings. One pattern must be the Penultimate's name or portrait . . . there, traces of a cartoon, very simplified, a style weirdly reminiscent of William Rotsler. The other would be speech.

He had guesswork for a Rosetta Stone. What would a protector say to an invader? That might be a pictograph pun: a word you could read as 'Enter' or 'Extinct'; 'Greetings' or 'Epitaph'. Could you extrapolate a language from that?

Nah.

Louis flew low, enjoying the skill it took to weave between trees. Maybe they'd conceal him if Proserpina came looking for him on her own turf. (Nah. She had his scent.) Hard turns and high gees and a brief freedom from intellectual problems.

Proserpina's sunfish ship rested among the trees near Proserpina's base. Lesser trees had grown up through the gridwork. Louis set the flying belt behind a thick trunk, stripped off his falling jumper, and left that too. He made his way forward on foot. *See the naked, limping breeder.*

Here was the ARM 'doc from *Gray Nurse*. Louis wondered what the diagnostic readings would say about him. Mutated? Not human? Dying? He walked past it without a pause. No time!

He stopped by *Snail Darter*'s library. *No time*, but protectors didn't always have a choice.

He'd watched Claus and Roxanny work this device. It wasn't hard to persuade it to summon up a roster for the Fringe War fleet. There were dozens of Wu, and six Harmony: his first daughter had married a Harmony. An ID number sequence would identify his line of descent—

A grandson and his daughter had joined the Navy decades ago. Wes Carlton Wu was Flight Captain aboard *Koala*, a lurker ship, with Tanya Wu as Purser. Another quick pass found no other blood relatives, and time was shrinking.

Louis approached the sunfish ship.

Think like a Pak. A protector might kill any breeder

who smelled wrong, to leave more space for her own breeders. But you're Proserpina. Accommodation has been your survival for a million years. You don't want to hurt a breeder. It might be some powerful enemy's N-child!

There were no steps up to the cabin. Louis climbed up like a Hanging Person.

It was roomy inside. There were handgrips everywhere, and footgrips: just how prehensile were Proserpina's toes? And sensors and touchpads and toggles and levers, randomly placed. There was a horseshoe of couch, but only one control chair, and it would not fit Louis. He'd have to change it – but he'd better give some thought to convincing the ship he was Proserpina.

Louis was disappointed in the Hindmost. He had steered the destiny of a species whose tools and learning beggared mankind's. Why couldn't he move a few kilotons of medical equipment? It would have saved Louis considerable trouble and two or three hours' time.

Maybe the Experimentalist faction on the Fleet of Worlds was more like New Orleans' traditional Fool King. Set them going, but watch them. Turn them off when they do something excessively expensive or dangerous. Sometimes they'll do something worthwhile—

He was getting distracted.

Thou shalt have no Proserpinas before me. She'd have set

defenses to prevent a protector from manipulating the ship. Unless – would Proserpina really set a death trap for someone like Tunesmith, acknowledged as brighter and more dangerous than Proserpina herself? Retaliation could be terminal.

And what about protector slaves? This chair looked like it had been altered to fit a Hanging Person, then adjusted for Proserpina again. Hey, she must have let Hanuman fly it!

Futz! The ship wasn't defended. She *was* the defense. Who would dare steal Proserpina's ship? – and that was the point: *risk* for Louis Wu was *do nothing*. He adjusted the chair and sat down, strapped himself in, and lifted.

Trees had grown into the ship's metal lacework. They tore loose. Louis lofted the ship above the atmosphere, then turned toward the rim wall.

Was the sun starting to roil? He'd burn his eyes out if he looked hard. There must be a way to dim the glass, right? And Tunesmith would have the meteor defense going. Louis zigzagged his path a bit, and studied the controls. Here?

It didn't just darken the view; it was light-amplification too. He turned it very dark, and looked up.

A solar prominence was reaching out and out.

Louis jogged the ship at high gees. The ground flared below him. He could see the beam tracking and avoid it, even guide it a little to miss a populated spill mountain, and then he was off the Ringworld and dropping, easing back and under the Ringworld floor.

He had to follow the arc halfway around, three hundred million miles. Now the nontrivial danger was alien ships. Louis zigged along the magnet grid, accelerating hard, hearing a *toc, toc* of multimolecule-sized cameras hitting the skin of the ship. The Fringe War would be after him soon enough.

Something flashed on the Ringworld's underside. Louis zagged almost into another flash. Maybe he'd started a war himself.

Tunesmith's Meteor Reweaving System had closed Fist-of-God. Louis came up around the rim instead. He made for the Map of Mars, a little over half a million miles away. The sun was roiling again.

A spark struck upward: a launch from Mons Olympus. Louis slid the sunfish ship beneath the path of the meteor package, just for a moment. Tunesmith wouldn't have set the meteor defense to fire on those! He slowed, descended through the crater, and set the ship to hover.

He crawled halfway out of the cabin and shouted down. 'Hindmost! Close it!'

The crater's lid began to close.

Louis began to play with the sunfish ship's controls. The 'doc's Intensive Care Cavity rose, twirled in the air, and settled a bit jerkily into the bay in *Long Shot*. Then the Service Wall, trailing loose cables. Then other, smaller components. Then the lifeboat.

Then a tank Louis had identified earlier.

The puppeteer was shouting something. '—tied down?'

Louis settled the tank in with the rest of the 'doc. He brought the sunfish ship down and got out.

The Hindmost came trotting up. He asked, 'How will you tie these components against shock of takeoff?'

'Tunesmith was using a tank of foam plastic. Let's set it going and close the ship up, then board.'

The tank was spraying foam plastic as Louis closed the lid on it. He'd taken the pilot's seat without comment. Hey, it was built for humans. The Hindmost asked, 'Shouldn't we open the crater again?'

'Hindmost, let's try something else.' He activated the hyperdrive. The cavern disappeared. The Q2 ship launched itself straight down into a boil of colors.

Map of Earth. Shortly after nightfall Acolyte begged audience with Chmeee.

One of the guards said, 'Play elsewhere, child. Your father is busy.' And grinned.

'I bear a message from Tunesmith.'

'An odd name.'

'Chmeee will know it. Tunesmith who lives under the Map of Mars.'

The guard was bored, and he toyed with Acolyte a bit longer. Then he went into the tent. When he came out, he asked, 'How did it come, this message?'

'There were flashes of light from the mountains to starboard.'

Acolyte was allowed entrance. He groveled before his father, who asked, 'Is this the Tunesmith who wants to give me the Map of Earth? I've heard nothing since you delivered his message.'

'He says you may take the Map yourself, after the other prides have gone mad.'

It had gone quiet: Chmeee's courtiers were paying attention.

Chmeee asked, 'Mad?' and studied his son, whose subservience seemed laid over a whiplash eagerness. 'Lecture me, then.'

'Tunesmith instructs us to hide ourselves from the sky for two full days. We must be under a roof or tent, all of us, even females and kits. We should sleep if we can. We must all be under cover, or blindfolded, before shadow reveals the sun.'

'So soon? How shall I manage that?'

Acolyte dared to grin. 'What would Louis Wu say?'

'"That's why I get the big money." What is to happen to the sky?'

'That was not told. You have seen ships leaving tracks

of light across the sky. You have heard talk of the Fringe War. I watched it in Tunesmith's Meteor Defense Room. It is told that Tunesmith will end the war.'

Chmeee nodded. 'Are you ready to run? It is well.' His voice rose to a bellow. 'All in my hearing, you are each an emissary to my far provinces! Divide the contents of my kitchen to feed yourselves. Go where I send you. Carry a blindfold ready to use. You will know when to use it. Fools will go blind or mad.

'You are each more valuable than those you will speak to, and you will be under cover before the shadow square passes. Two days hidden, or answer to me. The rest of us may conquer the Map of Earth if we so choose.'

The boy Kazarp was gazing open-mouthed at the sky. Shadow had covered the sun, but the shadow squares were glittering in a way he'd never seen. Presently he raised his instrument and began to play.

Over the music he heard a stealthy shift in posture, too close for any stranger, and he said, 'I knew you were there.'

'Don't turn around. I am become Vashneesht.'

His father had disappeared falans ago, and now this: a thing out of fantasy, awesome and terrible. Kazarp didn't turn. 'Father? Does mother know?'

'You must tell her. Tell her gently. Then tell her she

must hide from the sky for two days, and you too, for fear of going mad. Spread the word. A burrow would be better than a roof. Afterward there is a world of mad folk to care for, and far more feasting than our folk will ever want.'

'Will you stay?'

'Not now. I will visit when I can.'

Long Shot's cabin was at the bottom of the sphere, between four fusion-drive nostrils. In hyperdrive *Long Shot* flew ass-backward into the unknown. Louis launched straight down, into and through the Ringworld floor – feeling a touch of drag from the superdense scrith – and out into space.

He was moving away from the sun and straight into the thickest gathering of Fringe War ships. Not that that mattered. Those ships were all in Einstein space, this close to a large mass. Louis was flying blind, of course, through hyperspace. What he hoped was that this faster ship would outrun the eaters.

The puppeteer was wound into a tight knot. *He* wouldn't be of much help.

How fast would *Long Shot* move near this great a mass? He'd wondered if it would even exceed light-speed. Tunesmith might have worked out the QII system's behavior, but Louis didn't have enough clues. He'd learn soon enough. When the crystal sphere that was the mass detector began working, he'd be outside the 'singularity.'

Eleven hours later, Louis knew that even protectors could grow tired. He could ignore that, and hunger and thirst, and pain in guts and joints, headache and sinus ache, that properly belong only to an aging savage. It didn't matter. He'd got clear of the Ringworld. Of thirty trillion Ringworld hominids, a fat percentage would survive. Wembleth and Roxanny and their child were lost in noise. If Tunesmith worked out what they truly were, he wouldn't even search. With luck, though, he'd think Louis had taken Wembleth to the stars.

Winning could compensate for a lot of pain.

The window was the floor, and it would darken, light-amplify, record and display recordings, or zoom. Louis watched flow patterns of colored light, and a dark comma zipping past.

He saw the view change. The window wasn't there: his eyes slid around it.

Louis looked at the mass detector. There should have been lines of light crawling toward him. Nothing showed. It was just doped crystal.

Louis hit the cutoff.

He saw showers of stars. The universe was wide and beautiful below his feet. He was in Einstein space.

It would have pleased him to sell *Long Shot* to some band of freebooters in human space. Or form his own! Now that looked unlikely. Louis set the window to zoom, then darkened it a little against the zodiacal glare. The Ringworld eclipsed the sun except for a tiny sliver of light.

Six light-hours from Ringworld system – he measured it – the sun wouldn't light up *Long Shot* very much, but putting the ship in the Ringworld's shadow would leave it black as space. He hadn't used fusion motors at all: nobody would find him via neutrino flux. The rest of the electromagnetic spectrum might reveal him to the Fringe War if they happened to look. Louis thought they'd be too busy for that. They'd hunt for Proserpina's sunfish ship until something more interesting happened . . . real soon now.

The rec room above was as tiny as the cabin below, but there was a game-room wall, food dispenser, and a shower bag. He noticed also the hatch in the ceiling. That was new. It led into a maze of man-wide access tubes he could see through the wall. They were hard to follow, a neat puzzle, but one led to the storage room where he had stowed the lifeboat and autodoc. *Good.*

He took time for a shower. Hey, if he missed the event, *Long Shot* would catch the light wave further out.

Nothing had changed when he'd dried himself. He sank his fingers in the Hindmost's mane and dodged a hind leg kick – almost. 'Wake,' he said.

'Did I hurt you?'

'Doesn't matter.'

'Why are we at rest?'

'I want to watch something. Also, I can't use the mass detector.'

'Eee!' the Hindmost whistled.

'It's a psionics device. You'll have to fly the ship yourself. But we're loose, everyone I love is safe, the Fringe War won't be looking for us, and the way lies clear to Canyon.'

'To Canyon?'

'Well, or the Fleet of Worlds, if you like. I just assumed you'd brought your mate and children with you when you left the Fleet.'

'Of course.'

'If we can work out details, there's something I need.'

'You're bluffing, Louis, as you did once before. You're dying, aren't you?'

'Yah. I was too twisted up when tree-of-life started to change me. I'm dying, stet, but not bluffing. Everything's worked out fine. But I'd be pleased if we could get Carlos Wu's autodoc running again.'

'That would take . . . mmm.'

'Considerable trouble. Hard physical labor. What can I offer you?'

'*Long Shot* moves too fast. Collision with some star is nearly certain. I don't have the nerve to fly us to Home.'

'Not Canyon?'

'Home,' said the puppeteer. 'I didn't think I could hide us on Canyon. Too small. Home is very like Earth, Louis, and has a wonderful history.'

'Home it is,' Louis said agreeably. 'Hey.' The magnified sun glared, etching the control room with sharp-edged shadows.

The puppeteer turned one head, then both. The pupils irised nearly shut. His voice was a monotone: the Hindmost was upset. 'Where is the Ringworld?'

'Yah.'

'Yah?'

'Yah. Tunesmith used nanotechnology to change the entire superconductor grid to the configuration he found in *Long Shot*. He's off like a bunny under Quantum II hyperdrive, and he took the Ringworld with him.'

'How far?'

'What?' But this was the only ship that could catch it. A little more than two thirty-hour days at Quantum II hyperdrive . . . a light year in 5/4 minutes . . . 'Three thousand light years before Tunesmith runs out of power. That's *way* out of human space. Telescopes won't see anything for a hundred generations. You might catch that much mass shifting around with a gravity-wave detector. What were you going to do, chase it down?'

'The wealth,' mourned the Hindmost. 'All gone. I lost my place as Hindmost chasing the Ringworld's wealth of knowledge. And those you spoke of, those you love, Louis, what of them?'

'I'll never find them. Hindmost, that's the point.

Now let's fix that autodoc before something intimate tears loose inside me.'

'I think we can ignore the tidal effect,' Tunesmith said. 'Don't you?'

Proserpina's fingers danced. The wall display – which showed nothing, a kind of curdled gray everywhere – went black. White hieroglyphs danced across it in a Pak mathematical system millions of falans old. 'The sun's gravity pulled up and a bit inward along a very narrow angle, when the Ringworld had a sun. With the sun gone,' she said, 'all the seas will tend to flow toward the rim walls. We're in flight for two days? Stet, that's negligible. What I'm worried about,' hieroglyphs danced again, 'is the approach.'

The sky had gone crazy. Roxanny and Wembleth wriggled out of the tent, Roxanny a little clumsy, and stared into a light-show that would have won awards. Wembleth asked, 'What is happening?'

'I swear I have no idea. Some supersecret weapon. Futz, I hope it isn't Kzinti. I don't see any ships at all, unless – what was that?' A little black comma fell wiggling across the sky, starboard to port. It left a pockmark near the top of the rim wall, visible through mag specs.

'I don't know,' Wembleth said.

'A ship bigger than *Long Shot*? No species *I* know makes one.'

'It's changing again, Roxanny.'

For an instant the colors faded, and then the whole *sky* was gone, and they were both blind.

It was hard to remember that there had once been sight. 'It's the Blind Spot,' she said. Roxanny had been trained: she looked at her feet. Yes, there they were. 'Futz, I can't believe it. We're in futzy hyperdrive! Look down. Lower your—' Wembleth was wandering off, still blind. Roxanny followed him and, still without looking up, felt her way up his body and tilted his head down.

'Let's get into the tent,' she said.

They lived in the pressure tent for two days. When they had a sky again, it was stars glaring on black. 'This is going to drive a lot of your people crazy,' Roxanny said. 'The Ringworld was never this dark. The headlights on the flycycle are going to be priceless.'

'I never saw stars so bright,' Wembleth said. 'It's a whole new age, Roxanny. You said there are Ball Worlds around most stars? They could be our children's inheritance.'

One bright star was growing brighter above the portward rim wall.

*   *   *

The sky had returned to the Meteor Defense wall display.

Proserpina said, 'We'll have to find us a sun, stet? And shift the whole Ringworld sideways to get to it. The mag fields are useless without something to push against, so we'll be using just the attitude jets. Line up with a sun, fall toward it, use the fields to stop ourselves. The seas will shift, Tunesmith.'

'I know. I've found a yellow-white star with nearly our own velocity. There, the bright one, do you see it?'

'Yes. Zoom.'

The star expanded, and darkened. 'Increased X-ray output in this region,' she said. 'We'll need to boost the ozone layer until we can build a shadow square system.'

'Yes.'

'I'm more worried about tides.'

'Yes, there will still be stress on the seas and oceans.'

'I thought of letting them freeze, but we can't. We—'

'Of course not, but we can use magnetic effects on the sun itself. Look, I found a way to skew our path so the star comes straight down the axis. We'll ring the sun. We'll bob a few times stabilizing ourselves; that sends the seas back and forth, not just all in one direction, which would be disastrous.'

White hieroglyphs danced across the starscape. 'It would work,' Proserpina said. 'We'll lose much of our population, even some species.'

'I know.'

'I have a request. Tell me if it's feasible.'

'See if you can describe it.'

'Leave the sun bobbing back and forth along the Ringworld axis. We'll get tides. We'll get seasons, changing weather.'

'What, like a Ball World?' Tunesmith laughed. 'Like your world, the Pak world. What about breeders? Won't they go crazier yet?'

'Anyone who kept his mind through these last two days will get used to anything,' Proserpina said.

CHAPTER 22

Breeder

Louis Wu woke aflame with new life. Cautious in free fall, he waited for the coffin lid to move aside. A hologram Hindmost was looking down at him.

Louis wriggled out. 'Nothing hurts.'

'Good.'

'I was used to it. Oh, futz, I've lost my mind!'

'Louis, didn't you know the machine would rebuild you as a breeder?'

'Yah, but . . . my head feels futzy. Full of cotton. I never felt so much *myself* as when I could think like a protector.'

'We could have rebuilt the 'doc—'

'No. *No*.' Fist against coffin lid. 'I remember that much. I have to be a breeder, or dead. If I'm a protector, I *will* track down Wembleth and Roxanny, and Tunesmith and Proserpina *will* follow me.'

'But they would certainly protect your blood line.'

'They would, yes. But if Wembleth is loose on the Ringworld, his luck . . . hey.'

'You don't believe in Teela Brown's luck.'

'I didn't. But when I was a protector . . . it's not good science, stet? Because it's not falsifiable. But look at the pattern. He stole my woman, stet? She fell into his lap. The only woman in reach who could make Wembleth young again, and bear his children too. He's the only survivor of a village that died of asphyxiation, and he'd be dead if rescue hadn't fallen on him from interstellar space!'

'Louis! Teela wasn't lucky!'

'Stet, and Wembleth lost all his friends, and ended up a hunted refugee. What if it's the genes that are lucky? Teela's genes want to reproduce. You can always argue either way.

'It could still be all moonbeams. Anything that doesn't make predictions that can be disproved isn't science. Maybe Teela was only a statistical fluke until we found her. After that, whatever happens to her, you can always explain it as luckier than something else that might have happened. Read *Candide*.'

'I'll look it up.'

'Unfalsifiable. If it's wrong, you can't prove it. When I was a protector, I didn't *dis*believe. Maybe Teela's children are the Ringworld's luck. If their location is uncertain, they protect the whole Ringworld. Basic quantum mechanics. And it's going to need that! They've all gone out into the universe at a minute and a quarter per light year—'

'Louis.'

'What?'

'We haven't moved since you went into the 'doc, two months ago Earthtime. We're a warm spot on the sky. Sooner or later the Fringe War will notice us. What else has that heterogeneous mob got for entertainment but to track us down and take our ship?'

'Right.' Louis climbed back through the maze of access tubes, getting lost once, guided by the puppeteer behind him. He set himself in the pilot's chair and jumped to hyperdrive. Radial lines indicating stars edged out of the mass detector, and Louis turned *Long Shot* toward Home.

Glossary

Aerobrake: To shed velocity by passing through a planetary atmosphere.

Antispin: Direction opposite the Ringworld's direction of spin.

Arch: The Ringworld as seen from anywhere on its surface.

ARM: Once the Amalgamation of Regional Militia; for several hundred years, the United Nations armed forces. Jurisdiction was originally limited to Earth-Moon system.

Autodoc: Any system built to perform automated medical operations.

Belter: Citizen of the asteroid belt, Sol system.

Canyon: A world of human space, once Patriarchy property.

Carlos Wu's autodoc: An experimental medical system first seen in 'Procrustes'.

Droud: A small device that plugs into the skull of a current addict. Its purpose: to meter a current flow to the pleasure center of the user's brain.

Elbow root: A ubiquitous Ringworld plant. Grows as a kind of natural fence.

Experimentalist: A Pierson's puppeteer political faction now out of power.

Eyestorm: The pattern of winds that forms above a puncture in the Ringworld floor. A tornado on its side. (Hurricanes and tornadoes are impossible on the Ringworld's flat surface.)

Fleet of Worlds: The homeworld of the Pierson's puppeteer species, and four more worlds sequestered for farming, all occupy a Kemplerer rosette moving at near lightspeed.

Flup: Seabottom ooze.

Flycycle: A one- or two-LE flying device.

Fringe War: All the spacegoing species of known space seem to have sent ships to Ringworld system. Bram, when he was in command of the Repair Center, shot them down if they approached too close. Tunesmith hasn't done that, and the Fringe War is currently in a cold state.

General Products: A company owned by Pierson's puppeteers that sold mostly spacecraft hulls. Dissolved two hundred years ago.

The Great Ocean: One of two salt seas on the Ringworld,

measuring six hundred times the surface area of the Earth.

Grippy: An all purpose hand tool.

Home: A world of human space, unusually Earthlike.

Hot Needle of Inquiry: Second ship (of Experimentalist design) to reach the Ringworld.

Human space: The region of stars explored by humanity.

Known space: The region of the universe known to explorers who communicate with humanity.

LE (*Legal Entity*): Any entity (human or not, organic or not) legally entitled to civil rights.

Long Shot: Prototype Quantum II hyperdrive spacecraft, first ship to visit the galactic core.

Lying Bastard: First ship (of Experimentalist design) to reach the Ringworld.

Map of Earth (or *Mars, Kzin, Kdatlyno, etc.*): The Great Ocean is scattered with maps of nearby inhabited worlds at one-to-one scale, complete with local ecologies as of the time the Ringworld was built.

Meteor defense: Ringworld systems can cause a solar flare, and a superthermal laser effect within the flare. Energy output is awesome, but the effect is slow.

N-child: Lineal descendant.

Outsider hyperdrive or *Hyperdrive:* A means of faster-than-light travel common in known space.

Patriarchy: The Kzinti interstellar empire.

Port: To the left as one looks spinward.

Quantum II hyperdrive: An advanced experimental

faster-than-light system, puppeteer designed, first seen in 'At the Core.' One Ringworld day under QII hyperdrive = 1440 light years.

Repair Center: The ancient center of Ringworld repair, maintenance, and control, housed beneath the Map of Mars on the Great Ocean.

Rishathra (reshtra, etc.): Sexual practice outside one's own species but within the intelligent hominids.

Scrith: Ringworld structural material. Scrith underlies all the terraformed and contoured inner surface of the Ringworld. The rim walls are also of scrith. Very dense, with a tensile strength on the order of the force that holds an atomic nucleus together.

Sheathclaws: A world held by humans and Kzinti together.

Spill mountains: Mountains standing against the rim wall, the outflow of the rim spillpipes. One stage in the circulation of flup.

Spin or *Spinward:* In the direction of rotation of the Ringworld. (Against the rotation of the sky.)

Starboard: To the right as one looks spinward.

Stasis field: Human technology. An induced state in which time passes very slowly. Ratios can be as high as a billion years of real time to a few seconds in stasis. An object in stasis is very nearly invulnerable.

Stepping disks: Puppeteer technology, an advanced form of teleportation.

Stet: Leave it alone; accept as written; make no change; restore.

Tanj: An expletive, once shorthand for 'There ain't no justice.'

Thruster: Reactionless drive. In human space, thrusters have generally replaced fusion rockets on all spacecraft save warcraft.

Vishnishtee (Vashneesht, Vasnesht, Vasneesit, etc.): Wizard or protector.

Webeye: Puppeteer technology, a multisensory transmitter.

Weenie plant: Ubiquitous Ringworld plant. Edible.

RINGWORLD
Parameters

30 hours = one Ringworld day
1 Ringworld rotation = 7½ days
75 days = 10 turns = 1 falan
Mass = 2 x 10exp30 grams
Radius = .95 x 10exp8 miles
Circumference = 6 x 10exp8 miles
Width = .997 x 10exp6 miles
Surface area = 6 x 10exp14 square miles = 3 million
   times the surface area of the Earth
Surface gravity = .992 *G* (spin)
Spin velocity = 770 miles/second
Rim walls rise inward, 1000 miles.
Star: G3 verging on G2, barely smaller and cooler than
   Sol

THE ALGEBRAIST

Iain M. Banks

It is 4034 A.D. Humanity has made it to the stars. Fassin Taak, a Slow Seer at the Court of the Nasqueron Dwellers, wil be fortunate if he makes it to the end of the year.

The Nasqueron Dwellers inhabit a gas giant on the outskirts of the galaxy, in a system awaiting its wormhole connection to the rest of civilisation. In the meantime, they are dismissed as decadents living in a state of highly developed barbarism, hoarding data without order, hunting their own young and fighting pointless formal wars.

Seconded to a military-religious order he's barely heard of – part of the baroque hierarchy of the Mercatoria, the latest galactic hegemony – Fassin Taak has to travel again amongst the Dwellers. He is in search of a secret hidden for half a billion years. But with each day that passes a war draws closer – a war that threatens to overwhelm everything and everyone he's ever know.